Praise for the

KAREN E. QUINC

## Satin Doll

"Gritty, haunting, and hypnotic . . . powerful and provocative . . . Will keep you on the edge of your seat for days to come."
—*Essence*

"In addition to its fast pace, drama, sizzling sex, and domestic fireworks, *Satin Doll* raises deeper questions about class issues."
—*Virginian-Pilot*

"Energetic, fast-paced, and provides intriguing action."
—*Black Issues Book Review*

"A real page-turner . . . Karen Quinones Miller navigates this dilemma of two worlds with skill and passion."
—*Albany Times Union*

"A literary asset; an inspirational, gutsy story with a tough and endearing main character."
—*Philadelphia Tribune*

"Marvelous . . . A skillful blend of romance, violence, and family bonding."
—*Booklist*

## Ida B.

"Miller has transported readers into a small community unbeknownst by many, but respected by all who come in contact. Filled with comedy, drama, heartfelt scenes, and realism, *Ida B.* is truly an enjoyable, self-relating, and, most of all, an unforgettable novel."
—Monique Baldwin-Worrell, founder of A Nu Twista Flavah

*more . . .*

## Using What You Got

## I'm Telling

# satin nights

## KAREN E. QUINONES MILLER

**WARNER BOOKS**

NEW YORK    BOSTON

This book is a work of fiction. Names, characters, places, and incidents are the product of the author's imagination or are used fictitiously. Any resemblance to actual events, locales, or persons, living or dead, is coincidental.

Copyright © 2006 by Karen E. Quinones Miller
Reading Group Guide copyright © 2007 by Hachette Book Group USA
Excerpt from *Passin'* copyright © 2007 by Karen E. Quinones Miller
All rights reserved. Except as permitted under the U.S. Copyright Act of 1976, no part of this publication may be reproduced, distributed, or transmitted in any form or by any means, or stored in a database or retrieval system, without the prior written permission of the publisher.

Warner Books
Hachette Book Group USA
237 Park Avenue
New York, NY 10169
Visit our Web site at www.HachetteBookGroupUSA.com.

Warner Books and the "W" logo are trademarks of Time Warner Inc. or an affiliated company. Used under license by Hachette Book Group, which is not affiliated with Time Warner Inc.

*Book design by Giorgetta Bell McRee*

Printed in the United States of America

Originally published in hardcover by Warner Books, an imprint of Warner Books, Inc.
First Trade Edition: April 2007
10 9 8 7 6 5 4 3 2 1

The Library of Congress has cataloged the hardcover edition as follows:
Miller, Karen E. Quinones.
    Satin nights / Karen E. Quinones Miller.— 1st ed.
        p. cm.
    Summary: "The sequel to 'Satin Doll,' continuing the story of Regina Harris and her three girlfriends, dealing with divorce, single parenthood, and romance in Harlem"— Provided by the publisher.
    ISBN-13: 978-0-446-57844-8
    ISBN-10: 0-446-57844-4
    1. African American women—Fiction. 2. Female friendship—Fiction. 3. Harlem (New York, N.Y.)—Fiction. I Title.
    PS3563. I41335S284 2006
    813'.6—dc22

                                                                    2005035340

ISBN: 978-0-446-69604-3 (pbk.)

*Maferefun Olodumare*
*Maferefun Egun*
*Maferefun Oshun*
*Maferefun bobo Orisha*

I lovingly dedicate this book to both my spiritual and physical family.

# acknowledgments

*Satin Nights* was the toughest book I've had to write, not because the material or content was difficult, but because I was diagnosed with a brain tumor in the middle of the writing—which, of course, meant I had to have brain surgery. Needless to say, I turned this book in late. <smile>

I want to give a very sincere and appreciative shout-out to my editor, Beth de Guzman of Warner Books, who often called me during my illness and recuperation period—never to ask me when I was going to get the book in to her, but to make sure that I was okay and to let me know that she was there for me in whatever way I needed her. Beth, I'm so glad we're working together, and I hope we have an everlasting relationship.

My agent, Liza Dawson of Liza Dawson Associates, proved that she isn't only a super agent, but a super angel. What other agent would not only travel two hours to visit me in the hospital, but also make another trip to babysit me while I was recuperating. Liza, I truly love you!

Of course, I want to thank Dr. Kenneth Judy and the wonderful staff at the University of Pennsylvania Hospital, because

# prologue

1991

"So you going to miss me?"

Sixteen-year-old Regina Harris turned her head to stare out the window so he wouldn't see the tears in her eyes. She nodded her head. "Yeah," she said in as cool a voice as she could muster. "But I still don't see why you have to go."

Little Joe sat up in the bed and gave an expansive stretch accompanied by a loud yawn. He scratched his bare chest and threw his legs over the side of the bed, scrunching his toes on the plush white carpet in the hotel suite.

"Girl, you done wore me the fuck out. I'm too old be trying to keep up with a young-ass girl like you," he said as he stood up and put on his black silk pajama pants. "You know I gotta go. I got no choice. You hungry? We can go over to Tavern on the Green before I take you home if you want."

Regina reached over and grabbed his arm before he could move away. "Yes, you do have a choice. You're not in custody, and I don't see why you have to turn yourself in to go to prison just because they say you do."

"Hey, hey, hey," Little Joe said as he sat down on the bed beside her. "Look at you, getting all worked up. I ain't never seen you this sentimental and shit. Someone would think it's you being sent to the slammer 'stead of me. You need to—"

"No, Little Joe." Regina jumped up and knelt in front of him. "Please. I don't want you to go. Please. Let's just get on a plane and go somewhere. Me, you, and Ray-Ray. We can change our names and live in California, or South America, or anywhere they can't find us."

"Aw, isn't that sweet? You wanna run off together, huh?" Little Joe chuckled as he caressed her face.

"Little Joe, please. You're laughing, and I don't see anything funny." Regina didn't bother to hide her sobs as she buried her head in Little Joe's bare chest. "I don't want you to go. And you don't need to go. Please don't leave me. I won't know what to do without you."

"You'll do what you've always done, Regina. You'll survive," Little Joe said gently as he rocked her back and forth and stroked her back.

"No, I won't," Regina moaned. "Please, Little Joe. Let's just get on a plane. Let's just go."

"I can't, baby. First off, they've already confiscated my passport."

"Can't you get a fake one?"

"Yeah, maybe, but I ain't inclined. I'm going to beat this bum rap. My lawyer's already working on an appeal, and he thinks he can get me sprung in like a year. Shit, I can do a year standing on my head. Ain't like I ain't never did no time before. And if I run now, I'm gonna be running the rest of my life, and I ain't down for that shit. I got all my business handled already, so I can be outta the life and legit by the time I get sprung. Just live off the investments I've already made. Let me just do this, and I'll be out before you even realize I've been in, okay?"

"No." Regina sobbed hysterically. "It's not okay. I don't want you to go. I don't want you to go."

"I know you don't, baby, but I'll be okay, and you will, too," Little Joe said as he continued to rock her back and forth. "And you'll be the first person I'll find when I get out. I promise." He wiped some of the tears from her cheek and kissed her lips tenderly. "Now, stop all this crying before you make my dick hard again."

# chapter one

2005

*S*o you're saying you don't feel guilty?"

"Nope. Not in the least."

"Okay, Puddin', let me get this straight." Regina put her elbows on the table in the snazzy Manhattan restaurant and cradled her face in her hands. "You mean to tell me that you hit a complete stranger with your car, in front of his three grandchildren, and you don't even feel the slightest bit guilty?"

"Why should I?" Puddin' picked up a shrimp and lavishly dipped it in cocktail sauce. She took a large bite, then threw the tail back on the saucer. She licked her long tapered fingernails before continuing. "The car skidded on black ice. Even the police put that shit in their report. It wasn't my fault, so why the fuck should I feel guilty? They better hurry with our meals, I'm about through with these little-ass shrimps."

"Oh my God!" Regina banged her fists on the table, rattling the dishes and silverware. "Forget about the shrimp! You should feel guilty because you killed a man!"

Puddin' shrugged and said with a half-smile, "No, I didn't. The car slid on ice, then slid into him. I ain't had nothing to do with it, except I was there. It was an act of God. Blame it on Him." She dipped another shrimp in the cocktail sauce, and this time popped the whole thing in her mouth.

"But it was a sixty-five-year-old man. And his grandchildren were right there!" Regina said. She knew Puddin' was callous—hell, everybody knew that—but this was just a bit too much.

"Oh please! Will you just stop?" Puddin' sucked her teeth and waved her hand in the air. "For all you know, the man was a pervert and molesting those kids."

"What? How can you say that?" Regina sputtered. "You knew him? You didn't tell me that."

"No, I ain't know him." Puddin' shrugged. "But I'm just saying, you're making like it was worse 'cause he's a granddaddy, but what if he was fucking them kids? You wouldn't be trying to make me feel bad then."

"Puddin', come on, girl!" Regina cocked her head to the side and studied her friend of twenty years. "You don't have anything to base that on. You don't know that he was a pervert."

"And you don't know that he wasn't. So let's drop it." Puddin' looked around for the waiter and snapped her fingers to get his attention. When he ignored her, she shouted, "Hey! I know you saw me!"

"You know you just . . ." Regina's face tightened as she glared at Puddin'. "You just . . ." She suddenly sighed, unclenched her fists, and leaned back in her chair. "You're right. Fine. Let's just drop it." She pulled her shoulder-length hair up into a ponytail, then released it, letting it fall around her oval-shaped face. *I should be home at my computer writing that article for* Essence, she thought, glancing out the window, *or calling up sources for the* New York Times *story that's due next week, or putting the finishing touches on Camille's birthday party next week.* She smiled at the thought of her daughter, who was about to turn four. Her smile turned to a grimace as she looked at Puddin', who swilled the last of her drink. *But no, instead I'm here* if they hadn't done their thing, there would be no book because there would have been no more me.

I would like to give special thanks to Dr. Andrew Quint, the only medical practitioner who seemed to care that my medical problems were not only affecting me physically, but also mentally and emotionally, and preventing me from doing what I care about most—writing. His understanding and compassion were essential to my recovery.

My brother Joseph T. Quinones and my new sister-in-law Ayoka Wiles were there with me every step of the way, lying and telling me I looked beautiful when I knew I looked like hell, and catering to my every whim. May the Orisas bless the two of you always.

I have to give thanks to Baba Facundo and his wife, Valerie, who marked the spiritual ebos and cleanings I needed to ensure a full recovery.

I also need to thank all of the members of the Eveningstar Writers Group, who showed their support in a million different ways. And especially to Bahiya Cabral-Johnson and Sherlane Freeman, who sat with me for hours and helped outline this book when I was still too unfocused to do it myself.

And, of course, I want to thank all of my readers who found out about my little medical trauma and sent their love and well wishes.

But my biggest and loudest shout-out has to go to my daughter, Camille. My poor baby was in the middle of preparing for her senior prom and high-school graduation, and filling out college applications, when I was diagnosed, and she put everything on hold to make sure I was okay. She never once complained, and never let me see her cry. She was, is, and will always be my biggest source of inspiration. I love you, Love Girl, and I'm proud to be your mother. Thanks for being my daughter.

# author's note

Dear Readers,

I've often been asked which of my novels was the hardest to write, and up until recently I've not been able to answer. None of the novels were *hard* to write. Writing has always been a fun, relaxing endeavor for me. Some novels have taken longer than others because of the different things going on in my life, but I can't say that any have been hard.

Until *Satin Nights*, that is. This was an extremely difficult book to write, and for the longest time I couldn't figure out why. But eventually I did learn the reason.

I had a brain tumor.

The first indication I had that something was wrong was when all of a sudden I seemed to stop dreaming. And I always had such interesting dreams—many times they became the inspirations for my novels. But then, nothing!

I was actually upset enough to go my doctor to find out what was going on. The doctor gave me a checkup, said nothing was medically wrong with me and that maybe I just wasn't remembering my dreams anymore. Not unusual, he said to me. BS, I said to myself.

Then I found I'd lost my desire to write. I couldn't believe it! All my life I couldn't wait to get a pen in my hand or a keyboard under my fingers, and all of a sudden I was making up excuses not to open up my already started manuscript for *Satin Nights*. I'd sit in front of the computer, play Solitaire until I won a game, then play Hearts until I won two games, then play Spider Solitaire advanced level until I won three games. After that I'd be so tired I would just go to bed and sleep a dreamless night away.

I, of course, went back to the doctor. It was one thing for me not to be dreaming, but a whole other thing for me to lose my desire to write. Again, the doctor found nothing.

The completed manuscript for *Satin Nights*—which I had estimated would be 75,000 words—was due to the publisher by May 2005. By January 2005 I had only 10,000 words written. I was in trouble.

I started having headaches and eventually partial complex seizures, and the doctor ordered a CAT scan and later an MRI. Come to find out that I had a small tumor on the left frontal lobe of my brain. The creative area of the left frontal lobe arranges words and concepts into new patterns—in effect allowing us to think of new things to say. This is essential for a writer. It was also probable that the tumor is what caused my inability to remember dreams.

I didn't panic. In fact, I felt a certain sense of relief. I'd finally found out what was wrong with me. I talked to my family and assured them I'd be okay, talked to my publisher and told them that my manuscript was going to be late, then scheduled my brain surgery for mid-May. For various reasons, it was pushed back to June 29, 2005.

The surgery went well, and I was back home (under supervision) in just three days. Ten days after my return I woke up from a deep sleep and couldn't wait to tell someone about my dream! I was so excited. Just a few days later, I was panting to get to my computer; every minute away began to seem like torture. I had only 23,000 words of *Satin Nights* written when I was admitted to the hospital. I started writing again on July 15. By August 14 I turned in a 78,000-word manuscript to my publisher.

I've now completely recovered from the brain tumor and surgery. Well, I get tired a bit faster than I did a couple of years ago, and I can't remember things as quickly as I once did. But those things are not much of an issue to me. What is important is that I've just completed a new novel, *Passin'*, which will be out in February 2008, I've already started on my next book, and I've come up with an idea—based on a recent dream—for yet another book.

Yeah. The kid is back.

Sincerely,
Karen E. Quinones Miller
authorkeqm@aol.com

*wasting my time talking to Puddin', who doesn't have a care
in the world and doesn't even know the meaning of the word "respon-
sibility."*

Puddin's mouth curled as she looked up at the waiter, who
had finally sauntered over to the table. "Oh, you finally decided to bring your ass over here, huh?"

"Did you need something else, ma'am?" he asked in a heavy
Jamaican accent.

"Yeah," Puddin' snapped. "I need you to be hovering over
this table like you hovering over those white folks' table." She
lifted her butt up slightly and pulled a credit card out of the
back pocket of her skintight jeans. "See this? The bitch is a
Platinum American Express, got that? Like the Reverend Jesse
Jackson said, I am some-fucking-body, okay?" She threw it on
the table. "Now, maybe you think you should be bowing and
kowtowing elsewhere, but as long as I got my little platinum
bitch here"—she tapped on the credit card—"you better act
like you know. Now, take your ass to the kitchen and find out
why our food is taking so long."

The waiter gave her a nonchalant nod and started walking
away.

"Hold up." Puddin' snapped her fingers, and the waiter obediently turned back around, his eyes saying he wanted to kill
her. "Bring me another apple martini. You want another one,
Gina?"

Regina shook her head.

"Bring her another one just in case," Puddin' said to the
waiter, who was tapping his foot impatiently. "And do me a
favor? Put some fucking glide into your stride. This is supposed to be a high-class place. I don't appreciate having to wait
forever for my shit."

Regina waited until the man shot Puddin' a dirty look and
hurried off before reaching for the credit card still lying on the
table. But Puddin' was too fast and snatched it up.

"Mind your business," she said as she slid it back into her pocket.

"Puddin', whose card is that?" Regina said in a loud whisper.

"What I just say? Mind your damn business." Puddin' grinned, and took a bite of the last shrimp.

"Yeah, all right. But I'm telling you right now, I'm leaving before you pay the bill, 'cause I don't plan on getting caught up in your shit." Regina gave a little chuckle. "That's if you haven't gotten our asses thrown outta here already, breaking on that guy like that."

Puddin' let out a loud laugh. "Wouldn't be like you ain't get me thrown out a fancy restaurant before. I ain't never forget the time you and Yvonne was—"

"She and Yvonne was what?" a young red-haired woman wearing a mint-green Liz Claiborne business suit asked as she sat down in the chair next to Puddin'.

"Oh, you finally decided to drag your ass in, Yvonne? Twenty minutes late." Puddin' rolled her eyes. "Heifer."

"I love you, too," Yvonne said lightly as she placed her clutch bag on the table. "Hey, Gina. You look nice. I like that color on you."

Regina smiled and shook her head. Here she was wearing a black leotard top and black jeans, and Yvonne was saying she looked nice. That's Yvonne, giving compliments to get some in return. Regina considered saying nothing, but then decided, *What the hell.*

"Thanks, sweetie, but look at you! I love that suit," Regina said graciously.

"Oh, this old thing?" Yvonne waved her hand in the air. "I've had this for—"

"Oh fuck, will you give us a break?" Puddin' snorted. "Don't try that shit, saying you had it forever. The fucking price tag is still on your sleeve. Fucking show-off."

Yvonne jerked her hands off the table and looked at her

cuffs, then glared at Puddin'. "You ain't shit, Puddin'. I don't have any damn price tags. And lower your damn voice before they throw your ass out for disturbing the peace."

"Now, see," Puddin' said with a giggle, "that's just what I was talking about when you sashayed your yellow ass in here. Remember the time you and Regina got us all thrown out of a restaurant because y'all were fighting in the bathroom?"

"It was just a little argument," Regina broke in.

"And blown totally out of proportion. Anyway, that's ancient history," Yvonne said dismissively as she picked up a napkin from the table and placed it on her lap. "Although," she said with a slow smile, "if we did fight, I woulda kicked Regina's ass."

"Oh, shut up," Regina said with a grin. "You've never had a fight in your life. I was the one who always had to fight for you when we were kids."

"Well, didn't either one of us fight as much as hot-tempered Puddin' over here," Yvonne said with a laugh. "She fought every day when we were back in school."

"Yeah." Regina nodded. "Sometimes twice a day." In fact, right after they met, she and Puddin' fought three fights in two days—one the day they met and two the day after—because Puddin' pushed in front of her while she was waiting in line to jump double Dutch. Regina wound up with a black eye and bloodied nose, but she came back after Puddin' the next day, and they fought twice more. It was only after Yvonne managed to broker a peace between them that they all became friends, but mostly because Puddin' was tired of Regina coming after her.

"Yeah, Puddin' was a terror."

"Well, finally," Puddin' said to the waiter, who was placing her drink in front of her. "Took you long enough."

"The food will be right out, ma'am," the waiter said, addressing Regina. "I trust the martini is to your taste?"

"Now, see, why you ain't ask me that?" Puddin' snapped.

"I'm the one paying, and I'm also the one who ain't tipping your ass."

"Yvonne, we already ordered. Do you want something?" Regina asked, ignoring Puddin', as the waiter also seemed to be doing.

"No, I'm fine. I can use a cosmopolitan, though."

"Very good, ma'am." The waiter gave Yvonne a slight bow and headed off.

"And bring me another one, too," Puddin' shouted to his back. "Now, y'all seen that shit, right?" she said with a chuckle. "I tell you I don't get no fucking respect. I'm like the black Rodney Dangerfield or something."

*Drama, drama, drama,* Regina thought as she took a sip of her martini. But that was to be expected whenever they got together with Puddin'. The girl prided herself on "keeping it real," and she did, although reality for Puddin' often turned into a nightmare for everyone else. But still, Puddin' had her good points. Great points, actually. If you were ever in trouble, Puddin' would be the first one by your side, to either throw a punch on your behalf or drag you to a quick getaway.

And Yvonne was a good friend, too, Regina thought as she glanced over at the woman. Her best friend, in fact. True, they had their ups and downs, but there were a lot more ups than downs. She was the one who Regina could talk to when she felt she couldn't talk to anyone else. The only one she could cry to. Who welcomed her into her own family after Regina's mother died when Regina was thirteen. Yvonne could be a real bitch sometimes, but she could also be a saint.

And of course, Tamika, the last and the sweetest of the Four Musketeers. Little Tamika . . . Regina shook herself slightly as if to wake herself up. Why was she getting so sentimental about her friends all of a sudden? she wondered. She pushed her drink away from her. Three apple martinis obviously exceeded her limit.

"So, Puddin', what's this big news you made us come down

here for?" Yvonne asked after the waiter brought Puddin' and Regina their food. "You finally get a job?"

"Yeah, right. That'll be the day," Puddin' answered with a mouthful of food.

"Oh, she already told me," Regina said nonchalantly. "She killed a man yesterday. And right in front of his grandkids."

"Oh please, I already know about all that. Puddin' called me last night after it happened."

"She did?" Regina was surprised. Usually, she or Tamika was the first person Puddin' turned to, since she knew Yvonne always had a lecture prepared.

"Yeah, she had to. The heifer had my car," Yvonne said dryly.

"What? You didn't tell me that," Regina said as she slapped Puddin's hand. "I thought you had Jimmy's car."

"Naw, I dropped that cheap-ass mofo."

"Oh really?" Regina raised her eyebrow. "So then, that's not his platinum card you flashed, huh?"

"Puddin' got a platinum card?" Yvonne said in astonishment. "Now, ain't that some shit? Here I am an executive assistant in the NBA public relations department and I only have a gold card, and you ain't never worked a fucking day in your life and you're pushing platinum? Shit!" Yvonne downed her drink and signaled for the waiter. "I'd like another one, please," she said when he strolled over.

"What I wanna know is *whose* platinum card," Regina said with a chuckle. "She won't let me see the name on it."

"Oh really?" Yvonne put her hand out in front of Puddin'. "Okay, chickie, unass the damn card."

"Fuck you," Puddin' said with a wave of her hand.

"Look, don't make me and Regina jack you up in this place," Yvonne said as she moved her chair closer to Puddin's. "Hand it over."

Puddin' chuckled and shook her head at Yvonne, then looked at Regina. "Why come all of a sudden girlfriend's thinking she can thump? Which reminds me, I almost had to give someone else a beat-down yesterday."

"Yeah, who?" Yvonne asked.

"The old man's daughter. The one that got killed."

"What?" Regina's jaw dropped. "You killed her father, and then you were gonna give her a beat-down?"

"I ain't kill him. The car killed him. And when I got out the car to see if he was okay, this bitch came flying at me screaming and shit. I ain't know who she was, so I decked her."

"God damn it, Puddin'," Yvonne said in a hoarse voice, "why did you have to hit her? Was she threatening you or something? Did she hit you?"

"No, but she came flying out on me, and like I said, I ain't know who she was. For all I know, she was gonna hit me. And you know me, I ain't waiting around for someone else to throw the first punch. Fuck that. Sometimes that's the only punch thrown."

"You are such a mess." Regina shook her head. "The man's dead, his three grandkids are on the sidewalk next to him crying, and then you beat up their mother."

"I ain't say I beat her up," Puddin' said in a hurt voice. "I only hit her once. And I ain't even had my roll of pennies in my hand."

"But why did you have to hit her at all?" Yvonne broke in. "You know, all kidding aside, you're too old for this fighting shit."

"Ain't that the truth?" Regina nodded. "Here you are thirty-one years old, and you're still fighting in the street. You need to get ahold of yourself. Show some self-control."

"I agree," Yvonne added. "I'm not saying you should let someone hit on you, but you didn't know if that woman was going to do that. She was just hysterical because her father was killed. And rightfully so. Wouldn't you be in the same situation?"

"Yeah, well, she got in the wrong person's face," Puddin'

grumbled. "It wasn't like I aimed the car at the man. It just happened. And I ain't gonna let no bitch just scream on me like that."

"Puddin', do me a favor," Regina said with a sigh. "In the future, just try to show some self-control. Take at least a couple of deep breaths before you swing on someone, okay?"

"You expect me to flip my script this late in my life? Yeah, right." Puddin' snorted.

"It's supposed to be about evolvement," Regina said as she finished her martini. "It's never too late for us to work on our shortcomings, you know."

"Oh?" Yvonne grinned at Regina. "Does that mean you're going to work on yours?"

Regina raised her left eyebrow. "What shortcomings do you suggest I have, *dearie*?"

"Your crazy-ass need to get revenge anytime you think someone's done you wrong, *sweetie*," Yvonne said smugly. "We don't call you the Queen of the Get Back for nothing."

"I don't consider that a shortcoming," Regina retorted. "I'd be stupid to let someone think they can fuck over me and get away with it."

"It's the lengths you go to get back at them that makes it so ridiculous, Gina," Yvonne said lightly.

Regina tossed her head. "Yeah, well, when people fuck me over with their actions, they can't very well complain about the extent of my fucking reaction."

Yvonne winked at Puddin'. "Ever notice, when Regina gets put on the spot, she starts sounding like you?" Puddin' laughed in response.

"Ah, fuck you and go to hell," Regina sneered.

"All I'm saying is that if you want Puddin' to take her two breaths before kicking somebody's ass, you should take a couple before you go after someone."

Regina glared at her friends for a moment, then waved her hand in the air dismissively. "Okay, I'm game. Puddin', if you start controlling your temper, I'll start controlling mine. Deal?"

"Yeah, well, fuck it, okay. Deal." Puddin' shrugged. "I'll at least try."

The two women reached over the table and shook hands.

"And back to the original subject, Puddin'. Whose card is it?" Yvonne demanded.

Puddin's grin grew wider as she slightly raised from the chair and pulled the card out, then threw it on the table. "Check it out."

Regina reached for the card, but Yvonne was quicker.

"Who the hell is Leslie Cranston?" she asked as she peered at the card.

"Leslie Cranston?" Regina ran through the file cabinet in her mind but came up empty. "Is that someone we know?"

"Yeah, if you listen to the radio," Puddin' said nonchalantly. "Ever heard of Rob-Cee? Well, that's Leslie."

"What?" Yvonne hooted. "That gangsta mofo's real name is Leslie? I don't believe it. Why his mama do some shit like that?"

"I got a better question." Regina started waving her finger in the air. "What the fuck are you doing with his card? And does he know you have it?"

"Oh, calm down. He's still passed out from all that coke we was sniffing this morning. The wimp can't hang," Puddin' said with a laugh. "I'm timing it just right. Dude told the hotel to give him a wake-up call at seven, and it ain't even five yet. I'll have this card back in his wallet before he even knows I lifted it."

Regina's eyes widened in disbelief. "You stole his card?"

"Borrowed it," Puddin' answered. "It's no big deal. He don't probably even look at his credit card bills. And it's not like I went out shopping. I'm just taking my best friends out for lunch and drinks."

Regina shook her head and looked at Yvonne. "I already told her I'm leaving before she pays the bill."

"Ditto," Yvonne said with a nod. "But I still want to hear the big news Puddin' dragged us out here for."

Puddin's face fell. "Well, it *was* big news. Real big news. But it ain't shit now."

"What do you mean?" Regina asked.

"Well, I found out this morning I picked the winning six numbers for the Mega Millions Lottery last night—"

"What!" Regina and Yvonne said at the same time.

"Yeah," Puddin' said simply.

"Girl. You're rich!" Yvonne started pounding Puddin' on the back. "What was it worth? Fifty million? One hundred million?"

"Oh, Puddin', this is just so damn great!" Regina's shoulders were wiggling with excitement. "You're a millionaire."

"And I want my cut!" Yvonne all but shouted.

"Same here," Regina added.

Puddin' pushed Yvonne's hand away. "Well, ya'll can get a cut of the twenty-five bucks I got in my pocket, 'cause that's all that I got."

"Not for long," Yvonne said as she grabbed her pocketbook. "We'll come with you to take the ticket to Albany. That's where it's gotta be validated, right? Come on, let's get outta here and drive up there right now. We can spend the night at a hotel and get to the Lottery Commission in the morning."

"I think you'd better slow your roll, Yvonne," Regina said as she noticed the crestfallen look on Puddin's face.

"Yeah, you can just back that shit up. All the way up," Puddin' said with a sigh. "Like I said, I picked all the right numbers for the Mega Millions, but I didn't realize until after I told you guys to meet me here that I played the New York Lotto. I ain't win shit."

Regina sank back in her chair. "You've just got to be kidding." She paused for a moment and then let out a deep sigh. "That's some real tough shit."

"Aw, man, Puddin'. You got us all excited for nothing." Yvonne sucked her teeth.

"How excited do you think *I* was?" Puddin' took another sip of her drink. "And how the fuck do you think I felt when I found out how I fucked up? I ain't wanna cancel on you guys after I made such a big deal about you coming out here, so I decided we should all just go ahead and have some food and some martinis and have a good time."

"Yeah, I hear you," Regina said. She reached over and patted Puddin' on her shoulder.

"Damn. What a bummer," Yvonne said as she let her head loll on the back of her chair.

"Man, I had it all planned what I was gonna do with that damn money. The Four Musketeers were about to come off big-time. I was gonna buy you your own magazine, Gina, so you wouldn'ta had to write for anybody but yourself. And I was gonna pay for Tamika's medical school. Then I was gonna buy you a husband, Yvonne."

"Thanks, heifer," Yvonne said, not bothering to raise her head.

"Well, I'm doing quite well with my freelancing, and with the alimony and child support from Charles I'm more than okay," Regina said. "And David's doing pretty well in his new law practice, so I'm sure he'll be able to pay Tamika's school bills. And with the raise Yvonne just got with her job promotion, she should be able to buy her own man."

"Thanks, skank," Yvonne said.

"Yeah, but still, it woulda been nice," Puddin' said sullenly.

"What were you going to buy yourself?" Regina asked gently.

"Me? I was gonna buy Harlem. Or a whole fucking block of it. A whole block of brownstones, and I was gonna move all my friends in and let them live rent-free."

"And that's it?" Yvonne asked.

"Yeah, that and a cocaine farm in South America and a private jet with a pilot to bring me fresh stash every week."

"You're ill." Regina giggled.

"Yeah, I woulda been one ill-assed millionaire. Better than being an ill-assed broke bitch," Puddin' said with a shrug.

Regina sneaked a peek at her watch and saw it was almost five-thirty. She really needed to get home soon and start work on some of those magazine articles. She figured she'd stay another half hour or so to make sure Puddin' was all right, then say her polite good-byes.

"You know what I'ma do tomorrow night?" Puddin' said suddenly.

"What?" Regina asked.

"I'ma go to that Usher concert and after-party with Rob-Cee, and then I'ma drop his ass and hook up with Usher."

"Oh really?" Regina said with a smile. "And what makes you think youngblood's gonna go for the hookup? You're at least five or six years older than him."

"What's age got to do with it?" Puddin' chuckled. "My shit is tight. And remember, he was fucking around with that chick from TLC for the longest, and she was older than him, too. If he went for her, I know he's gonna ape-wild over me. All I gots to do is meet him, and Rob-Cee is my ticket to do just that."

"Okay, well, you go do that tomorrow, sweetie," Yvonne said. She straightened herself up in her chair and dabbed the corners of her mouth with her napkin. "But come spend the night over at my place tonight. The kids are over at my mother's, and I don't have anything to do."

"You got any coke?" Puddin' said with a grin.

"You know I don't do that shit anymore."

"You got any reefer, then?"

"Yeah, I got enough for a couple of joints."

"Yeah, all right, then, I might do that." Puddin' shrugged and then looked at Regina. "You know she's only doing this 'cause she thinks I'm depressed or some shit, right? Mother Yvonne to the rescue."

"Now, see, I'm just doing it because I'd thought we—," Yvonne started.

"I'm only teasing," Puddin' interrupted with a wave of her hand. "Yeah, that's cool. I could use a break from Rob-Cee, anyway. Just drop me off at his hotel when we leave here so I can slip this card back in his shit, and we'll head uptown."

"Why don't you let me pick up the tab this time?" Yvonne asked.

"Because I'm the one that asked you and Regina out," Puddin' answered.

"Yeah, but . . ."

"Regina, could you please tell Mother Yvonne to shut up before I kick her ass?"

"Come on, Yvonne." Regina got up from the table. "Let's wait outside while Puddin' commits larceny."

It was drizzling outside, and Regina started to pull the hood of her bomber jacket over her head but changed her mind. She needed to get a perm, anyway, so the rain wasn't going to do any damage. She grimaced as she saw Yvonne pull a gold cigarette case out of her pocketbook.

"Girl, you've been quitting for ten years now and haven't missed a day smoking yet." Regina snatched the cigarette out of Yvonne's mouth before she could light it. "And don't think I'm not going to tell Mama Tee you're out here trying to smoke right out in the street. She'll lose her Trinidadian mind."

"Here we are, thirty-odd years old, and you're still threatening to tattle on me to my mother," Yvonne said with a smile.

Regina broke the cigarette in half, and seeing no trash can in close proximity, put it in her pocket.

"Guess who's moving to New York?" Yvonne said, looking straight ahead as if the traffic on 57th Street was fascinating to her.

"Who?"

"Robert."

"Robert who?" Regina said suspiciously.

"That Robert."

"Shit."

"He called me last week. I didn't tell you because I knew you'd have a fit, but he broke up with his wife a couple of months ago, and he's got a job with the Bronx District Attorney's Office."

"And you're going to start going out with him again, right?"

"I didn't say that."

*And you haven't said that you're not,* Regina thought grimly. Yvonne's relationship with Robert had almost broken up their friendship five years before, and it had taken nearly two years for Yvonne to stop crying over the relationship, which had been fucked-up from the start. He had lied to her about not being married; he had her move to Philadelphia to be close to him, then ignored her; and he fully kicked her to the curb when he got tired of her.

"But whether I see him or not, I want you to know I'm in control. He's out of my system, and I'm not going to let myself get caught up like that again, okay?" Yvonne said, still looking straight ahead.

"Whatever, Yvonne." Regina shrugged. "Whatever."

# chapter two

$\text{W}$hat had been a gentle shower when she left the restaurant had turned into a downpour by the time she got out of the taxi on the corner of 119th and Lenox Avenue. It was only seven o'clock, but it was already getting dark as Regina stepped into the corner bodega.

"*Buenas noches, Pepe. Cómo estás?*" Regina addressed the wizened old man partially covered by the supposedly bulletproof Plexiglas surrounding the cash register area.

"*Bien, chachi,*" Pepe answered with an almost toothless grin. "*Y tú?*"

Pepe, like most of the Puerto Ricans who owned bodegas in Harlem, spoke perfect English, but since he'd been around long enough to remember her father, who was originally from San Juan, Regina always greeted him in Spanish, though their conversation would quickly switch to English, since Regina's Spanish was spotty at best.

"Can I get a Revlon perm kit?" Regina asked as she snapped open her pocketbook to take out her purse. "Mild, please."

Pepe turned around in the partition and looked at a shelf. "No Revlon. We got Ultra Sheen, though. Want it?"

Regina nodded and handed him a twenty. "So what number played today?" She didn't really care, but she knew that Pepe, like many of the old-timers in Harlem, still followed the numbers game fanatically, even though most of the younger people, like Puddin', had long switched over to the legal lottery.

"Five two seven, *chachi.*" He motioned her to come close to the opening in the partition and told her in a low voice, "I hit for five dollars."

"Straight?" Regina whistled. "What's that? Three thousand dollars?"

Pepe put his finger to his lips and winked, then nodded to make sure she understood she was right. He straightened up and put the perm kit in a brown paper bag and handed it to her. "Carlos is taking over for me for a week or so. I'm taking the wife to Las Vegas to live it up a little bit."

*"Está bien,"* Regina said with a smile. "That's real good. I guess I'll see you when you get back. *Hasta la vista.*"

Outside, Regina glanced over at the bistro on the corner of 118th as she crossed the street. Things had sure changed since she had lived on that block as a kid. There used to be a hardware store on that corner that served as the neighborhood meeting place for old men playing checkers. Now it was the hangout for apple martini–drinking yuppies and buppies who had recently moved to Harlem after Bill Clinton decided to open an office on 125th Street, suddenly making Harlem cool again.

She walked past the row of brownstones on 119th Street before she finally reached her home in the middle of the block.

The rain finally began to let up as Regina fumbled in her pocket for her keys. The familiar musky odor of wood greeted her when she opened the door, a smell that a lot of people who owned brownstones tried to get rid of with incense and air fresheners, but which Regina considered a sign that she had made it. Better the smell of musky wood than the smell of chicken and pig feet in the apartment buildings she'd always lived in.

She shook her umbrella out and placed it in the stand in the vestibule, carefully rearranging the other four or five umbrellas to cover the baseball bat she kept in there for protection.

"Hey, Ray-Ray, when did you get here?" Regina asked as she walked into the living room.

"Hi, Aunt Gina. I got here a couple of hours ago," the teenage girl answered from the floor where she was lying with a textbook open in front of her.

"I hope you haven't been blasting this music the whole time." Regina walked over and turned off the CD player, which was playing Michael Jackson's "Beat It." "We do have neighbors, you know. And God knows I don't want them to actually think I still listen to 'Beat It.' I have a reputation to uphold, you know."

"Yeah, but that's my song," Renee said. "And they can't hear it. At least they ain't knock on the door to say anything."

Regina smiled as she looked lovingly at her niece. "You probably don't remember, sweetie, that's the song that—"

"I know, I know, you used to play that song to put me to sleep when I was a kid." Renee scowled. "Where's Camille, anyway? I came over to ask her what she wants for her birthday."

"Tamika's babysitting her for the night. I was supposed to pick her up a little while ago, but Camille whined that she wanted to stay. She would have wanted to come home if she knew her big cousin was here to see her, though," Regina said as she started sorting through the mail Renee must have put on the coffee table. Con Edison, Verizon, AT&T, and Saks. All bills. She breathed a sigh of relief when she saw an envelope with *People* magazine in the return address. She quickly opened it and pulled out a check for six thousand dollars for the two pieces she did for them the month before on E. Lynn Harris and

Halle Berry. Enough to pay the mortgage and the down payment on a new car, she thought with satisfaction.

"So I came all the way over here for nothing? She's staying with them for the weekend?" Renee asked as she got up from the floor and adjusted the blue Yankees ball cap on her head. "By the way, I ordered a pizza. I don't know why, though. As much as I hate living in Queens, they got better pizza than they do here in Harlem."

"Yeah, well, I didn't move back to Harlem for the pizza," Regina shot back. "And stop acting so damn shitty. You can carry your ass back to Queens and play that teenage-girl-attitude crap with your mother, 'cause I'm not having it."

Ray-Ray sucked her teeth. "All I was saying was—"

"Did you suck your teeth at me?" Regina said, striding across the room to her niece.

"No, Aunt Gina," Ray-Ray said quickly as she backed up. "I didn't suck my teeth at you. You know I would never suck my teeth at you."

"Oh?" Regina crossed her arms and looked at Ray-Ray. "So you're trying to tell me I didn't hear what I just heard, huh?"

"Well . . ." Ray-Ray batted her eyes. "You know they say when you hit thirty, your hearing is the second thing to go."

Regina struggled to hide the smile that was threatening to appear. It was an old trick Ray-Ray was pulling—trying to make Regina laugh when she was mad at her. "Oh really? And what's supposed to be the first thing?"

"Your sense of humor?" Ray-Ray grinned.

"You couldn't come up with something better than that?" Regina teased.

"Well, I had to think of something quick to make you smile." Ray-Ray chuckled. "I ain't want you playing 'Beat It' on my head." She moved closer to her aunt. "I 'pologize," she said in a baby voice.

Regina gave a little laugh. "Yeah, well, just watch your

mouth, okay? I love you, but you know I'm not one for putting up with a lotta nonsense."

"So is Camille gonna be at Tamika's for the whole weekend?"

"No. I'm picking her up tomorrow. You wanna spend the night and come with me to pick her up in the morning?"

"Nah." Renee shook her head. "I'm going out with Liz. She's gonna pick me up in about a half hour, and we're going to a party in the Bronx."

Regina looked Renee up and down and shook her head. Oversize gray sweatshirt, baggy jeans, and white Adidas—her regular uniform for the past six months. The eighteen-year-old had a wonderful shape, but you wouldn't know it by looking at her. "You're going to a party dressed like that?"

"What's wrong with what I'm wearing? It's clean, ain't it?"

"You're still a size five, aren't you? Why don't you come on upstairs, and I'll hook you up with something more, you know, partylike?"

"No thanks, Aunt Gina. You know I don't care about fashion and all that." Renee pointed to a colorful painting on the wall of two teenage girls in cheerleading outfits jumping up and down holding pom-poms. "I see you got a new one. Don't you already have the print, though?"

"Um-hm, I do." Regina smiled and walked up to her latest Annie Lee painting. "But the October Gallery called me to let me know the original was available, so I had to get it."

"Aunt Gina, you could open up your own art gallery with all these paintings you have."

Regina looked around the large living room, covered with paintings of Robert Goodnight, Ernie Barnes, Brenda Joysmith, and Charles Bibbs. She'd spent the better part of her first check from freelancing eight years before on a signed Annie Lee print, and had been buying African-American art ever since. One of the reasons she bought a brownstone, rather than an apartment, was so that she would have room to hang all of her paintings. Some people bought art that would complement their furniture; Regina had done it the other way around. The plush sofa and chairs and lamps in the living room were all different shades of brown and gold but with no discernible designs that might clash with her paintings. Even the expensive throw rug on the floor was brown and gold, with no ornate design—although the open can of grape soda perched precariously on the coffee table threatened to create one.

Regina grimaced as she moved the almost full can. "What are you studying, Ray-Ray?" she said, pointing to the open textbook on the floor.

"Trigonometry, and it's kicking my ass. I mean, butt. Sorry, Aunt Gina." Renee suddenly looked contrite. "But it's really hard as sh—as crap."

"I'm sure you can handle it." Regina smiled. "And what's this your mother was telling me about you getting a 1500 on your SATs?"

"Yeah, ain't that something?" Renee brightened back up. "I knew I did good, but I ain't think I did that good."

"Would you please stop saying 'ain't'? How can someone who scored a 1500 have such bad grammar? But seriously, I'm not the least bit surprised," Regina said as she sat on the couch and took off her sneakers. It had broken her heart when Renee was left back in the eighth grade, not because of academics, but hookying, but it had made Renee hit the books with a vengeance. And now it had paid off. She was going into her senior year of high school with a 4.0 GPA. "You can get a scholarship to just about any university with scores like that. Even the Ivy League schools."

Renee shook her head. "I'm going to Temple."

"Temple's a good school, but you should at least consider—"

"If it was good enough for you, it's good enough for me."

"Renee, that doesn't even make any sense," Regina said in an exasperated voice. "Like I said, Temple's a good school, and

I don't regret going there, but I didn't have the options you have."

Renee dug her hand deep into her jeans pocket and fished out a wrinkled five-dollar bill and two singles. "Um, Aunt Gina? Can you spot me a couple of bucks to pay for the pizza?"

"So you're just going to change the subject, huh? Okay, I'm going to let it go for the minute, but don't think I'm going to drop it for good. You still have almost a year before you make your final decision." Regina pointed to her purse lying on the coffee table. "I only have tens, and I want my change, missy."

"Oh but of course!" Renee pulled out a ten-dollar bill just as the doorbell rang. "Coming!" she called out, and hurried to greet the deliveryman.

꒰ꇐ꒱

"So Mom told you she's studying to become a Buddhist?" Renee said as she chomped on her third slice of pizza.

"You're kidding." Regina put aside her book and looked at Renee. "When did she decide that? She just became a Jehovah's Witness a couple of months ago."

"Yeah, but she didn't want to go around knocking on people's doors anymore."

"So, let's see, in the last seven years my sister has been a born-again Christian, a Hare Krishna, a Hebrew Israelite, a Muslim, and a Jehovah's Witness, and now a Buddhist," Regina said with a laugh. "I guess she's covering all bases."

"Yeah, I really thought the Muslim thing was gonna stick. But she got all bent outta shape after the World Trade Center attack."

"That's so ridiculous." Regina shook her head. "Blaming all Muslims because of the attack. It's like turning your back on Christianity because the Germans tried to conquer Europe."

"Yeah, I told her that, too. But you know Mom. 'Sides, I think she was just looking for an excuse to make a change. I mean, she was Muslim for like three years. That's a record for her. I'm just waiting for her to decide to become Jewish," Renee said with a giggle.

Regina shook her head and said nothing. She wasn't going to share it with Renee, but Regina's opinion was that as long as Brenda didn't go back to worshipping the crack pipe, she could claim any God she wanted. She'd wasted eight years of her life on that junk, and when they found out Brenda was pregnant, they had prayed to any God they thought would listen that Renee wouldn't be another crack baby. When their mother died, it was left up to thirteen-year-old Regina to raise Brenda's infant child while Brenda roamed the streets—lying, stealing, and selling her body to make enough money for her next hit. It took Regina being shot and almost killed for Brenda to snap out of her crack-addicted haze and finally become a mother to her then eight-year-old child. Regina looked over at Renee and smiled. *But still, she's like my child, too. My first baby.*

"What are you smiling about, Aunt Gina?"

"Nothing. Are you spending the night?"

"You asked me that already, remember? Liz's gonna be picking me up in about a half hour, and we're gonna go to a party in the Bronx," Renee answered with a mouth full of pizza. "Aunt Gina, I know you're gonna give me the Mustang when you get your new car, right?"

"Who said I'm getting a new car?"

"I ain't stupid. I saw all them car catalogs in the kitchen. What kind you gonna get?" Renee's eyes suddenly widened. "Ooh, get the Acura. A gold joint. That way I can borrow it sometime!"

"Girl, please. First off, didn't I just tell you about saying 'ain't'? Second off, I'm probably going to get a Camry. And third, I don't know how you're talking about getting my old car or borrowing my new one when you don't even have a driver's license." Regina tried to paste a frown on her face, but Renee seemed to see right through it.

"So you are thinking about giving me the Mustang, huh?" she said excitedly.

"I didn't say anything like that," Regina retorted.

"Aw, come on! That could be my graduation present! My early graduation present!" Renee got up from the floor and plopped down on the couch next to Regina. "Aw, come on, Aunt Gina. Please?" She laid her head on Regina's shoulder. "Pretty please?"

"You are such a baby, Ray-Ray." Regina pushed Renee's head away. "We'll see, okay? And that's all I'm going to say right now."

"So then—," Renee started excitedly.

"Ah!" Regina pointed her finger at Renee. "One more word, and I'm not even going to consider giving you the car."

"Okay, okay, not another word," Renee promised as she threw her arms around Regina's neck and kissed her on the cheek. "But, just so you know, if you put a banging stereo system in there, I'll consider that my early 'congratulations on getting into college' present."

"You are a mess. Didn't I tell you—"

*Ring.*

"I'll get it." Renee jumped up from the couch. "Hello," she said after grabbing the receiver. "Oh hey, Uncle Charles! . . . Guess what? . . . I got a 1500 on my SATs! . . . For real." She pulled the receiver away from her ear. "Aunt Gina, would you please tell him I got a 1500?"

"She got a 1500," Regina obediently shouted loud enough for Charles to hear.

"See, I told you!" Renee said triumphantly into the telephone. "No, she's not lying for me." She pulled the telephone away from her ear again. "Are you lying for me, Aunt Gina?"

"No, I'm not lying for her," Regina shouted as she stretched her legs out on the couch and laid her head on the armrest.

"And I'm thinking about going to Temple, so I can babysit Camille for you when you have her in Philadelphia," Renee said into the telephone. "Yes, I am thinking about going to Temple . . . Yes, I am." She removed the receiver from her ear again. "Aunt Gina, will you tell him that I—"

"Give me the damn telephone, Ray-Ray," Regina said wearily.

"Hey, Charles," she said after Renee complied. "What are you up to?"

"Not much, baby," a husky voice answered. "Oops. I'm sorry. I'm not supposed to call you baby, right?"

"Right." Regina smiled to herself as she twirled a lock of hair. They'd been divorced almost four years now, and in every telephone conversation since, he said the same thing, and she gave him the same answer. It was a running joke between them now. She hated to admit it, but she'd probably be upset if it ended. The joke, that is.

"So then, how's my other baby? Is she all excited about her birthday next week?"

"Please. Every morning she gets up and asks if it's her birthday yet," Regina answered.

"That's my little impatient girl." Charles laughed. "Listen, I put a couple of hundred extra dollars in this month's alimony check to help out with her party. And guess what my mother's getting her."

"I don't even want to guess," Regina said dryly.

"A pony. Can you believe that? She didn't give me a pony when I was a kid."

"A pony? Where the hell is Camille going to keep a pony in Harlem?" Regina grimaced. Leave it to Mother Whitfield to do something stupid and extravagant.

"Don't get mad at *me*. I tried to talk her out of it," Charles said with another laugh. "But they're going to keep it at their place in Chestnut Hill, and Camille can ride it when she comes out to visit. Let me speak to her for a minute, okay? I'm at the airport, so I'm on my cell phone, and my battery's about to go dead."

"Ooh, sorry. She's spending the night over at Tamika and David's. I didn't know you were going to call. Where are you heading, anyway?"

"Mississippi, stumping for John Fennell. He's trying to get the Democratic nomination for the U.S. Senate next year, and he's starting his campaign early. Fat chance, of course. Can you imagine Mississippi electing a black senator? Not gonna happen."

"So why bother going out there?"

"Strategy, my dear."

"And what are you strategizing?"

"Well . . ." Charles paused. "Well, I have an idea that I'm kicking around, but I want to talk to you about it on a serious level before I make any kind of decision. I'm coming to New York next week. How about dinner?"

"Hmm, sounds important. Can't you just give me a hint?"

"I'd rather not."

"Oh, Charles, come on."

"Really, Regina, I'd rather wait until we can talk in person. How about dinner next Thursday?"

Regina sucked her teeth. "Yeah, I guess I'm free."

"All right, I've got to go. They're announcing my flight."

"Okay," Regina said, anticipating Charles's next, inevitable question.

"Is it okay if I tell you I still love you?"

"Nope," she answered lightly. "See you Thursday, okay?"

"Okay, Regina. Take care of yourself."

*Damn,* she thought as she hung up. Now she had to wait almost a week to find out this big secret. And she'd forgotten to ask him about Robert. He, David, and Charles had been best friends for years. Charles hadn't said anything to her about it, but she'd gotten the impression that he and Robert, who was still in Philadelphia, had begun to drift apart. But he had to know Robert was moving to New York, she thought.

"Y'all didn't even talk about me?"

Renee's exasperated question jolted Regina from her thoughts. "Um, no, he had to get off the telephone."

"Well, y'all had time to talk about everything else," Renee huffed. "I guess I'm just not important anymore."

Smiling, Regina got up and walked over to Renee, who was slinging her backpack over her shoulder.

"Stop being silly, Ray-Ray," she said, straightening the ball cap on the girl's head. "You know you're my girl. And you know Charles is crazy about you, too."

"I know," Renee said reluctantly. She paused for a moment and looked down. "Aunt Gina, I need to talk to you about something. But, I mean, just between us, you know? You can't tell my mother or anything."

"Well, sure, honey . . . wait a minute." Regina took a few steps back and looked at her niece, especially eyeing the over-size sweatshirt. "Renee, please tell me you're not pregnant."

"What?" Renee put her hands on her hips. "Now, see, Aunt Gina. Why you wanna try and go there? No, I ain't pregnant! I can't believe you asked me something like that."

"Okay, I'm sorry," Regina said soothingly. "What do you need to talk about?"

Their conversation was interrupted by someone leaning on a car horn outside the house.

"That's Liz." Renee gave her aunt a quick peck on the cheek. "I gotta go."

"But you said you had to talk to me about something important," Regina protested to Renee's back.

"I do, but I'll do it another time," Renee said, closing the door behind her.

*Damn*, Regina thought as she walked back to the couch and sat down. *Now what am I going to do for the rest of the night?* She should have started working on one of her articles as soon as she walked through the door, but she used Renee's presence as an excuse to put it off. Truth was she simply didn't feel like working. And she didn't feel like reading her book anymore. She didn't know what she felt like doing. She was actually feeling a little lonely.

She glanced at the clock. Almost nine, Camille's bedtime. She reached for the telephone to call Tamika and wish her daughter a good night, but the call went straight through to voice mail. Tamika's son, twelve-year-old Darren, was probably online playing Internet video games, Regina figured. She considered hopping into the car and going over there but decided against it. Maybe she'd head over to Yvonne's and hang out with her and Puddin' but decided against that, too. She wanted company, but those two were probably high as a kite by now and would be loud and silly. It was fun sometimes—most times, as a matter of fact—but she wanted something a little more sedate at the moment. *Damn,* she thought, *it would have been nice if Renee had stayed around for the night.*

Maybe she should call Brenda. It was about time for their once-a-week telephone call, anyway. With Brenda living in Queens and Regina in Harlem, and neither being crazy about the other's area of the city, they probably didn't see each other as much as they should. To be honest, Regina had to admit that their lifestyles also had something to do with their staying apart—and there might have been another reason, too.

Still, it was nice talking to Brenda on a regular basis. Yeah, she decided, she'd give her big sister a call. She reached for the telephone, but just before she could pick up the receiver, it rang.

"Hey, Aunt Gina. It's me again," Renee's voice greeted her.

"You okay, sweetie?" Regina said hopefully. Maybe she changed her mind and was coming back over.

"I'm fine, Aunt Gina. But I just wanted to tell you that . . . um . . . that I'm . . ."

"You're what?" Regina asked suspiciously. *Shit, she really is pregnant.*

"Aunt Gina, I like girls. I'm a lesbian," Renee said in a rush.

"What?" Regina shouted into the telephone. "What the hell are you talking about?"

"Oh man. I knew you was gonna be mad." Renee's voice had turned into a whine. "I gotta go. I'll talk to you tomorrow. Or soon. Or something. I gotta go."

"Ray-Ray, wait!" Regina said, but the phone went dead.

Regina sat on the couch in shock, still holding the telephone in her hand. Puddin' killed a man. Yvonne was getting back with a man whom she almost committed suicide over. Brenda was a Buddhist. Charles had some big secret. And her eighteen-year-old niece had just announced she was gay.

"Fuck it," Regina said as she got up from the couch and headed upstairs. "I'm going to bed before I find out that Tamika's really a man."

# chapter three

I don't know, Tamika. I guess I'm in shock is all," Regina said as she put her hand over her eyes to partially block out the sun shining down on Frederick Douglass Boulevard. "It's not that I have a problem with Ray-Ray being a lesbian, but I just wasn't expecting it when she told me last night. I mean, she's only eighteen—how does she even know for sure herself?"

"Well, has she ever had a boyfriend?"

"Not really. I mean, she's been out on dates with a couple of boys but nothing serious as far as I can tell," Regina said with a sigh.

"Does she have a girlfriend?"

"Hell if I know!" Regina threw her hands up in the air. "I'm telling you, Tamika. She dropped the news and then got off the telephone before I could ask her anything. When I called her at home this morning, Brenda said she'd already left for her part-time job." She squinted her eyes a moment, then shouted out, "Darren, don't walk so fast if you're going to hold Camille's hand. You're going to make her fall."

"I'm okay, Mommy," Camille called in a little singsong voice.

"Darren, slow down. You're getting too far ahead of us," Tamika called out.

"Okay, Ma," the boy answered sullenly.

Regina smiled. Tamika was such a good mother, insisting that she and Darren walk Regina and Camille to 125th Street, saying that she and her son both would benefit from a little fresh air. She was right: Darren did need to get out more. His ten-year-old sister, Sissy, had begged David to take her with him to the office, but if it were up to Darren, he would spend the whole day in the house playing video games. And now he couldn't wait to get back home to play more.

"So," Tamika said, turning back to Regina, "Ray-Ray has a part-time job?"

"Yeah, she's working as a security guard at Lord & Taylor."

"Really?" Tamika started to giggle.

"What's so funny?" Regina looked at Tamika in puzzlement, then she, too, began too giggle.

"It is kind of ironic, huh? I used to boost from there to support Ray-Ray when she was a baby, and now she's the security guard." Regina shook her head. It seemed so long ago, she thought, that other life.

Regina's mother had raised her to be "a good West Indian girl," but when she died, and Regina was left to take care of one-year-old Renee on her own, she had to find some way to support them, and no legitimate employer was hiring thirteen-year-olds—at least none that paid enough for her to pay the rent and utilities and buy food and clothing. She had lucked up one day when she went into Lord & Taylor for a job. She didn't get the job, but she met a young white girl there, Krystal, and the two became friends—and coworkers of a sort, once Krystal taught her to boost clothing. Regina was making money hand over fist stealing from fancy boutiques and high-end depart-

ment stores. Until both she and Krystal were busted at Bloom-
ingdale's.

She'd gotten off with probation, since she was only sixteen
at the time and had no record. But since Krystal was nineteen
and had been caught twice before, she was sentenced to three
years in prison. It was then that Regina decided to switch ca-
reers, becoming what she liked to call "a professional girlfriend." Meaning that she graced the arm and shared the bed of
big-time drug dealers and gamblers who didn't mind shower-
ing her with gifts and throwing money her way. When one got
tired of supporting her, she'd find another to take his place. It
was going well until someone put a contract out on one of her
sugar daddies, and she had the misfortune of being with him
when the contract was fulfilled. Her boyfriend was killed in
front of her eyes, and she'd been shot in the shoulder. It might
have been worse if Tamika hadn't rushed out the building just
then, forcing the assailant to run off, but it was enough to
make Regina realize that she had to make some serious
changes. After Brenda cleaned herself up and took in Renee,
Regina got her high school equivalency diploma and moved to
Philadelphia, where she attended Temple University and ob-
tained a journalism degree before returning to New York and
starting a freelance writing career.

And now Renee was working at the store where Regina's
shoplifting career began. "Life has a way of coming full circle,"
Regina mused aloud.

"Sure does." Tamika nodded. "In the most delightful way."

"So what did your sister say about Ray-Ray being gay,
Regina?"

"Huh? Oh, I didn't say anything about it because I got the
impression that Ray-Ray hadn't told her yet." Regina chuckled. "Brenda's going to have a fucking fit. You know how she
is."

"Oh but don't I?" Tamika said. "I remember how she used
to get on Ray-Ray for wearing clothes that had animals in the

print, because it was against Islamic tradition. And you know Muslims don't be playing that homosexuality stuff."

"She's not Muslim anymore."

"Oh, that's right. She's a . . ." Tamika's eyebrows furrowed in thought. "Right! Right! She's a Jehovah's Witness now. Well, I'm guessing they're not too keen on homosexuality, either, huh?"

"Don't know, and it doesn't matter. Brenda's a Buddhist this week."

"You're kidding."

"Nope."

Tamika shrugged. "Well, better her worshipping Buddha than a crack pipe."

"I thought the exact same thing. But then, you know, great minds think alike," Regina said with a grin. "Speaking of great minds, how are things at school?"

"They say the first year of medical school is supposed to be the hardest, and I hope that's true, because this stuff is killing me." Tamika sighed. "I've always been good at biology and chemistry, but I ain't never seen some of the stuff they're throwing at us now."

"But you can handle it," Regina said as she gently placed her hand on Tamika's shoulder. "Look at how far you've come already. From a high school dropout working as a supermarket cashier to medical student in only five years. Who would have thought our little sweet giggly Tamika would someday be studying to be a pediatrician?"

"Missy, missy. We do your hair real quick," a woman wearing colorful African attire said in a Senegalese accent as she motioned Tamika toward her small storefront with posters of women wearing cornrows. "We have two people do your head, make it real quick. You want microbraids? Box braids. We real quick. Very cheap."

"Thanks, but no," Regina said with a polite smile as she continued walking. "I've been considering getting micros, though," she told Tamika as they crossed the street. "Maybe it's time to get rid of the perm and go natural. Of course, I just bought a perm yesterday, which I plan to put in my hair tonight, so I obviously haven't decided for sure to go natural."

"Mommy, can I get some money to buy a Popsicle?" Camille said, running back toward her mother. "And can I get enough money for Darren, too?"

"Darren," Tamika said reprovingly.

"I ain't ask her to ask her mom," Darren said defensively.

"It's okay," Regina said, pulling a dollar from her purse and handing it to Darren. "I can treat both of you."

"Um, Aunt Gina," Darren said sheepishly, "they're sixty cents each."

"Well, you can dig in your pocket and come up with the other twenty cents," Tamika said sharply.

"But, Ma! I was just—"

Tamika's eyes narrowed. "Boy, don't you play with me."

"Yes, Ma." Darren poked out his mouth, turned around, and stalked off into the candy store, with Camille skipping behind him.

"Remember when Popsicles only cost ten cents?" Regina asked while they waited outside the store.

Tamika nodded. "Yeah, and we used to get the twin pops so we could break it down the middle and share it. And P.S., you know your four-year-old daughter has a crush on my twelve-year-old son, right?"

"That's pretty obvious." Regina pointed at the sidewalk. "Watch that dog shit, Tamika. I don't know why people have dogs in the city. All this dog shit is why we have so much pollution in Harlem."

"I don't like stepping over dog crap, but I really don't think it contributes to pollution," Tamika said as she sidestepped the brown pile. "After all, manure is nature's best fertilizer."

"Yeah, right. I guess the guy that let his dog shit there on the sidewalk was hoping to grow roses. Ooh!" Regina snapped

"Gina, she's going to have a fit." Tamika shook her head. "You know how crazy she was about that guy."

"Yeah, don't think I don't know it. Remember, we almost broke up our friendship over him," Regina said with a snort. "She was so stupid over him she actually thought I played her. Thought I knew he was married and didn't tell her."

"Yeah," Tamika said sadly. "I remember."

"Well, you know we gotta tell her," Regina said with a sigh. "What you doing tonight? Maybe we can go over there."

"I don't think I'm doing anything. David should be getting back from the office by about four o'clock, since it's Saturday. How about, say, six?"

"Yeah, that'll work." Regina peered into the candy store. "Let me go in here for a minute so I can get a newspaper."

Regina's brow furrowed as she walked into the store and saw Darren off to the side reading a comic book. She had to look around a few seconds before she spotted Camille, off in a corner talking to a middle-aged man who was wearing dark sunglasses and chewing a toothpick.

"Excuse me," Regina said as she snatched Camille by the hand and pulled her out the store. "Didn't I tell you about talking to strangers?" she said, kneeling down in front of her daughter once they were outside.

"But, Mommy, he was just telling me that I looked like—"

"Camille, did you hear me? I mean, never, never talk to strangers. Especially strange men."

"What happened?" Tamika asked in a worried voice.

"Darren is in there reading comic books, and Camille was off in a corner talking to some man she doesn't know." Regina's lip curled as she talked.

"What? I'm going to kill that boy," Tamika said before stomping off into the store.

"But, Mommy, for real, he was just saying—" Camille began again.

her fingers. "Talking about crushes, that reminds m
who's moving to New York?"

"Who?"

"Robert!"

"Robert who?"

"That Robert. Old married Robert who Yvonne w
love with. The one she almost killed herself over. Yo
Charles and David's friend in Philadelphia." Regina
pushed Tamika's shoulder. "According to Yvonne, h
left his wife, quit his job, and is moving to New York

"Oh, girl, stop!" Tamika's mouth opened wide in a
ment. "You know you're lying."

"I'm only telling you what Yvonne told me," Reg
with an exaggerated shrug.

"Well, honey, she obviously didn't tell you ever
Tamika leaned forward. "Because Robert didn't finally
wife, she threw his butt out. He didn't quit his job, hi
fired!"

"What!" Regina's eyes widened. "Girl, stop the ma

"I'm not kidding." Tamika continued, "David wa
me just the other day. But that's not even the worst of

"What do you mean? There's something else?"

Tamika paused and looked around as if to make sur
was within hearing range. "Gina, Robert is strung out

"No! Robert's a crackhead?" Regina asked in a hoar
per.

"Honey, worse! He's dusty."

"What!" Regina almost shouted. "Robert's smokin
dust? You're killing me here!"

"I kid you not. He called David to see if he could
partner with him in his law practice, and at first Da
going to do it, but then when he called down to Ph
found out the real deal."

"Shit," Regina said slowly. "We gotta pull Yvonne
because I know she doesn't know."

"He was just saying that she looked like someone he used to know," a man's voice cut in.

Regina stood up, trying to make herself look taller than five feet two.

"I beg your pardon?" she said coldly as her hand tightened around Camille's arm.

"I beg your pardon, huh?" The man chuckled. "You always was polite, though."

"Pardon me?" Regina said in a more cautious tone. The voice was familiar, she thought, but she couldn't place him. Then the man smiled, revealing a gold tooth with an embedded diamond. She gave a sharp intake of breath and released Camille's arm. "Little Joe," she said breathlessly.

"In the flesh," the man said with a quick smile. He bent down and chucked Camille under the chin. "Didn't I tell you that you look like a young woman I used to know?"

"You mean my mommy?" Camille said in an amazed voice.

"Yep. Your mommy." Little Joe straightened up, took off his sunglasses, and looked Regina straight in the eyes. "Prettiest girl I ever met in my life. My own little Satin Doll."

"I can't believe it's you," Regina said slowly. She couldn't help herself. She touched his arm to make sure he was real. He was. For some reason, tears sprang to her eyes and her knees began to weaken. His closely cropped hair and short beard were snowy white rather than the salt-and-pepper she remembered, but his face looked as smooth and his dark brown eyes were just as piercing as when they first met when she was fifteen. "When did you get out?" she finally stammered.

"Day before yesterday."

"But how . . ."

"It took sixteen fucking—excuse me," Little Joe interrupted himself as he looked down at Camille, who was staring into his mouth. "Sixteen years and a good two hundred thousand dollars, but my lawyer finally found an appeal that stuck. So here I am."

"So here you are," Regina said softly.

"And here you are." Little Joe stroked her cheek, causing Regina to blush. "Still smooth as satin," he said in almost a whisper. "My Satin Doll. Remember?"

"I remember," she said quickly as she grabbed Camille's hand in an attempt to keep from floating into the clouds.

"You've got a pretty little girl here," Little Joe said, chucking Camille under the chin again. "How long have you been married?"

"Oh, um, I was married. Only two years," Regina said. "I'm divorced now."

Little Joe looked down at Camille again, then leaned into Regina and whispered into her ear, "Lucky me."

"Everything okay?" Tamika's voice rang out before Regina could think of a response to Little Joe's statement.

"Everything's fine," Little Joe said, his eyes never leaving Regina's face.

"Tamika, you remember Little Joe—I mean, Joe Blayton—don't you?" Regina said quickly.

Tamika's eyes narrowed as she looked Little Joe up and down, and seconds passed before her face registered recognition. "Oh my God! Little Joe! Didn't you have the club on Lenox Avenue? Next to the Laundromat, right?"

"Yeah." Little Joe nodded and extended his hand. "JoJazz. And I remember you, too. You always was the sweetie in the bunch. And what were your other running buddies' names? One was Yvonne, right? And the other . . . what was her name?"

"Puddin'," Regina said with a laugh.

"Yeah, how could I forget her?" Little Joe responded with a laugh of his own. "That was one wild little girl."

"And she grew up to be one wild woman," Regina said.

"Dag, Little Joe, it's so good to see you again." Tamika shook his hand. "But I thought you were—"

"We covered that already," Regina interrupted. "I'll catch

you up later, okay?" she added, giving an almost imperceptible nod toward Darren.

"Oh of course," Tamika agreed. "Listen, Regina, why don't I go ahead and take Camille home with me and Darren, and you can pick her up later?"

"I wanna go with my mommy." Camille moved in closer to Regina, hugging her leg.

"Isn't that cute? She wants to go with her mommy." Little Joe gave a short laugh. "Well, maybe she'll let me borrow her mommy later on? Maybe for dinner?"

"That would be nice," Regina said demurely.

⌇

"Dag, prison must have suited Little Joe," Tamika said after she and Regina had settled on the couch in Regina's living room. "He's looking good. He musta been one of the guys who spent all his time working out. How old is he? About fifty?"

Regina shrugged. "Something like that. He was in good shape even before he went in. He used to take up karate and yoga. But his arms and chest are bigger than I remember, so you're probably right."

"Yeah, he's got a physique on him, and he can still dress his ass off, too," Tamika said. "Too bad he went back in the store, I wanted to see what he was driving. Didn't he used to have a Bentley?"

"He had a couple of cars. My favorite was his little red Porsche convertible. Back then all I cared about was whether a man had nice cars and nice money."

"And he obviously had both, but that's not all you liked about him, was it?"

Regina looked at her friend. "Why do you say that?"

"Girl, you're crazy about that man . . . even now. It's evident all over your face." Tamika started to giggle. "And it was evident on his face that he's crazy about you, too."

"You think so?" Regina said excitedly.

"Oh heck yeah. I thought he was gonna drop to his knees and ask you to marry him, the way he was looking at you," Tamika said with a wave of her hand. "Of course, I know you're not going to let it go there. I mean, like I said, I can see you really like him, but I know you're not really serious about going out with him."

"Why not?"

Tamika's jaw dropped. "You know good and well why not, Regina. That man was one of the biggest dealers in Harlem."

"That was twenty years ago. You don't know what he's up to these days." Regina crossed her arms and leaned back in her seat.

"And neither do you," Tamika answered. "That man was in the life for at least thirty years before he went away. I'm betting that's all he knows. And you've come way too far to get caught up in that shit again. Look at you." Tamika waved her hand in Regina's direction. "You're a successful writer. You were married to a U.S. congressman. You're a mother to a wonderful little girl. And you're going to tell me you're going to backtrack now because of some guy you had a crush on fifteen years ago?"

Regina tapped Tamika on the shoulder. "Excuse me, but you do remember who you're talking to, right? I mean, yeah, sixteen years ago Little Joe was dealing, but sixteen years ago I was boosting for a living, snorting more coke than kids eat candy, and spreading my legs for any man who had enough money to show me a good time. So if I was able to turn my life around after all that shit, why should it be hard for me to believe Little Joe could, too?"

"Regina," Tamika said through narrowed eyes, "you're my girl, and always been my girl, and you know I've always had your back. But I see you about to go down a road that you've already traveled. And if I remember correctly, that journey weren't shit."

"Tamika . . ."

"I said my piece, and I'm not saying anything more," Tamika said, throwing her hands up in front of her as if in surrender. "What did you always used to say when me and Yvonne or Puddin' hooked up with someone you thought was bad for us? If you love him, I adore him."

"Well, I got that from Mama Tee," Regina said defensively. "And remember, I didn't say anything about loving him, Tamika."

Tamika shrugged and turned away. "Well, you know, I guess I've always held out hope that you and Charles would get back together."

"Oh yeah, well, that's not going to ever happen," Regina said dismissively. "And I'm not going to get my hopes up about Little Joe. I mean, shit, like you said, I don't even know what he's into these days. I'm not trying to get caught out there like that."

Tamika nodded.

"And Little Joe always had a million women, and a wife, too, now that I think about it." She snapped her fingers. "Damn! I don't know how I could have forgotten to ask if he was still married."

"Maybe," Tamika said gently, "because you didn't want to know."

"Go to hell, Tamika," Regina said as she threw a magazine across the room.

"Yeah," Tamika said, picking up the magazine and flipping through it. "I love you, too."

# chapter four

"What the hell are you doing here?" Regina asked Puddin' as she and Tamika entered the living room of Yvonne's spacious Convent Avenue apartment. "I thought you were going to the Usher concert to snag yourself a new sugar daddy. Or should I say sugar baby, you cradle robber?"

Regina took a look around the room. A brand-new money-green leather couch, trimmed in chrome, sat to the left of the room, and across from it were a love seat and high-back swivel chair. On the wall, where Yvonne used to have a picture of her twelve-year-old son, Johnny, was a green and beige tapestry, which matched the Oriental rug on the floor. "Damn, Yvonne, when did you get all this new shit? And what did you do?"

"Fuck you and pipe down," Puddin' said as she aimed the remote control at the television and turned up the volume. "*Boyz N the Hood* is on."

"You're missing the concert for a stupid movie you've seen a thousand times?" Regina asked as she slipped off her coat. "Why don't you just invest ten bucks and buy the damn DVD?"

"Shut up a minute. It's getting ready to go off, and we can talk then," Puddin' spat at her.

"God, please leave her be," Yvonne said as she sat in the swivel chair and twirled around. "She's been glued in front of the TV hissing at me to shut up ever since it came on. You know how she is about that damn movie."

Regina turned to her. "The place sure looks different from when I was just here like a week ago. When did all this happen?"

"Yeah, Yvonne, when did you get this new furniture and stuff?" Tamika asked, running her hand over a four-foot-high mint-colored sculptured dog. "It must have cost you a fortune."

"It was delivered today, as a matter of fact," Yvonne said nonchalantly. "I just got a raise, so I decided to redo the place."

"It's beautiful, but it's a little, you know, well . . ." Tamika hesitated. "It doesn't really look like you. You've always gone for the traditional, homey kind of stuff. I never thought you'd go for the sleek modern kind of decor."

*Nope,* Regina thought, *but I'm betting Robert does. She probably ordered all this furniture as soon as she found out he was relocating to New York. I wonder if she told him that he could move in with her.*

"I just wanted to make a change." Yvonne shrugged, avoiding everyone's eyes. "Nothing wrong with that, is there?"

Regina started to answer her, but just then Puddin' clicked off the television.

"Okay, now I can talk," she said to Regina as she threw the remote down on the smoky-glass and chrome coffee table.

"Damn it, Puddin', if you break that glass, you're going to pay for it," Yvonne snapped.

Puddin' ignored her and continued to address Regina. "Like I was saying, I'm skipping the concert, but I'm gonna make the after-party. I'ma roll up in there about two a.m."

"So you're really serious? You're telling me you skipped an Usher concert to watch a movie that you've already watched fifty million times?" Regina chuckled. "I don't know what's up with you and that stupid movie."

"First of all," Puddin' said, stretching her long legs over the arm of the love seat, "*Boyz N the Hood* is probably the best ghetto film—scratch that, the best *film*—ever made, so you just can all that 'stupid movie' shit. Second, I'm not going down to Madison Square Garden to hear music, I'm going on a mission. I'll make my entrance at the after-party about two, blow Usher's mind about three, and be sporting his platinum card tomorrow night around seven."

"Well, I wish you luck," Regina said as she sat down on the couch next to Tamika and took off her shoes. She curled her toes on the Oriental rug. *Nice,* she thought, *and damn expensive.*

Puddin' stood up and stretched, then bent down and picked up a joint that had been lying in the ashtray, lit it up, and took a deep drag. "Well, I gotta split so I can change into a 'come over here and fuck me' outfit," she said through an exhale of wispy smoke. "I'll see ya'll tomorrow or something."

Regina looked up. "Wait a minute, I gotta ask you something real quick."

"What's that?" Puddin' said as she started putting her things in her big shoulder bag.

"You heard anything about Little Joe? Me and Tamika ran into him today on Frederick Douglass Boulevard. I didn't even know he was out."

"Get the fuck outta here! When did he get out?" Puddin' exclaimed. "Shit, I wish I'da known. I bet his buddies gave him a phat-ass coming-home party. Damn, and I missed it. I bet there was enough coke there to make it look like a fucking Harlem snowstorm. Is he dealing yet?"

Regina shrugged. "I was hoping you could tell me. I couldn't really get into it with him 'cause Camille and Darren was with us. But I gave him my number, so I'll get the 411 when he calls."

"You gonna start fucking around with him again?" Puddin'

asked. "Good," she continued before Regina could answer. "That motherfucker used to party us up in the day. And I could use some partying up."

Tamika giggled. "Girl, your whole life is a damn party, Puddin'."

"And may the party never end," Puddin' said with a grin.

"Naw, I don't think I'm gonna start messing with him again," Regina said.

"So why'd you give him your damn digits?" Yvonne asked teasingly.

"Well, you know he's an old friend," Regina said defensively. "I wouldn't mind getting together with him and, you know, catch up on what's going on in our lives."

"And?" Yvonne asked.

"And what?"

"And what else?" Yvonne replied. "You *know* I know how crazy you were about Little Joe. And he couldn't get enough of him some Regina." She turned to Tamika. "Remember the time we was all hanging out with him and Regina said she wanted a piña colada? He drove us to the airport and flew us to Puerto Rico to have piña coladas on the beach."

"Yeah, and if law had found out, they woulda put him under the jail," Tamika piped in. "What was we? Like sixteen or something?"

"Fifteen," Regina said. "By the time we were sixteen they put him under the jail on that conspiracy charge. Life without parole."

"Yeah, and you cried for like a whole week. Stopped eating and everything," Yvonne said.

Regina's eyes fell to the carpet as she remembered. She was fifteen when she went from boosting to support herself and Ray-Ray to using men for the same purpose. They all knew what she wanted, and they gave it freely, and although she never stayed long with one who treated her badly, none had really treated her well. The usual routine was they'd take her out to eat, party her up, and then take her to a hotel and screw her brains out, then slip her some money for her time and her body. Spending the whole night was never an option, and many took her to the hotel on St. Nicholas Avenue where the rooms had mirrors on the wall and were rented by the hour. It took a while for her to get used to it, but she did, telling herself it was only a job, and most people didn't like their jobs. All of the affairs were short, none lasting more than a few months. It would end when they got tired of her or she found a mark with longer money. But then she met Little Joe.

She had gone to a new club, JoJazz, on Lenox Avenue to scope the joint out for potential paychecks. She was there barely fifteen minutes when a man sidled up to her and asked if he could buy her a drink. It took only a quick look up and down at him, with his cheap clothes and bulging bloodshot eyes, for her to politely decline and turn away. The man then tugged on her shoulder and pulled a slightly bulging folded one-hundred-dollar bill from his pocket.

"Why don't you come on in the back with me and do some blow?" he said.

She again politely turned him down and tried to get the eye of the bartender so she could order a refill of her soda.

"Well, fuck you, then," the bloodshot-eyed man said.

She ignored him, but then Bloodshot took his drink and threw it on her, ruining the red suede pantsuit she'd boosted before she got busted. Before she could say anything, or pull the knife she always carried in her pocketbook, Bloodshot was surrounded by two burly men and a smaller dapper man wearing a gray sharkskin suit.

It was the little man who spoke. "Get the fuck out my bar."

Bloodshot opened his mouth to say something but quickly changed his mind when the smaller man pulled his jacket back a little, revealing a shoulder holster.

"You okay?" the dapper man asked her after Bloodshot had left. She nodded as she took a good look at him. His copper-colored face was unwrinkled, though his closely cropped hair was salt-and-pepper, as were his eyebrows. His small, slightly slanted eyes were dark brown, almost black, and were so piercing that she dropped her gaze. It was when she looked back up that his smile revealed a diamond-embellished gold tooth. That's also when she noticed that he seemed to have a halo around him, as if he were an angel. It made her feel comfortable and flustered at the same time.

"I'm fine," she told him.

"Excuse me, Little Joe," a tall burly man said as he tapped the dapper man on his shoulder. "You've got a long-distance call in the back."

"Cool," Little Joe said, though he was still looking at Regina. His gaze was cool and appraising, and made Regina a little uncomfortable, though she tried to act like she wasn't bothered. Finally, Little Joe smiled, once again revealing his expensive tooth, then turned and walked away. "Come to the club tomorrow afternoon," he said over his shoulder, "and I'll take you shopping for a new pantsuit."

That was it. She officially became his girl. While most of the men she'd been with would give her money, Little Joe did that and also spent big money on her. He delighted in taking her to fancy restaurants downtown, Broadway plays, and luxury hotels in midtown. Her mother, before she died, had always told her to act with class, and she did with Little Joe. He brought her around people with class and watched in amusement as she tried to emulate them. He was the one who turned her on to jazz, taking her to piano bars in Greenwich Village and jazz concerts in the Catskills, and told her that she reminded him of the Satin Doll in Duke Ellington's famous song. She never introduced him to Renee, but he was the only man she told about her precious toddler. After that, whenever he took her clothes shopping, he also made sure she bought clothes and toys for Renee.

Little Joe had money. Big money. She had once seen him

lose sixteen thousand dollars on a single craps throw without blinking an eye. But she knew never to ask how he got his money, and he never offered details. It was fast-assed Puddin' who told her that Little Joe was a big-time heroin dealer. Just a few weeks afterward the man he had introduced to her as his business partner—Natty Jones—was featured on the cover of *Time* magazine as the biggest drug dealer in Harlem. Two months later Little Joe was picked up on conspiracy charges, and she was back to scoping out clubs to find men to survive.

"Yeah," Regina said, turning to Yvonne. "I cried like hell. But I got over it, didn't I?"

"I don't know," Tamika said, looking Regina directly in the eyes. "Seems to me you never did get over him."

"Ain't that something?" Puddin' said as she reached for her jacket. "Regina getting back with cash-money Little Joe, and Yvonne getting back with lame-ass Robert."

Regina and Tamika shared an uncomfortable look, then both glanced over at Yvonne, awaiting her response to Puddin's remark. Regina's eyes widened when Yvonne simply shot Puddin' a dirty look and said nothing. *Damn! Yvonne musta fessed up to Puddin' that she's gonna get back with him.* She cleared her throat and looked at Tamika again before speaking.

"Hey, Yvonne, you know the word out is that Robert didn't quit his job, but that he got fired."

"Yeah, well, whatever," Yvonne said as she reached for the remote control on the coffee table, then clicked the television back on.

Regina nudged Tamika. "You're not even going to ask why?" she asked Yvonne.

"What the fuck do I care?" came the answer.

Regina noticed that Puddin' had dropped her shoulder bag to the floor and sat back down on the love seat. "What's going on?" she asked as she crossed her long legs.

Regina took a deep breath. "Yvonne, you're not going to believe this, but Robert's smoking dust."

"Get the fuck outta here," Puddin' said in almost a whisper.

"What?" Yvonne threw the remote on the coffee table. "Where did you hear some stupid shit like that?"

It was Tamika who answered. "David told me about a week ago. And just so you know, he didn't leave his wife, she threw him out after she found out he drained his kids' trust funds." Tamika wrung her hands as she talked. "I didn't think to mention it to you because I didn't know you two were still in contact."

"Oh come on," Yvonne said with a wave of her hand, "that bitch is probably just making all that shit up because she's mad he finally kicked her to the curb."

"Naw, sorry, Yvonne, but I called Charles and verified it this afternoon," Regina piped in. "He said that most of Robert's friends had cut him off because he was getting crazy with the stuff. And rumor is that his law firm fired him because he embezzled about sixty thousand."

"Sixty grand?" Puddin' let out a whistle. "That's a whole helluva lot of dust. You sure that's all he's using?"

"Well, this is the first I've heard of any of this shit." Yvonne slapped her hands on the arms of her swivel chair and started swaying around. "And I'm not saying I don't believe you guys, but at the same time, I'm just finding all this really, really hard to believe. I mean, I musta talked to him a hundred times over the last two weeks, and he sounded perfectly fine to me. And I know Robert takes a drink every now and again, but I ain't never known him to do any drugs. Not even marijuana. And now you're telling me he's a dusthead? I just find this shit hard to believe."

"Well, if you want to, you can call David yourself and talk to him," Tamika said. "You know that was his boy when him, Charles, and Robert were all at law school together, but when Robert asked him if he could join his practice, he turned him down."

Yvonne snorted and said in a low voice, "Some friend."

Tamika's jaw tightened. "I don't know how you can say that. It's not like he's turning his back on Robert, but he doesn't want a dusthead who stole from his last firm working with him. And you know what? I think he's right."

"Ooh, look at little Tamika basing up." Puddin' chuckled. "You should know better than trying to bust on her man like that."

"You know what?" Yvonne stood up. "I gotta go over to my mother's house to run some errands for her. I'll walk y'all downstairs."

*What the hell kind of errands does Mama Tee need done at nine o'clock at night?* Regina thought. *Yvonne's trying to cut and run.* Out loud she said, "Well, Tamika and I aren't doing anything. You want us to run with you?"

"Nope. I got this." Yvonne walked over to the coffee table and picked up the remote and clicked the television off. "Y'all ready?"

"Vonne, why don't you call Mama Tee and see if you can take care of her stuff tomorrow?" Puddin' asked as gently as possible for Puddin'. "Come on and hang out with me tonight. I'll pick up Usher, and you can pick up 50 Cent. We both can get some of that hip-hop cash."

"No, I gotta go take care of business," Yvonne said sharply. "Y'all ready or not?"

# chapter five

"You've really outdone yourself, Regina. That was one birthday party Camille won't forget."

"She'd better not," Regina grumbled as she slouched farther down on the love seat and kicked off her shoes. "I swear, Charles, those kids drove me crazy. I thought capping it at ten kids would make it easier to handle, but I feel like there were a hundred kids running around the park screaming, jumping up and down, falling and scraping knees, and crying 'cause they didn't think they got enough time on Barney's lap."

"That was an awful-looking Barney, by the way," Charles said as he swung his feet up so that he was lying on the couch. "Looked like he had fleas or something."

"The kids loved him, thank God, and that's what counts," Regina said with a sigh.

"Yeah, Camille was still mumbling his name in her sleep when I put her in her bed. That girl is knocked out for the night, you know."

"Yeah, well, I can use the break. It's not even six o'clock and I feel like it's past midnight, I'm so tired."

Regina sat up and stretched, then looked over at Charles. Even as worn-out as he was, the man looked good. His six-foot frame was just as trim and fit as it was when she first met him, and the shiny dark mustache he had grown was in fine contrast to his almond-colored skin. And now that he had let his hair grow out a bit, his protruding ears weren't as noticeable—not that they ever really detracted from his looks.

"Boy, I know you don't have your feet up on my couch," she said as she threw a pillow at him, then ducked just in time when he threw it back at her.

"Let's go get something to eat. I know I promised to take you to dinner Thursday, but since I couldn't break away to get to New York until today, let's do it now." Charles yawned. "Feel like Italian?"

"You really wanna wake your daughter up to take her with us?" Regina said with a grin.

"Dear Lord no." Charles grinned back. "And I probably couldn't wake her up if I wanted to. Wanna do takeout, then?"

Regina paused. What she really wanted to do was go to sleep, but at the same time, she really didn't want Charles to leave just yet, especially since it was so evident he wanted to stick around for a while. Probably, she figured, because he still wanted to talk to her about whatever it was he was alluding to on the phone the week before. And she really wanted to find out what it was. The suspense was killing her. "Yeah, I could go for a little something something. Maybe Chinese? I've got a menu around here for a place that delivers."

"No, that's okay," Charles said as he stood up. "Unless you know a liquor store that delivers."

"A liquor store?"

"Yeah, I thought we might have some champagne."

*Hmmm . . . whatever this little secret is, it must be good,* Regina thought. Out loud she said, "I still have that magnum of Moët you sent me for my birthday. How about we break that open?"

"Is it chilled?" Charles asked.

"Been in the fridge since you gave it to me back in June."

"Have I told you lately that I love you?" Charles asked as he leaned back on the couch. "Pass me the menu, and I'll make that call."

∽

"So, okay, remember when I said that I was kicking around an idea that I wanted to talk to you about?" Charles asked as he served himself another portion of Hunan duck.

"Of course," Regina answered expectantly.

"Okay, here it is." Charles paused, then let out a deep breath. "I'm considering running for the U.S. Senate."

Regina blinked a couple of times and leaned back into the couch. "Get the fuck out of here," she said in a low voice.

"I beg your pardon?"

"Sorry," Regina said quickly. "I mean, well, wow! I mean, how long have you been thinking about this?"

"Just a couple of months." Charles chewed his lip as he talked. "Right after old man Spetrum announced that he isn't running for a seventh term, leaving the office vacant and pretty much for the taking. And let's face it, one of the big things I have going for me is negotiating that hostage deal in Afghanistan last year. That's given me a wave of popularity that I'd be foolish not to take advantage of, wouldn't you agree?"

Regina nodded. Charles had made the cover of every news-magazine and been on all of the major Sunday morning talk shows after bringing home twelve soldiers who had been captured by the Taliban. Especially when it was found out that Charles had promised the Taliban nothing in return for the hostages besides the possibility that the United States would be willing to sit down across the table from them at some point in time. Many of the liberal news media outlets were already touting Charles as the first real potential African-American presidential candidate—though that really didn't mean much, since they had awarded that label to every African-American from Colin Powell to Barack Obama.

"I've already put out a couple of feelers, and I think I'd have some pretty strong support from party officials. They all think it would be a long shot, because you know Pennsylvania hasn't had a Democratic senator in almost twenty years. And at thirty-one I would be the youngest person elected to the Senate. But I think they're all keeping in mind that I was a long shot when I first ran for Congress, and we managed to pull that through."

Regina nodded again, remembering all too well. They had been married only a few months when a group of local politicians approached him about running for the House of Representatives. The campaign had gone well at first, but then his opponent, Richard Davis, found out about Regina's past—her shoplifting, her sugar daddies, her shooting—and leaked the information to the press. All hell had broken loose. Charles's campaign rushed to do damage control, and he was successful in his election run, but the ordeal had put a fatal strain on their marriage. That and, of course, Charles's affair with an old flame.

"I wanted to talk to you, though, before I made a final decision," Charles was saying. "Because you know this is going to affect you and Camille as well. I mean, of course, I wouldn't expect you to come out and campaign for me or anything." He paused and grinned. "I would appreciate your vote, though."

"Charles," Regina said slowly, "you do realize that my past is probably going to come up again, right?"

Charles nodded. "I do. But it won't be too damaging, since we're no longer married."

"No?"

"No." Charles shook his head. "And I think we can handle it the same way we did before—turn it to our advantage. I really believe the whole thing might have actually won me some votes. Made me seem more human."

Regina stood up and walked to the window, fingering her chin. "Yeah, but that was for the House. This might be a lot different. You only had to win over people in that congressional district, which is pretty liberal. Running for the Senate means you'd have to win votes statewide, and some of the cities in up-state Pennsylvania are extremely conservative. Pennsylvania might not be quite as bad as Mississippi, but remember, they've *never* sent an African-American to the Senate. My past is not going to play too well in Altoona, honey."

"Yeah, I thought about that. But—"

Regina cut him off. "And remember, too, if you do win the Democratic primary, there's a good chance you might get national media coverage, which would mean even more possible exposure of my past. I mean, you'd be only like the third African-American elected a U.S. senator."

"Yeah, well, since Reconstruction, but I did think about that, too."

"And?"

"And I think it's going to be hard, but, Regina, I can still win the election."

Regina walked over and sat in a chair facing Charles. "Really? Is that a fact?" she said slowly. "And what about—"

"What about you?" Charles finished the question for her. "That's why I'm coming to you." He leaned forward and grabbed her knees tightly. "This is something I really want to do, but there's no way I will if you think it's going to hurt you or Camille."

"I don't know, Charles. I don't think it would be a good . . ." Regina paused. "You know what? I guess, well, why not, huh?" She paused again. "I don't know, Charles. Let me think about it, okay?"

"Fair enough," Charles said, releasing his grip on Regina's knees. "I can't ask for more than that."

They sat in silence for a few minutes, not looking at each other.

"Well, how about we don't break open that champagne tonight, then?" Charles said finally. "I could use a drink, though. Do you have any Scotch?"

Regina nodded and got up to fix them both a stiff drink, when the telephone rang.

"Hello," she said rather distractedly.

"Hey you," the voice on the other end said.

"Oh," Regina said breathlessly as she recognized Little Joe's voice and his usual telephone greeting. "Hey you back. How you doing? I thought you lost my number or something."

"Been a little busy but doing okay. What you doing? Can you get out tonight?"

"You've got some nerve," Regina said in a teasing voice before remembering Charles was in the room. She looked over at him and noticed he was so busy looking the other way that he had to be listening intently. "Um, no," she said into the telephone. "I really can't. And I, uh, really can't talk right now."

"Why? Your man there?" Little Joe said with a chuckle.

"Very funny," Regina said, trying to keep her voice casual. "But could you call me back in a little bit?"

"Yeah. No problem."

She started to say "Make sure you do," but caught herself. She didn't want to sound desperate.

"Okay, then," she said instead.

"About an hour, then?"

"Yeah, that'll be fine."

"Okay," Little Joe said before hanging up without saying good-bye, which, Regina remembered, was how he usually ended telephone conversations.

She hung up and turned toward Charles with a weak smile. "I'm sorry. Let me get those drinks."

"No, that's okay," Charles said, looking at his watch. "I need to get out of here, anyway. So who was that on the phone?"

She wanted to tell him that it was none of his business, but she was feeling a little too guilty. Which, she reminded herself, was silly. After all, she and Charles had been divorced for about four years. "It was just an old friend," she said simply.

"Must be a pretty good old friend," Charles said as he put on his jacket. "It's been quite a while since you used that tone of voice with me."

"Charles . . ."

"No problem. I know it's none of my business." Charles leaned down and kissed her on the forehead. "I'm staying at the Plaza until Monday morning. Call me if you want to talk, okay?"

Regina rushed to the telephone after he left and looked at the number on the caller ID. It was a 917 number, which meant it was probably a cell phone. She hesitated a moment, then punched in the number.

"Hey you," Little Joe said.

"Hey you back. How'd you know it was me?" Regina said as she settled into the couch.

"Same way you got this number. Caller ID. You got rid of your man already?"

"Please. That was not my man," Regina replied.

"You got a man?" Little Joe demanded.

"None of your business. Are you still married?"

"None of yours. Now, can you get out tonight? I wanna take you to dinner."

"Aw, I wish I could, but I don't have a babysitter."

"Call your girlfriend. The one you was with the other day."

"Tamika? I can't. She's home with her own kids."

"Then drop your daughter over there. Come on, girl. I wanna see you. We got a lotta catching up to do."

"You still didn't tell me if you're still married."

"Come out to dinner with me and find out," Little Joe taunted.

Regina started thinking quickly. She wasn't tired anymore,

and she really wanted to see Little Joe. It had taken him almost a week to finally call, and she didn't want to wait another week before talking to him again. "Let me call my niece and get right back to you, okay?"

"Okay. Hurry up, though." The phone went dead.

*He's got a whole helluva lot of nerve calling me like this at the last minute and expecting me to just figure out a way to do what he wants me to do,* Regina thought as she once again punched numbers into the telephone.

"Hey, Ray-Ray? Can you do me a favor, sweetie?"

# chapter six

She'd been careful picking out her outfit—a pale yellow silk blouse and knee-length black suede skirt, topped with a black suede jacket—but still, she felt self-conscious as she entered the Flash Inn to meet Little Joe. It had been one of their favorite restaurants back in the day, and Little Joe even had his own table, which management kept vacant just in case he decided to show up. It was still a classy place, though a little worn from the years. The wallpaper was a little faded, and the clientele was a little older, but then, so was she.

She suddenly found herself comparing her present-day image to her fifteen-year-old former self. She still looked good, she thought, patting her waist and sucking in her slight belly, but she certainly didn't look like the teenager Little Joe had been so enamored with. He didn't seem to mind when he saw her in the street with Camille a week before, but perhaps he would while sitting across from her at a dinner table.

"And may I help you, miss?" the tuxedoed maître d' said in a slight French accent that she assumed was Haitian.

"I'm actually meeting someone," Regina answered as she

quickly scanned the restaurant for Little Joe. "I'm here a few minutes early."

"And your party's name?" the maître d' asked as he glanced down his nose at the reservation book.

"Joseph Blayton," Regina said, checking the bar to see if there was an empty stool she could occupy until Little Joe arrived.

"Ah yes. Mr. Blayton." The maître d' looked up quickly. "I was not aware he was honoring us with his presence tonight, but I will gladly show you to his table."

*Little Joe's only been out like a month, and he already has his own table at Flash Inn again?* Regina wondered to herself as she followed the man. *Hmph, it looks like he hasn't wasted any time reestablishing himself.*

"Hey, Jean-Paul, I got this," Little Joe's voice rang out behind her. He kissed her on the back of the neck before she could turn around, then pulled the chair out for her. "I thought I was early, but here you are beating me to the joint."

"You're looking good," Regina said as he sat down across from her. He was wearing a green cashmere V-neck sweater, with no shirt, so his fine, silky chest hairs peeked out.

"So are you," Little Joe said, flashing the diamond gold tooth. "Doesn't she look good, Jean-Paul?"

"The miss certainly does," Jean-Paul said, giving a slight bow in Regina's direction. "I'll send the waiter over with your menus. May I bring you something from the bar?"

"Just bring two of my usuals," Little Joe said, never taking his eyes off Regina. He was staring so intently she lowered her eyes.

"Stand up and let me take a good look at you," he said after the waiter left.

"Oh please." Regina gave him a little wave of her hand.

"I'm serious. Stand up so I can take a really good look."

Regina leaned across the table and said in a loud whisper,

"I'm serious, too. I'm not going to stand up to be appraised like some show dog."

"Why you always gotta be so damn obstinate?" Little Joe said with a chuckle. "I ain't seen you in, what, sixteen years? It don't make sense I wanna take a good look at you?" He put his hand over hers. "What if I say 'please,' huh? Will that help? Well, please, then. I ain't asking you to take off your damn clothes; I just want you to stand up, that's all. Please."

Regina gave an inward sigh and slowly stood up next to the table.

Little Joe smiled warmly as he languidly looked her up and down. "It's kinda warm in here. You don't wanna take off that jacket?" he said, leaning back in his seat.

Regina tried to shoot him an angry look when she took off her jacket, but as she walked over to the coat hook on the wall a few feet away, she was feeling a bit giddy about the approving looks she knew he was sending her way. She let her hips sway seductively but not too overtly when she walked back over and took her seat.

"Damn, it's good to see what I've been missing all these years," Little Joe said with a grin. "What are you, in your thirties, right? And a mother, too? You keeping yourself in real good shape, girl. What? You got a personal gym in that brownstone of yours?"

"No," Regina said. She opened the menu the waiter had brought to the table and flipped through the pages. "But I go to the spa a couple of times a week. I try to keep myself up. But you should talk. I mean, look at—" She suddenly squinted. "Wait a minute. How did you know I live in a brownstone?"

Little Joe chuckled. "Don't get paranoid. I lost your number and had to get it from information, and since there was more than one Regina Harris listed, the operator asked if I wanted the one in the one hundred block of 119th Street. So I took a guess and picked that one. And since there's mostly brown-stones on that block, I took another guess." He took a sip of the drink that the waiter placed in front of him. "I guessed right, huh?"

"Except one thing," Regina said as she twirled her drink with the plastic stirrer. "I'm not listed."

"Really? How come?"

"I like my privacy," Regina said with a slight shrug.

"Why? You got something you needing to hide?"

"No, but . . ." Regina paused. "Little Joe, back to the original point. How did you know I live in a brownstone?"

"The *new* point is why the hell you had ta go fuck up a perfectly good lie by being unlisted."

"That's not the point. Tell me how—"

"Stop arguing, woman, and let me just sit here and look at them beautiful eyes of yours," Little Joe said. "You always had the most beautiful eyes I ever seen on a woman. And damn if you ain't got more beautiful now that you got a couple a years on you. You are one amazingly beautiful woman, Regina. You are just amazing. My little Satin Doll."

Regina lowered her eyes and unsuccessfully fought back a blush. Why it was that Little Joe got to her the way he did, she couldn't understand, but there was no denying he did. Always had. He was rough, gruff, and so sweet all at the same time. Thug romantic. That's what Little Joe was. Thug romantic. And it was appealing. Maddeningly appealing. And hard as hell to resist. *But damn, I really should be trying harder,* she thought. *What the hell is wrong with me? I'm not fifteen anymore.* She shook herself and took a sip of the drink and grimaced. "What's this?"

"A whiskey sour," Little Joe said as he opened his menu.

"Yuck," she said, putting it down on the table. "Too strong for me."

"Maybe I'm trying to get you drunk." Little Joe grinned. "You know, you never used to complain about whatever I ordered. You used to just drink it and smile real pretty at me."

"Well, that was before—"

"See, like that little smile you're trying to fight right now." Little Joe leaned over and chucked her under the chin. "Stop trying to be a badass, Regina. You're too sweet."

"Well, I might not be as sweet as I was when I was a teenager, you know," Regina said, and leaned back in her seat. "Like you said, I'm grown now. People change."

"Yeah, okay, right." Little Joe signaled for the waiter, who hurried over to the table. "Pierre, my date has decided she doesn't like her drink. Bring her whatever she wants."

"Of course, Monsieur Blayton." The waiter turned to Regina. "If you please, *mademoiselle,* what is it I can bring for your pleasure?"

"An apple martini, please," Regina said as she pushed the whiskey sour away from her.

"Very good, *mademoiselle,*" the waiter said, removing the drink. "And are you ready to order your meal?"

"We'll need a few minutes. Just get her her drink," Little Joe said before she could answer.

"Very good, *monsieur,*" the waiter said, and turned to hurry away.

"Pierre," Little Joe said before the man could leave. "Yo, man, look, man, I ain't mean to be rude and shit. Everything okay?"

"Everything is doing so very fine, *monsieur.* Thank you so much for asking. And I thank you again for being so kind to my son. I trust you've received his note of thank you?"

Little Joe gave a slight nod. "I haven't checked my mail lately. But that's good. Shows he's got good breeding. I'm glad I could help. Tell him I said to bring home good grades and we'll call it square."

"What was that all about?" Regina asked Little Joe after the waiter left.

"What was what all about?"

"Um, his son," Regina said. "He was thanking you about something regarding his son."

"His son was on the waiting list to get into Grays University. I made some calls and helped him out," Little Joe said nonchalantly. "Let's drop it."

"Grays? You got connects at Grays?" Regina said incredulously. "That's one of the top schools in the country!"

"I thought we decided to drop it."

"*You* decided. I didn't agree to anything," Regina said with a laugh.

"Look at you, getting all assertive and shit." Little Joe raised an eyebrow. "I'm have ta get used to this new Regina, huh?"

Regina put her hand over Little Joe's. "Yeah, but it's gonna be okay."

"Promise?" Little Joe asked with a smile.

Regina nodded.

"Yeah, well, remember that kid Warren that used to be a bartender at my club, JoJazz, back in the day? Well, he was working his way through school. When I went over, I tried to hit off my employees, and him I made special arrangements for. I gave my lawyer money for him to get his master's if he finished his bachelor's. He did, and damn if he didn't go on to get his doctor's degree . . ."

"His doctorate?"

"Yeah, well, doctor's, doctorate, what the fuck, whatever. Anyway, now he's head of the Political Studies program at Grays. So about a week ago . . ." Little Joe paused and looked at Regina. "In fact, that day I saw you on Eighth Avenue, ain't that some shit?" he said, using the old name for Frederick Douglass Boulevard. "That day, I came in here and Pierre was telling me about his son on the waiting list, so I gave Warren a call. School was starting the next week, and he managed to get the kid in. That's all." Little Joe chuckled. "Maybe Pierre should be thanking *you,* shit. I was in such a good mood after seeing you I woulda done anything for anybody."

Little Joe opened his menu again. "You wanna get calamari for an appetizer? You see I'm asking, right? 'Cause I don't want you making no sour-ass face like you did for the damn drink I ordered."

"No, calamari's cool," Regina said. *It wasn't my imagination,* she thought. *Little Joe really is cool as all hell. How many people would bother taking care of his people like that before they went up the river? But isn't that something? Some kid from Harlem made it through college, got his master's degree, and made it to PhD level because of the heroin that Little Joe was selling back in the day, and was now helping other kids make it. It's a crazy-ass world.*

There was a twinge of something . . . something she couldn't name . . . but she tried to ignore it as she looked over the entrées. It was just a really small twinge, but one that refused to go away. *After all, I was supposed to be his girl. Why hadn't he—*

"But, you know, I gotta give it to Warren," Little Joe cut into her thoughts. "I was away, what, sixteen years? And that kid Warren did my whole bid with me. I mean, he wrote me letters from day one. Well, a lot of people did from day one, but after two, three, four, or five years people stop, you know? I know I've done some shit in my life, but I did good by a lotta fucking people, don't ya think? But it's always about whatcha done for me lately, ain't it? Warren stuck with me the whole time. All damn asshole, motherfucking, bitching, goddamn years, he kept in contact, ya know? Even came out to visit me a few times after they transferred me to Lewisburg. Anyway, I'm gonna have the rack of lamb. Whatchoo gonna have?"

Regina face turned crimson as the twinge of resentment quickly turned into a twinge of guilt and then from a twinge to a pang and then to an overwhelming wave. "Lewisburg? That's in Pennsylvania, isn't it? I thought you did your whole time in Leavenworth. In Kansas."

"I got transferred ten years in."

Regina bit her lip as she studied her menu, speculating about what Little Joe was thinking but not saying. That she would have known had she stayed in touch. *But Christ,* she thought, *I was only sixteen when he got sent up. And I may have been his girl, but I was only one of them. And maybe I would have tried to visit him if I didn't have to worry about running into . . .*

"So how's your wife?" she asked out loud.

Little Joe guffawed and signaled the waiter over. "Pierre, bring me another drink. I'll wait for the lady to make up her mind before I order my food."

"So," Regina said after the waiter hurried off, "what about your wife? How's she doing?"

"What wife?" Little Joe asked, and drained the little bit of liquid left in his glass.

"The wife you had the whole time you were messing around with me," Regina said. "You know, the one who was sitting in the front row of the courtroom when I went to your first day of trial."

"Don't act like you ain't know I was married," Little Joe said with a growl in his voice. "I told you that shit the first time I took your little ass out."

"I didn't say I didn't know," Regina said huffily. "I'm just asking how's she doing."

Little Joe shrugged. "Far as I know, she's doing fine. I heard she moved up to Syracuse."

"You *heard* she moved to Syracuse?"

"Yeah, well, we got divorced after I had been up eight years."

"Oh damn, I didn't know." *But I would have, had I stayed in touch,* Regina thought again.

"I ain't mad. Shit just works out like that sometimes. She was a good woman and all, but you know a woman's got needs. And you know"—Little Joe gave a little chuckle—"you don't get conjugal visits when you're doing time with the feds."

"No, I didn't know that." Regina didn't know what else to say.

"Of course, it would have been nice to get any kind of visit from just any-old-body. But what the fuck, ya know?"

"Little Joe . . . ," Regina started, but was startled by someone coming up and bumping her chair.

"What's up, my ace? My boon! You old gray dog!" a huge man with a booming voice yelled as he snatched Little Joe up from his chair and pulled him into a bear hug. "What's up, pimp!"

"Get the fuck offa me, motherfucker. You trying to smother me or some shit?" Little Joe laughed as he struggled free. "What's up, Hulk? Damn if it ain't good to see you, you old ox. How you doing, man?"

"I'm wishing I was looking good as you, bro. Man, you are a sight for sore eyes," Hulk said as he pounded Little Joe on the back. "Yo, Little Joe, man, I just got back in town, else you know I woulda found your ass before now. How long you been out? Two weeks? And looking sharp as shit. Don't tell me you back in the game already. And hey, man"—Hulk pulled a white envelope from his pocket—"you know I got a little something for you. A little WAM for my man."

WAM? Regina inwardly whistled. She wondered how many envelopes of "walking-around money" Little Joe had collected from his old hustler friends?

"Hulk, man, you know you ain't have to do that," Little Joe said. He quickly took the envelope and slipped it into his jacket's inside pocket. "But I heard you been coming off like a kingpin. Holding it down and shit. I wanna be like you when I grow up."

"Shit, man, I'm still trying to be like you, Joe," Hulk said, eyeing Regina approvingly. "What I gotta do to pull something like that?"

"Yeah, Hulk." Little Joe's voice suddenly turned cold as he folded his arms over his chest. "You remember Regina, right?"

"Oh yeah. Hell yeah. How you doing, girl?" Hulk nodded at her. "I ain't seen you in a minute, but you looking good."

Regina was sure she'd never met him, but before she could say anything to the man, he turned back to Little Joe.

"So where you staying, man?" he asked.

Little Joe stood there for a moment, not saying anything. "Yeah, man, we'll talk, but right now you messing up my game," he said finally. "Why don't you give me your number, and I'll give you a call later tonight or something? Aight?"

Hulk looked crestfallen but said, "Well, yeah, man, make sure you do that, okay? 'Cause I really wanna get with you about some stuff. You know, pull your coat about some shit. You sure you okay and shit?"

"Yeah, man, I'm tight." Little Joe stood there, his arms still folded, a dismissive tone in his voice.

"Well, okay, man, here's my numbers. Make sure you call me before you make any moves, okay?" Hulk reached out to give his card to Little Joe, then placed it on the table when Little Joe refused to unfold his arms. "I'm out, then. See ya later."

Little Joe waited until the man was out of sight before sitting back down, his jaw tight and his eyes hard. Regina reached over and patted his hand. "You okay?" she asked softly.

"I'm fine. I just ain't like the way the motherfucker was looking at you."

"Don't tell me you're jealous," Regina said in a teasing voice.

Little Joe shook his head. "Naw, it wasn't even about you."

"Well, what do you mean, then?"

"The motherfucker disrespected me," Little Joe said through clenched teeth. "He ain't know if you was my wife or my sister, talking shit like that to you."

"Or your daughter," Regina said as she reopened her menu. She knew she was just being mean, but she didn't care. Little Joe could have played it off a little bit and at least pretended it was about her instead of about him. But then, it was always really about Little Joe, wasn't it?

"Very funny. You ready to order?"

"You know what?" Regina closed the menu, placed it on the

table, and picked up her purse. "I'm not even hungry. Why don't we just call it a night?"

Little Joe's face tightened even more before his lips curled into a sneer. His body language relayed that he was going to tell her to go to hell, but suddenly, he took a deep breath and shook his head.

"You know what, Regina? We're not going to call it a night. Because I've been thinking about you for the last sixteen years, wondering how you were doing and if you were making out okay," Little Joe said in a soft voice. "We're not calling it a night because I've missed you, and when I saw you the other day, all the feelings I had for you rushed back and almost choked me. We're not calling it a night because we owe it to ourselves to get reacquainted, and see if what we had was real or just a man with some money buying some tight pussy. We're not calling it a night because we need to see if what we did all those nights together was just fucking or making love. We're not calling it a night because we need to see why after all these years I'm still crazy about your crazy ass, and why you're still crazy about me. 'Cause you are, aren't you? Or are you gonna play like you're not."

Regina sat frozen in her seat.

"You can't play it off, can you?" Little Joe reached over and held her hand. "You want to find out the same things I do, don't you? Ain't no shame in admitting it."

Regina lowered her eyes and said nothing.

"Don't let the stupid muthafucka Hulk ruin our evening, Regina, okay? I'm sorry if I was acting cold or some shit, but you gotta remember I've been away a long time, and I'm just getting used to being out here and trying to figure out all over again how to protect what's mine. And shit, even trying to figure out what *is* mine, you know? Still trying to figure out the boundaries."

Regina nodded. "I know," she said softly.

"So are you mine, Regina?" He gently stroked her cheek. "Are you still my Satin Doll?"

"Little Joe," Regina said softly, tears in her voice, "I'm so sorry. I'm really so very sorry. Can you ever forgive me?"

"For what, doll?"

"I'm sorry I didn't write or visit you while you were away, but—"

"Shh." He put his finger against her lips. "That's water under the bridge, okay? You wanna make it up to me? Then stay and have dinner with me tonight. Can you do that for me?"

Regina nodded. "But just dinner, okay, Little Joe? Let's take it slow."

Little Joe grinned. "If there was one thing sixteen years in the pen taught me, it was patience, doll. We'll take it as slow as you want. 'Cause in the end I know you're gonna be mines."

# chapter seven

It was the sun sneaking through the slats of the wooden shutters that woke Regina, but it was the empty spot next to her that made her jump up in the bed.

"Little Joe," she called out as she walked to the small bathroom that adjoined her master bedroom suite. There was no answer, but the damp towel on the rack and the raised seat on the commode testified that he had been in there. She blinked rapidly to try to clear her head and went downstairs, still wearing the shirt and skirt from the night before, now rumpled and askew.

"Little Joe," she called again. She padded barefoot into the living room and looked around. Her jacket was still thrown over the couch where she left it the night before, and she tried to remember where they had put his. Had she hung it up? She walked to the hallway to check the coat closet and almost bumped into Little Joe coming from the kitchen, bare-chested and carrying a wicker breakfast tray with two cups of coffee and a saucer with four slices of toast.

"Damn if you ain't ruined it," he said with a wide smile. "I

was going to bring you breakfast in bed. Not much of a breakfast, though, 'cause you ain't had shit in there I knew how to
cook. How come you ain't got no eggs?"

"I must have run out. I don't like eggs, anyway," Regina
said, trying to keep the surprise out of her voice. "And since
when did you start cooking people breakfast?"

"Don't get used to it. This is a one-shot deal," he said, jig-
gling the tray. "You wouldn't give me none last night—making me sleep in my clothes and shit—so I'm trying to sweeten
you up to try and maybe get some nookie this morning. Now,
hop back in the bed so I can do this up right."

"Can I at least take a quick shower before I eat?"

"Nope. Your coffee'll get cold. You can shower when you
finish." He balanced the tray with one hand and with the other
pulled her to him for a kiss. "Damn," he said, quickly releasing her. "On second thought, maybe you should hurry up and
brush your teeth."

"You're so romantic," she said with a laugh as she ran up the
stairs.

౿

"Will you please stop that?" Regina asked as Little Joe
flicked the remote from one channel to another.

"I'm trying to see what guests they got on the news shows,"
he said. "I'm looking for someone in particular."

"Who?" Regina asked, and stretched out in the bed.

The two of them lay on top of the satin champagne-colored
bedspread. Little Joe was still bare-chested, but Regina had
changed into sweatpants and a tank top after her shower. It was
almost 1 p.m., but she had told Ray-Ray that she wouldn't be
picking Camille up until four or five, so she was in no rush. She
was enjoying herself lying next to Little Joe, snuggling close to
him and pushing him away when he got a little too frisky. It
was good feeling like she was actually in control, something

she'd never felt with Little Joe before. Surprisingly, he was being good-natured about the whole thing, though he had swatted her with a pillow a couple of times and almost thrown her out of the bed a couple of other times. He'd finally given up and started concentrating instead on the television.

"Congressman Charles Whitfield," Little Joe said as he flicked the remote once again to a different channel.

"What?"

"I'm looking to see if your ex-hubby is on television. They got big shots like him on these programs all the time, and I wanna see what he looks like. Check out my competition."

"I never said he's a big shot." Regina nudged Little Joe on the shoulder, but he ignored her. "And I certainly never said anything that should make you think he's competition. We've been broken up for years now."

"Yeah, well, we been broke up for sixteen years, and damn if I ain't in your bed trying to get some." Little Joe casually put his hand on her thigh and started kneading it.

"Well, that's different," Regina said as she moved his hand. "We broke up because you went away. Charles and I broke up because we couldn't make it together."

"So why'd you get married? Was you pregnant?"

"No. We married because we were in love. But sometimes love just isn't enough, you know?"

"I don't know shit except that you shouldn't be laying in bed with one man and talking about being in love with another," Little Joe snapped. "What you tryin' ta do? Make me jealous?"

Regina elbowed him. "If you were listening, I said we *were* in love, not we still *are* in love. And anyway, how do you know he's a big shot?"

"You said he's a congressman, right? And congressmen are big shots. And shit, once you told me his name, I recognized him right away. Shit. Almost everybody's heard of Congressman Charles Whitfield since he negotiated that deal to get those guys out of the Middle East a couple of years ago. Made the cover of *Time,* right? Or was it *Newsweek?* We be keepin' up with the news in the joint, ya know. He's such a hero they're talking about him being the first black president."

*I wonder,* Regina thought, *what Little Joe would think if I told him that Charles has decided to run for the Senate.*

"How old is he, anyway?"

"Same age as me."

"And how old is that?"

Regina snatched the pillow out from Little Joe's head and hit him with it.

"Come on now, how the hell am I supposed to know how old you are?" he said, grabbing the pillow and hitting her back.

"I know how old you are. Forty-nine. And I even know your birthday. May 12."

"I'm only kidding. I know how old you are. Thirty-five."

"Wrong."

"Thirty-six?"

"No, and I'm getting upset here."

"Thirty-seven? Thirty-four?"

"Stop! I'm thirty-one, okay?"

"Get the fuck outta here," Little Joe said with a snort as he flicked to yet another channel. "I don't know why women always gotta be lying about their age."

"*You* get outta here. I'm thirty-one years old," Regina said angrily, and propped herself up on one elbow. "I was fifteen years old when you started messing around with me, remember? And that was seventeen years ago. I'll be thirty-two next month."

"You was fifteen?" Little Joe turned and looked at her. "Get the fuck outta here."

"Oh, like you didn't know," Regina huffed.

"What? You know goddamned well you ain't told me you was no fifteen."

"Well, I don't know if I actually told you, but I would have, had you asked. And you goddamned well knew I was just a kid."

"But damn, I ain't know you was jailbait!"

"Yes, you did. You were just a pervert. A thirty-two-year-old man screwing a fifteen-year-old," Regina teased.

"Yeah, well, if I remember correctly, I wasn't your first," Little Joe said in a harsh voice. "So don't throw around words like 'pervert' if you don't wanna get words back like—"

"Whoa! Why don't you just stop right there!" Regina sat up in the bed. "I was just kidding with you. You don't have to be coming out at me like that. What the hell is wrong with you, anyway?"

"Yeah? Well, bad fucking joke." Little Joe threw the remote on the bedspread and climbed out of bed. "Look, I gotta split, anyway. I'll call you later."

"Don't bother," Regina spat.

"Shut up," Little Joe said as he laced up his shoes. "You gonna come downstairs and lock the door after me, or do you have a slam lock?"

⌇

"And that was it. He walked out. I don't know what the hell was wrong with him." Regina sighed as she stirred her cappuccino. "All I know is I can't be bothered. I'm through with his ass."

"I can't believe you're sitting here lying like that," Tamika said, tapping her fingers on the table. "You dragged me out here to talk about all this, and then you're gonna sit here and not even be honest with yourself?"

"What are you talking about?" Regina raised her eyebrows and crossed her legs.

"One, you know what was wrong with him. You baited him, and you went too far. Two, you know you're not through with him because if you were, we wouldn't be sitting here talking about him, now, would we?" Tamika said in an irritated voice.

"Dang, Tamika, you don't have to act all stink and stuff." Regina rolled her eyes. "If you didn't want to come out, you shouldn't have come out."

"I'm sorry, Regina. I didn't mean to snap at you. Okay?" Tamika put her hand over Regina's. "But it's just that I feel like you're playing a really dangerous game. I don't know Little Joe well, but I know him well enough to know he's not a man to be trifled with. I don't want to see you get hurt."

"Hurt? Give me a break. I mean, you may be right—I may still have some feeling for him, but not so much that I would be torn up or anything over him."

Tamika sighed. "You're lying again. But that's not even what I'm talking about."

"What? You mean hurt physically, then?" Regina's head jerked back in surprise. "That's ridiculous. In the whole time I've known Little Joe he's never raised his hand to me. Never even threatened me. He—"

"It's not so ridiculous," Tamika interjected. "You've heard the rumors about Little Joe just like I have. Remember back in the day . . . what was it . . . like 1980 or so . . . when those stickup kids from 138th Street hit up the old heads' crap game on St. Nick Avenue? Rumor has it that it was Little Joe that had all those kids killed. And they were just kids. Teenagers. Babies."

"Those were just rumors—"

"And everyone knows that he was one of the people on the council that had to give a thumbs-up or thumbs-down when drug dealers encroaching on other people's territory were to be killed."

"There's no proof to—"

"And that it was Little Joe himself who killed that dude from 117th Street who ratted out one of his friends. Beat him to death with a baseball bat. Beat him so bad that his own mother couldn't identify him. And I know you remember that, because you were with him later that night and saw him when he put his bloody clothes in the incinerator."

Regina shifted uncomfortably in her seat. "Okay, we've established Little Joe is a dangerous man, but like I said, I've never had any reason to be afraid of him. He was nothing but kind to me. Or don't you remember that, Tamika? He was a friend to me when I needed a friend. He looked after me."

"Gina, you don't know what this man is capable of except that he's one dangerous motherfucker."

Regina winced. It was unlike Tamika to curse, so she knew how serious her friend was. And she knew she was right.

Tamika continued, "One of David's new clients reminds me a little of Little Joe. An old-time drug dealer. He's supposedly clean now, and David's defending him on an arson charge. And he's probably innocent on that charge, but he still gives me the creeps. Dangerous men don't change, Gina. They're always dangerous."

"I know, but—"

"You're infatuated with him because of the way he treated you when you were a helpless teenager who needed help. But that was seventeen years ago. That's your past. Leave it in your past. Why are you jeopardizing your family by letting someone like him back in your life? Have you lost your mind?"

"I'm not planning on bringing him around Camille," Regina protested weakly. "I'm not even planning on seeing him again. I told you that."

Tamika paused, then shook her head wearily. "All right, Gina. There's not too much more I can say, is there? I'm going to have to hope you come to your senses before it's too late."

# chapter eight

"Renee's bags are packed. I guess I'd be smart to assume she's going to be moving in with you, huh?" Brenda said after she opened the door to let Regina in.

"Huh? What are you talking about?" Regina quickly scanned the living room as she entered the house. Renee was sitting in a chair in the corner, bent over sobbing, and Camille was gently rubbing her back. Furniture in Brenda's usually neat home was upturned, and Renee's junior prom picture, which had hung on the wall, lay smashed on the floor.

"Tell her not to cry, Mommy. She can move in with us, can't she?" Camille said as she ran to her mother.

"What's going on?" Regina picked up her daughter and wiped her tearstained face. "What happened?"

"Nothing," Brenda said sullenly. "Except that my daughter is a dyke. A butch. A lesbo. A freak."

"Mom . . . ," Renee wailed from the corner.

"Don't call me Mom," Brenda snapped. "You're not my daughter. No child of mine would lay down with someone of their own sex. It's unholy, and this is a holy house, dedicated to Jesus, son of God."

"Wait a minute, wait a minute, Brenda. Hold on." Regina put Camille down and walked over to Renee. "Let's everybody calm down here, okay?" She bent down and cradled Renee in her arms and looked at her older sister. Brenda stood in the middle of the room, her arms crossed, her face tight and hard. Regina had never seen Brenda like this, and it almost scared her.

"What the hell is going on?" Regina asked again.

"Stop the act." Brenda almost spat as she talked. "Renee told me she already told you. Thanks for letting me know what's going on in my daughter's life. She is *my* daughter, you know. Not yours."

"Well, I mean . . . ," Regina stammered as she tried to think of something to say. "I was going to say something, but I thought I would give Ray-Ray a chance to tell you herself."

"Well, she didn't! I had to hear her on the telephone with the girl . . . that Liz . . . talking about how much she loved her. Talking all that homo shit with Camille right there."

"Camille wasn't in the room, Aunt Gina. She was downstairs with Mom," Renee wailed.

"She was in the house, wasn't she? If you don't have any respect for me, or respect for yourself, you couldn't even respect your own little cousin enough not to be talking blasphemy in this house while she's in here? At her tender age?" Brenda walked over and slapped Renee in the face hard enough to leave a red handprint on her cheek.

"Whoa!" Regina caught Brenda's hand before she could hit the screaming girl again. "Just calm down. You don't have to be hitting on her. Let's talk this out."

"Damn it, Regina, don't tell me how to chastise my child," Brenda said. She snatched her hand away and swatted at Renee's head.

Regina stood up and grabbed Renee close to her, shielding

her from her mother. "Brenda, stop it. You need to calm the hell down. You don't need to be hitting on this girl."

"Didn't I just tell you not to be telling me how to chastise my own daughter?" Brenda said, struggling to get at Renee.

"But you said she's not your daughter," Camille said in a teary voice as she tried to maneuver herself between Brenda and Renee.

"Camille, stay out of this." Regina pushed her out of the way.

"But, Mommy, she was beating Ray-Ray with an extension cord before you got here." Camille started crying full force.

"She what?" Regina swung back to face her sister. "Brenda, have you lost your fucking mind? Beating her with an extension cord? What the hell is wrong with you?"

"I'll beat her with anything I want," Brenda shrieked. "I'm gonna beat Satan out of that child if it's the last thing I do."

"Not while I'm here, you're not." Regina pushed Renee and Camille behind her. "You're gonna have to hit me before you hit her."

"Oh really?" Brenda put her hands on her hips. "Well, don't think I won't. You've spoiled that child, and that's probably why she thinks she can do whatever she wants in my house. Including sleeping with her girlfriend right here in my house."

"I never did that, Aunt Gina," Renee said through her sobs.

"Shut up!" Brenda yelled. "Nobody was talking to you, now, was they? Get up in your room and wait there until I come up and finish with you."

"Get your stuff, Ray-Ray. You're coming home with me," Regina countered.

"She's not going anywhere with you! You think you're her damn mother? Well, I'm the one who gave birth to her."

"Didn't you tell me when I walked in here that you have her stuff packed and for me to take her?" It was Regina's turn to put her hands on her hips. "Well, that's what I'm going to do."

She turned back to Renee. "Get your stuff and let's go," she said, pointing to the door.

Renee moved toward the door, but Brenda darted around Regina and grabbed the girl. "Well, I changed my mind. Don't think I don't know that it was her being around you with your loose ways that made her like this in the first place."

"Get the fuck off her." Regina wrapped her hand around Brenda's long hair and yanked her off Renee.

"You get the fuck off of *me*!" Brenda yelled as she swung at Regina but missed. "This shit is all your fault. If you hadn't been screwing around with—"

"Renee," Regina called out, tossing her niece a set of keys, "you and Camille get in the car. I'll bring your stuff out with me."

"Don't you dare walk out of this house!" Brenda stomped toward them, but Regina blocked her path, pushing her back.

"Go ahead and get outta here now!" Regina told them.

"Have you lost your mind?" Regina demanded after they left.

"I'm serious. I don't want my daughter around you anymore. You're a bad influence on her. It's probably because of all the men she saw you running in and out of the house with when she was a kid that made her hate men and think she wants to be with women. Selling your body to men for money like a whore." Brenda turned and spat on her own floor, then turned back to glare at her sister.

"Oh really? Is that a fact? Well, first of all"—Regina put up one finger—"I never brought any man to our house. Second"—Regina added another finger—"I may have been selling my booty for money, but it was to support the daughter you abandoned. *You* were out there selling pussy for crack. And for all the shit I've done, I never sunk as low as you. Or do I have to remind you about the time you put on a show with a German shepherd for three bags of crack?"

"That's a lie!" Brenda said, advancing toward her.

"No, it's not, and you know it. Puddin' used to mess around with the guy who paid you for the night's entertainment." Regina snickered. "Now, I didn't wanna go there, but don't you ever—you hear me, ever—put on a holier-than-thou act with *me*. You may have pulled your act together now, but I know the real deal. Okay?

"And third," Regina continued, "you need to get over your resentment of the fact that I raised Ray-Ray instead of you. It's not my fault you chose a crack pipe over your own child."

Brenda stood in the middle of the room, facing her sister, her eyes brimming with tears as she bit her lips. "Well, to hell with you, Regina. You accuse me of resenting you, but why don't you admit that you resent me because I am her mother and you want her to think you are? You resent me fulfilling my God-given role, and you've done nothing but try to undermine me all these years."

Regina sneered. "You know what? You need to get a fucking grip. Now, I'm taking the kids home, and I'll call you tomorrow to see if you've regained your senses." Regina took another long look at her sister, then turned and walked out the door.

She took a deep breath to collect herself before getting in her car. Renee was sitting in the passenger seat with Camille in her lap. The two were crying and holding each other as they rocked back and forth.

Regina reached over and pulled Renee into her arms.

"Don't worry, sweetie, everything's going to be okay," Regina said soothingly. "Your mother's just upset now, but you know her. She'll calm down in a couple of days and then she'll be calling my house begging you to come home. You just watch."

Renee shook her head. "Aunt Gina, I'm so sorry. But I swear Camille wasn't in my room when I was talking to Liz. She was downstairs with my mom. And I didn't know Mom was gonna pick up the phone and listen in on the extension."

"She did, Mommy," Camille said through her tears. "I saw her."

"I believe you, honey." Regina kissed Camille on the cheek and then Renee on the forehead. "And I believe you, too, Ray-Ray. And even if Camille was in the room, I wouldn'ta been mad, baby. But we don't need to talk about this right now. I want you both to calm down, okay? Everything's going to be all right, I promise. Now, did you guys eat? You wanna stop and get some pizza on the way home?"

"Oh, Mommy, no." Camille started crying louder, then buried her head in her mother's lap. "No, no, no."

Regina tried to lift her daughter up into her arms, but the little girl resisted and continued sobbing.

"Camille, what's wrong?" Regina said frantically. "No what?"

"Mommy, please, I don't want pizza," Camille said in near hysteria. "You said when you picked me up from Aunt Brenda's you was taking me to McDonald's."

Regina and Renee looked at each other for a moment, then exploded in laughter.

"Okay, Camille. You're right—I promised," Regina said, rubbing Camille's back. "So stop crying and we'll go get you a Happy Meal, and Ray-Ray and I are going to split a large pizza, and then we're all going to stay up all night and watch old movies on TV."

Camille looked up and wiped her eyes. "Or maybe we can watch *The Little Mermaid* on the VCR?" she asked in a tiny voice. "That's me and Ray-Ray's favorite movie. Right, Ray-Ray?"

Renee smiled and nodded. "It sure is."

Regina started the car. "Okay, McDonald's, pizza, and *The Little Mermaid* it is, then. Anything to make my little girls happy. So, Camille, get in your car seat and let Renee buckle you up, and let's get the hell outta here."

"I love you, Mommy," Camille said with a yawn after she was settled in the car seat.

"Me, too," Renee added as they pulled off.

"And I love you both," Regina said. "And always will."

# chapter nine

"Shit, here I am trying to tell you the shit that went down between Brenda and Ray-Ray last week, and you're in there trying to sniff a snowstorm up your nostrils," Regina said when Puddin' emerged from the bathroom stall. "I'm surprised you don't have a nosebleed."

"Gina, when the fuck you ever seen me get a nosebleed from a little coke?" Puddin' dipped the miniature straw into a compact filled with snowy powder and brought it up to her nostril for another sniff, as if to prove her point. "And I was listening. Yeah, that was fucked-up what Brenda did. I mean, hell, I'm surprised as shit that Ray-Ray's a butch, but Brenda didn't have to beat the fucking kid and throw her out." Puddin' licked her lips, then took another hit of coke. "Damn, this is some good blow. Rob-Cee always gets the good shit."

Regina knew when she agreed to meet Puddin' at the club for Rob-Cee's listening party for his latest CD that Puddin' was gonna have some coke with her. She always had blow on her when she went out, to make sure she had a "good time," but

Puddin' had been holed up in the bathroom for at least twenty minutes before Regina came looking for her.

"Yeah, well, it's been a long time since I've seen you do this much," Regina said as she leaned forward into the mirror to check her lipstick.

"Yeah, well, it's been a long time since I could get my hands on this much on a regular basis." Puddin' snapped the compact shut and dropped it in her pocketbook, then leaned against the dirty bathroom door, sniffing a few more times as if to make sure all the granules went straight to her brain. She opened her eyes wide and shut them quickly a few times, then fished out the compact again.

"Girl, would you put that away, and come on, let's get outta here. You don't think your boy Rob-Cee ain't wondering where your ass is?" Regina gave her hair a quick pat in the mirror.

"He should know," Puddin' said. "He's the one that gave me the shit. Probably wanted me out the way so he could get his rap onto one of them groupies that be pulling on him all the time." She opened the compact, but before she could dip her straw in again, the door opened, bumping her and sending the compact flying to the floor.

"My shit," Puddin' cried, getting down on all fours and trying to scoop the powder back into the compact.

"Sorry," a young woman with a short-cropped platinum-blond Afro said as she stepped over Puddin' and hurried into one of the stalls.

"Yeah, right, sorry," Puddin' muttered.

"Puddin'," Regina said in a warning voice, touching her friend's elbow. Puddin' was skied up from the coke; add that to her tendency toward violence, and Regina knew anything could happen. "Remember what Yvonne and I were telling you about your temper. Just let it go, okay?"

"I ain't say I was going to do anything." Puddin' shot a dirty look at the stall the woman had disappeared into. "Bitch coulda at least said sorry like she really meant it, though."

"Well, it is a public bathroom, you know," the woman called out above the sound of her tinkling urine. "You should have expected someone would come in."

"Was I talking to her?" Puddin' grumbled to Regina. She looked at the clumps of damp and dirtied cocaine she had scooped back into the compact. "Look at this shit." She shot another dirty look at the stall, then threw the compact into the trash can.

"That had to be a good three hundred dollars' worth of blow in there," Regina said, following Puddin' out the bathroom. As soon as she said it, she wished she could force the words back into her mouth. In her cocaine-agitated state it was a wonder that Puddin' hadn't already gone off the girl. She didn't want to add fuel to the fire.

"Yeah, well, there's plenty more where that came from," Puddin' said simply, and made her way back to a booth in a corner of the noisy club. A tall, thin, dark-skinned man wearing dark glasses and a white derby sat there, his neck laden with heavy diamond-encrusted gold chains; but not heavy enough to stop him from bopping his head to the music.

"It's about time you brought your skinny ass back here," he said, reaching out and grabbing Puddin' by the hips and drawing her to him.

"You miss me, baby?" Puddin' patted his hand as she winked at Regina, who had slipped into the other side of the booth. Puddin' grabbed the glass in front of the man and drained its contents in one gulp before sitting down next to him.

"You missed my standing ovation," Rob-Cee gushed. "I knew my shit was hot. I bet I'm gonna hit platinum the first week."

"Rob, you gonna order us some more drinks? My girl Gina likes apple martinis, and you can go ahead and order us another bottle of Cristal."

Rob-Cee grinned and bit Puddin' lightly on the neck, then put his hand up to signal a passing drink waitress.

"Excuse me, I believe you're in my seat."

Regina looked up, and her eyes widened as she saw the platinum blonde from the bathroom standing over Puddin'.

"Excuse yourself, bitch. Your hot young ass mighta been keeping it warm for me while I was occupied, but your services are no longer needed. Dig?" Puddin' said with a wicked grin. Still looking at Blondie, Puddin' licked her lips, then took Rob-Cee's hand and guided it down her blouse and into her bra. "Ain't that right, baby?"

"I'll let you two work it out," Rob-Cee said with a laugh. He gave Puddin's breast a quick squeeze before pulling his hand away.

Puddin' turned in the booth to face Rob-Cee, an incredulous look on her face. She was silent for a moment, then put her hand in front of his face. "I'll get with you in a moment." She swung back toward the woman. "And you . . . how 'bout you get the fuck out my face?"

The girl put her hands on her hips. "And how 'bout you get the fuck out my seat, you old-ass bitch? Rob-Cee don't want no dried-up prune like you," the blonde said in a voice loud enough to draw attention.

Puddin' tapped her long fingernails on the table and looked at Regina. "You believe this shit?" she said, nodding her head toward the blonde. "But I guess I'm still supposed to hold my temper, huh?"

Regina shook her head, then looked at the blonde, who still had her hands on her hips. "Why don't you just step off?" she said in a low voice.

"Like your cokehead girlfriend said in the bathroom, was I talking to you?" The girl almost shouted as if to make sure she could be heard over the music. People were staring, and some walked closer to the booth to make sure they got ringside spots in case something jumped off. A photographer scurried over and crouched down with his camera ready to get pictures.

"What's going on here?" Tamika said as she walked over with Yvonne right behind her. "You guys okay? Regina? Puddin'?"

"What's up? I thought you guys weren't going to be able to make it out tonight," Puddin' said, twirling her fingers at them.

"Looks like it's a good thing we did," Yvonne said, eyeing the blonde up and down.

"Oh what? Now y'all gonna try and jump me?" The blonde slid her hands up to her side and did a slow twirl.

"Yo, mama." Rob-Cee snapped his fingers at the drink waitress. "Can you bring over a magnum of Cristal?"

"What, Rob, you getting champagne ready for the winner?" someone from the crowd shouted out.

"You know it, man," Rob-Cee shouted back.

"You motherfucker," Puddin' said before Regina put her hand over Puddin's and leaned over the table to make sure she wasn't heard by anyone else. "Puddin', this man ain't even worth it," she said soothingly. "Remember what we talked about holding your temper, okay? Take a deep breath. Why don't we just get outta here?"

"Um, how about 'cause I ain't gonna give this bitch"— Puddin' pointed at the blonde—"the fucking satisfaction."

"I know y'all ain't whispering about me," the blonde all but shouted. "What y'all got to be whispering about? If you wanna say something, say it loud enough for me to hear. You old bitches gonna try and jump me or some shit? Come on with it. I'll kick all y'all old bitches' asses."

"Yeah, well, I wish you'd get to it instead of just talking about it," Rob-Cee grumbled. "I'm ready to see some shit jump off up in here."

"What the fuck?" Yvonne asked Regina, pointing to the rapper.

Regina glared at the man. "He's just an asshole."

"Little girl, ain't nobody gonna jump you," Puddin' said, turning to the blonde. "Ain't nobody even thinking about your stank ass. Now, why don't you take your bottle of peroxide and go somewhere so grown folks can talk?"

"Why don't you make me?" the girl said, bobbing her head and shaking her shoulders.

"'Cause I don't put on shows for free," Puddin' said calmly. "And this pencil-dick muthafucka ain't worth it."

"Oh, now you gonna try and play me because some bitch is threatening your ass," Rob-Cee said.

"She ain't threatened me," Puddin' said with a shrug. "She's just blowing off a little steam."

The whole thing suddenly struck Regina as hilarious. Here was Puddin', the most fiery-tempered woman she'd ever met, playing the levelheaded one and pulling it off well. Regina couldn't help herself. She started laughing. Which made Tamika and Yvonne start giggling.

"Come on, Judy." A woman with long burgundy braids grabbed the blonde by the shoulder. "This shit ain't worth it. Let's go to the bathroom so you can cool off."

As the disappointed crowd dispersed, Puddin' kept her eyes on the two women until they disappeared into the bathroom. "Okay," she said, and finally stood up. "That's my cue, wouldn't you say, Regina?"

"I would certainly say so," Regina said with a smile. *Shit,* she thought, *the deal was Puddin' was supposed to take a couple of breaths before going off on someone. No one could say that Puddin' hadn't done at least that.* "Give her an extra kick on my behalf, okay? Old bitches, my ass."

"There's two of them in there, so I'll go in with you," Yvonne said, passing Tamika her pocketbook.

"Yvonne, will you stop that shit? You know your ass can't fight," Puddin' said with a chuckle. "Besides," she said as the burgundy-braided woman sashayed out the bathroom, "she's in there alone. Y'all just stand by the door and make sure no one comes in till I'm finished."

Regina, Yvonne, and Tamika took their posts outside the door, and Puddin' disappeared inside.

"Sorry, they're in there mopping the floor," Regina said when a woman tried to push past them. "You'll have to use the men's room."

It took only five minutes for Puddin' to emerge from the bathroom. There was a small scratch under her left eye, and her hair was slightly disheveled, but otherwise she looked none the worse for the wear. The girls silently followed her back to the club area and the booth.

"Hey, baby, you miss me?" Puddin' said as she leaned over the table toward Rob-Cee and his two friends.

"You know it, babe." Rob-Cee grinned up at her. "I just opened the Cristal and was waiting on you before I poured myself a drink."

"Well, we can't have you thirsty, now, can we?" Puddin' grabbed the bottle off the table and poured the contents over Rob-Cee's head. She jumped back before he could connect with a punch to her face, then she grasped the bottle by the neck and brought it full force against his forehead.

"Damn, he's out cold," Tamika said. She grabbed his wrist and felt for a pulse. "But he'll be okay."

"Like I give a fuck," Puddin' said, straightening her clothes. She turned around just in time to be blinded by a flash cube as a photographer snapped her picture. "Hold up, man, hold up." Puddin' put her hand over her face. She turned to Yvonne. "Let me get a comb real quick." She quickly combed out her weave so it lay perfectly over her shoulders. "Okay, now you can take my picture."

"All right, let's go," Regina said after two or three photographers shot Puddin' posed next to the table where Rob-Cee lay sprawled facedown.

⧸⧹

"That was some crazy shit, and you know there's going to be hell to pay," Yvonne said after she took a deep drag off the joint Puddin' passed her. They were lounging in Yvonne's living room, listening to one of the free CDs Rob-Cee had given out at the listening party.

"You think he'll give the police your name?" Regina asked, twirling her rum and Coke.

"No, he'd lose his street cred behind doing some shit like that," Puddin' said, using the remote to turn up the stereo.

"Well, it's his street cred that's gonna make sure he's come after your ass," Tamika said, then took a sip from her drink. "Hell, he might come after all of us."

"I don't think y'all got anything to worry about. He doesn't know your names or where you live. And I can lay low until I can figure out how to handle the shit," Puddin' said dismissively.

"Well," Regina said slowly, "I've been thinking about that. And I might have an idea."

The women looked at her expectantly.

"Didn't you say he's supposed to have another listening party tomorrow night?"

Puddin' nodded. "Yeah, at a club in Brooklyn. Why?"

"I say we all show up," Regina said, smiling.

"Get the fuck outta here. You done lost your mind, for real." Puddin' started laughing.

"Girl, put down that drink," Yvonne said with a snort. "Your ass is drunk."

Regina waved them quiet. "Hold on now. I didn't say we'd show up alone. We'd show up with our secret weapon."

Tamika's eyes widened. "Ooh, Regina, ooh. I know you're not gonna say what I think you're gonna say."

"Yeah." Regina nodded. "I'm gonna say it."

"Well, hurry up and say it so me and Yvonne can know what the fuck you're talking about," Puddin' said.

Regina took a sip from her drink, then said, "What if we casually stroll in there with Little Joe?"

"Get outta here," Yvonne said in disgust. "That mighta worked back in the day, but these young punks don't even know who Little Joe is."

"Uh-huh, they know who he is," Puddin' said slowly. "In fact, if I remember correctly, Rob-Cee even mentioned him in one of the songs they played tonight."

"Sure did." Regina started wiggling her shoulders to imaginary music. "How'd it go? 'Fuck with me, nigga, and I'll be on you like Satan, do you up right, like Little Joe Blayton.'"

"That was the best cut on the whole CD." Puddin' hit the remote button to find the song.

"Yeah, that muthafucka knows who Little Joe is," Regina said as she bopped her head to the beat. "Just listen to it. They idolize the old-time gangstas like him and Nicky Barnes."

"Will Rob-Cee recognize him, though?" Yvonne said skeptically.

"I don't know about that, but he will if we walk up to him and introduce them to each other," Puddin' said excitedly. "Rob-Cee would be scared as shit to do anything to any of us then."

"You think you can get Little Joe to do it?" Yvonne's voice was a little less skeptical now, but she still didn't sound totally convinced.

"Yeah, Gina, you think that's a good idea?" Tamika added, "I mean, do you fight a demon by bringing in Satan?"

"I think I can," Regina said, addressing Yvonne and ignoring Tamika. "In fact, I know I can. It'll give me an excuse to call him."

"You still ain't talk to him since he walked out on you last week?" Puddin' asked. "Shit yeah, he'll come. He'll jump at the chance to get that pussy he didn't get that night."

"You going to tell him why you want him to go to the listening party?" Tamika asked in a concerned voice. "I think you'd better, 'cause if Little Joe found out later you played him—"

"I'ma tell him," Regina cut her off. "But I think he'll go for it. It'll give him an opportunity to flex his own street cred. And a chance, in his mind, for me to be in his debt."

"Okay," Tamika said with a frown. "But be careful you're not writing a check your ass ain't ready to cash."

# chapter ten

I hate going to Brooklyn, I hope you know that," Little Joe said as they entered the crowded club with Regina on one arm, Puddin' on the other, and Yvonne trailing not far behind. "And I hate going into clubs where I can't even get my lady into a booth. We're gonna have to sit on fucking barstools."

As they approached the bar, Regina looked around trying to spot Rob-Cee, and noticed that Puddin'—who was wearing dark glasses and her hair tucked under a big floppy hat—was doing the same. She knew Puddin' well enough to see that no matter how cool she was pretending to be, Puddin' was at least a little bit nervous. Tamika was so nervous about what might happen that she had decided not to go. Regina had to admit that even she was having doubts now. What if someone got hurt? And she knew that if Rob-Cee didn't back down, there was going to be real trouble, because there was no way Little Joe was going to be the one to back up.

She followed Puddin's gaze and saw Rob-Cee on a small stage at the front of the club, rapping on the mike to a music track coming out of giant speakers placed around the club. Even from the bar the knot on his head was noticeable.

There was a no smoking rule in New York, but it seemed it was being ignored that night, at least as far as reefer. The smoke was so thick Regina was sure they were all going to get a contact high. Little Joe led them to two empty seats at the bar, ignoring the fact that there was a drink in front of one of them and a jacket strewn across the other. He picked up the jacket and threw it across his arm, then pushed the drink aside and motioned for Puddin' and Yvonne to sit down. He grabbed Regina by the waist and squeezed against the bar between Puddin' and Yvonne while waving for the bartender. Regina was amazed. They hadn't been there two minutes, and already Little Joe had made himself at home.

"That your boy on the mike?" he asked, pulling Regina in close for a quick kiss.

"Yeah, that's him," Puddin' answered for her. "The fuck-faced muthafucka."

"Girl, you got the nastiest fucking mouth," Little Joe said with a chuckle. "You ain't changed a bit."

Puddin' grinned. "Why fuck with perfection?"

"Cursing like a sailor and conking people over the head with champagne." Little Joe shook his head. "Yeah, you're still the same old perfect Puddin'." He stroked Regina's face. "You need to be more like Regina. A lady."

"Man, I bet I can take you in the bathroom right now, and in five minutes you wouldn't even remember who Regina is," Puddin' retorted.

"Ho," Yvonne and Regina said simultaneously.

Little Joe threw his head back and laughed. "Damn, Puddin'. I swear to God, you are one nasty little—"

"Yo, man, these are me and my girl's seats," a short dark-skinned man with a derby and ropes of chains around his neck said in a threatening voice. His uniform told Regina that he was one of Rob-Cee's boys, but she didn't remember him from the night before, and there was no recognition in his eyes, so he probably didn't remember them, either. Which could only mean that, for some reason, he hadn't been there.

"Yeah, well, like what's up?" Little Joe answered in a nonchalant voice. "No disrespect, man, but the seats were here, and you weren't, and we needed to sit down. And it's not like you had your names on the stools, you know what I mean?"

"Man, I got my drink right there, and my girl's jacket was on the stool, so you know we was coming back," the man said in a growl.

"Yeah, well, I ain't know shit," Little Joe said in a deeper growl. "And here's your girl's jacket." He handed the man the jacket along with a look that definitely said, recognize, muthafucka, I'm not the one.

And sure enough, if the man didn't recognize Little Joe, he recognized the look. He stepped back and crossed his arms, as if trying to figure out his next move.

Regina wouldn't have admitted it to anyone, and probably would have denied it if anyone asked, but she suddenly got a tingle. It started in her head and spread down to her toes, and then fled back up to give her a warm—no, a hot—tingle in her private parts. This was the Little Joe she knew from sixteen years ago, the one who turned her on so much that she wanted to take him home and ravish him, or have him ravish her. The Little Joe who was always in control and controlled every situation.

Puddin' chuckled and handed the man his drink. "Maybe some introductions are in order. Actually, we don't give a fuck what your name is, but—"

"I'm Benny D., Rob-Cee's bodyguard," the man said.

"Yeah, well, like I just said, we don't give a fuck," Puddin' stated flatly, but this"—Puddin' pointed to Little Joe—"is Little Joe Blayton."

The man squinted his eyes as if trying to remember where he'd heard the name, so Yvonne decided to help him out by singing out, "Fuck with me, nigga, and I'll be on you like Satan, do you up right . . ."

The young man snapped his fingers and finished the lyrics for her. ". . . like Little Joe Blayton. Oh shit, man, this is a fucking honor," he gushed. "Shit, man. Let me buy you a drink. What you having?"

"A whiskey sour. Tell them to make it a double." Little Joe turned to the girls. "What do you ladies want? He's buying."

"Sure, man. I got it covered." He threw a fifty-dollar bill on the bar and told the bartender, "Give my man here a double whiskey sour, and these ladies anything they want." He pounded Little Joe on the shoulder. "I'll be right back, man," he said before scurrying off toward the stage.

Regina watched as the man whispered something in Rob-Cee's ear, and Puddin' ducked behind Little Joe just as the rap-per turned toward them.

"Hey y'all," Rob-Cee shouted into the mike. "I just found out we got a real celebrity in-house. Please give a big hand to one of Harlem's original gangstas, Little Joe Blayton."

Oohs and aahs filled the club along with applause, and peo-ple strained their necks to get a good look at Little Joe. He simply held his drink up in acknowledgment, then turned back toward the bar as Rob-Cee started singing the song with Little Joe's name. People came up to the bar to shake his hand, and soon a row of upside-down shot glasses were lined on the bar, signifying the number of drinks people bought for him. Little Joe seemed indifferent to the attention—he would say only a few words to his admirers, then go back to his drink, which he nursed throughout the song. One man tried to hand him a bulging piece of aluminum foil.

"Man, I don't do that . . . ," Little Joe started.

"I'll take it for him," Puddin' said, snatching the coke from the man's hand.

"You still got a big nose, I see," Little Joe said when the man left.

Yvonne took a sip from her drink. "She's like a damn elephant."

"I'll sniff to that," Puddin' said as she tucked the coke in her pocketbook.

As soon as Rob-Cee finished the song, he rushed over to Little Joe.

"Yo, man, this is a real honor," he said. "I've been hearing about you since I was a kid. My uncle used to run with you, man. Maybe you remember him. His name was Ricky Burnett."

"Yeah, yeah, I remember him." Little Joe nodded slowly. "He was a good man. I heard he got shot a couple of years ago. His wife or something, right?"

"Yeah, man. That was some wicked shit. She's still doing time for that shit. Hey, why don't you and your ladies come sit with me?"

"Hey, Robbie, baby," Puddin' said as she took off her dark glasses and grinned at him. "How's your head?"

Rob-Cee stepped back as if in shock. "What the fuck are you doing here, bitch?" He advanced toward her threateningly, but Little Joe stepped between them.

"Yeah, man, I heard you know my niece," he said calmly.

Rob-Cee's mouth dropped open. "Your niece?" he finally sputtered.

"Yeah, my niece. My favorite niece," Little Joe continued. "I heard there was some shit that jumped off between you last night, but you know that shit's squashed now, right?"

Rob-Cee chewed on his lip for a minute before saying, "Look, man, I don't mean no offense, but—"

"Then don't fucking offend me." Little Joe crossed his arms over his chest as he fixed a stony stare on the rapper.

"Man, I know you're not threatening me."

"I don't remember threatening you, but what the fuck are you gonna do if I am? Don't try to be playing with the big boys, you punk-ass muthafucka. You're out your fucking league. Way out." Little Joe cocked his head to the side and gave Rob-Cee an up and down look while barely moving his eyes. "Now, get the fuck out my face before I show you what I mean."

Rob-Cee stared at Little Joe for another minute, then turned and walked away without saying anything.

Puddin' picked up her drink, slid off the barstool, and started after him before Little Joe caught her by the arm.

"Where the fuck are you going?" he demanded.

"Come on, Uncle Little Joe," Puddin' said with a smirk. "Didn't you hear him invite us to go sit with him?"

"Girl, sit your ass back on that barstool and shut the fuck up."

"Aw, Uncle Little Joe. Is that any way for you to talk to your favorite niece?" Puddin' said with a pout.

"Excuse me, Mr. Blayton? I'm Tecumseh Joseph, and I was hoping we could speak for just a moment."

Regina looked up to see a twenty-something man wearing a dark blue suit and a closely cropped haircut extending his hand toward Little Joe.

"Yeah, well, I'm kinda busy right now," Little Joe answered as he took the man's hand.

"Well, I'll be real quick. I'm with Fox Searchlight, and I would like to talk to you about the possibility of turning your life into a movie."

"A movie?" Yvonne said quickly. "Are you for real?"

"Yes, ma'am, I am." The man took out a gold business card holder and handed her a card and another to Little Joe. "I'm a producer, and while I live in Los Angeles now, I'm originally from Harlem, and I've heard a lot about you. I think your story would make a fascinating film."

Little Joe stroked his chin. "Ain't you kinda young to be a producer?"

"Have you done any movies?" Yvonne asked before the man could answer. "Anything we might have heard of, maybe?"

"Well, I am a bit young, but so was Spike Lee when he made his first movie. And yes, I've done two feature films. *Chasing It* and *Going for It All,*" Tecumseh answered.

"I saw those movies," Yvonne gushed. "They were great. What did you say your name was?" She looked down at the card before he could answer. "Tecumseh Joseph. Oh man. This is really cool."

"Can I be in your movie, Uncle Little Joe?" Puddin' asked, nudging Little Joe on the back. "Please? Pretty please?"

"Get the fuck outta here," Little Joe answered. "I ain't doing no damn movie."

"Well, I hope you'll at least think it over," Tecumseh said calmly. "I have to get back to L.A. in the morning, but if you're interested, I'll be glad to fly you out there sometime next week so we can sit down and have a full discussion about the project."

"This is so exciting," Yvonne said after the man walked away. "Can you imagine? A movie about Little Joe. Ooh, are you going to have someone playing Regina?"

"Shit. Me and Regina are going to make our own movie tonight," Little Joe said as he pulled Regina toward him. "Ain't we, baby?"

&#x223D;

It was 3 a.m. by the time Little Joe and the girls left the listening party, and another hour by the time Little Joe had driven to Harlem and dropped off Yvonne and Puddin'. Regina was asleep when the car stopped again, and she was surprised when she opened her eyes to find that instead of pulling up in front of her house, Little Joe was parked on a hill overlooking St. Nicholas Park.

She wiped her eyes and looked at him questioningly, but he seemed lost in thought. "Is something wrong?" she finally asked.

"No." Little Joe shook his head. "I just wanted to get out and have a smoke."

"Okay." Regina settled back in her seat. It wasn't unusual for Little Joe to pull over for a cigarette. He didn't smoke in his car, so anytime he drove for more than an hour or so, he had to pull over.

"Listen, why don't you come out with me?" Little Joe said as he turned off the ignition. "We can take a walk. How about it?"

Regina looked over at him, wondering about his contemplative mood. "Um, sure," she said, then opened the door and stepped out onto the sidewalk.

After beeping on the lock and alarm on his car, Little Joe walked over and tucked her hand into the crook of his arm and started walking but saying nothing. They walked almost a block before they stopped at a concrete inlet in the park, and Little Joe removed her hand and took out a cigarette. With one foot on the small concrete wall, he inhaled slowly and looked up at the sky, then down below the hill. Regina stood next to him saying nothing and not knowing what to say.

"I missed this. I missed Harlem," he said finally. "I missed the air pollution, the jazz clubs, I missed the dirty streets, the beautiful women, I missed the crime, and I missed the culture. This is my Harlem, and they took me away from it to lock me up on some bullshit tip."

He took another puff on his cigarette and looked at Regina. "You do know I got sent up on some bullshit, right?"

Regina sat on the concrete wall, which was slightly damp as if from dew. "I can certainly believe it."

Little Joe took another puff from his cigarette, then threw it on the ground, not bothering to stub it out. "No, you can't. You figured, and still figure, that the charges were legitimate. Tell the truth."

Regina looked at Little Joe but said nothing.

"Yeah, right. Well, then, I won't make you feel bad by making you admit it," he said in a disgusted tone. "They sent me up for sixteen years on a bum rap. Took me away from everything I love for something I ain't do."

"So you mean you weren't involved in dealing heroin?" Regina asked, avoiding his eyes as she spoke.

"No, I ain't say all that. You know I'd be lying if I did." Little Joe shrugged. "Yeah, I was down with the crew, I was even on the council, but the specific charges that they sent me up for was bullshit. They had wiretaps with everyone else on tape, but they ain't had my voice on any of 'em. They had most of the other guys dead to right, but they ain't had me. All they had was a bunch of paid snitches who ain't even know me, saying I was in charge of laundering money."

"Um, were you?"

"Yeah, I was the laundryman, but they ain't know that shit," Little Joe snapped. "Didn't you just hear me say they ain't know me?"

"Sorry." Regina turned her head away.

"And you know, for real fucking real, the only reason the feds involved me in that shit was because they wanted me to roll on Natty. That was my man, but he didn't know how to keep a low profile, being on the cover of *Time* and shit. That's when they really decided they had to get his ass. I heard the word came down from the fucking White House that he had to be made an example of. It wasn't like they didn't have enough on him to send him up for life, but those muthafuckas wanted to get him sent up for triple life or some shit," Little Joe said as he lit up another cigarette. "I told them to kiss my ass."

Regina nodded. "I remember reading it in the paper. The headline said 'Little Joe says he ain't no rat.' Page three in the *Daily News*."

"Of course, the ironic shit is Natty rolled on damn near everybody else after he did twelve years. Not to get a reduced sentence, but 'cause he was fucked-up about one of his so-called friends sleeping with his wife. He rolled on the people who were already doing time on shit, and almost everyone still on the outside. He was out his fucking mind with anger and just started ratting everybody out. Everybody but me." Little Joe gave a little chuckle. "Me and Natty go way back. Grew up in the river projects together. Started stealing cars together when we like eight or nine. And it was me and him that put the organization together and headed the council. If he wanted, he coulda made sure I never got out. But he ain't roll on me. He ratted everyone else out, but he never gave 'em shit on me."

"Why do you think that was?"

"I think it was because we go so far back," Little Joe said slowly. "Me and him used to always look out for each other. And he knew that if there was no one else he coulda trusted with anything, even his woman, it was me. So he was showing me the same loyalty. He knew I loved him like a fucking brother, and he showed me he loved me the same way."

Little Joe went silent again. Regina hugged her arms, hoping to signal to Little Joe that she was cold and wanted to get back to the car, but if he noticed, he ignored her as he continued staring into the air. Minutes passed before he let out a wistful sigh. "I missed watching the sun rise over St. Nicholas Park, too. It's beautiful." He sat down next to Regina, though he was still watching the sunrise. "Almost as beautiful as you."

"Aw, thanks," Regina said lightly.

Little Joe went silent again for a few minutes, and Regina had to resist the temptation to look at her watch. It would be nice to get home before Ray-Ray woke Camille up for breakfast.

Little Joe stood up and put his foot on the concrete barrier again, staring off into space. "Regina," he said slowly, "I need you to believe me on something else."

"What's that?"

"I ain't know you was fifteen when we first started fucking around. I swear I didn't. I knew you was young but not that goddamned young." Little Joe closed his eyes and shook his head as he talked. "And I know what you mean when you said I shoulda known, but I gotta tell you I never even gave it a thought."

Regina stood up and touched him on the arm. "Little Joe, it doesn't matter."

"You made me feel like a fucking pedophile when you said that shit the other day," he said, jerking his arm away. "Like a child molester or some shit."

Regina shifted her feet. "I really didn't mean to. I was just making a bad joke."

Little Joe suddenly swung toward her. "Regina, you know you was the person I missed most while I was away?"

"What?" Regina jerked her head back at the urgency in his voice.

Little Joe grabbed her by the shoulders. "I need you to believe me on that, too. I shoulda told you before I left that I was falling in love with you, but I ain't know until I was gone and you was all I could think about. I know I was married, and I ain't saying I ain't love my wife, but I had fallen in fucking love with you. You was so sweet, and so funny and so pretty. You were so tough and so innocent at the same time. I had never met anyone like that. You had my nose wide open, and you ain't even know it."

"Little Joe, I—"

"But you never even sent me a fucking postcard," Little Joe said, abruptly letting her go. "It hurt the shit outta me the other day when you told me you knew my birthday, ya know. 'Cause how come then you never bothered to send me a birthday card? I thought about you for sixteen years constantly. And that whole time I know I ain't never even crossed your mind."

Regina turned her head away so that Little Joe wouldn't see the tears that had sprung to her eyes. "Little Joe, that's not true. I did think about you. A whole lot. But like you said, I was a kid when you left, and you were married."

"You wanna know some funny shit?" Little Joe asked, ignoring her apology. "When I ran into you and your daughter that day on Eighth Avenue, I felt like I had died and gone to heaven. And then when you told me you was divorced, well, I tried to play it off, but that shit kinda hurt."

Regina's brow furrowed. "Why?"

"Because even though I wasn't the first man you was with, it woulda been nice if I was the first man you married. The only man, shit." Little Joe shrugged. "It was one of the things that kept me going while I was away. Thinking about finding you, sweeping you off your feet, and carrying you over the doorstep." He chuckled. "That's old hat for you now, huh?"

"Uh-huh, for both of us," Regina gently reminded him.

"That night you let me stay in your house, then wouldn't let me make love to you, you know what? If it had been anyone else, I never woulda standed for that shit. I either woulda taken me some pussy or gotten my ass out there after fifteen minutes." Little Joe cocked his head and smiled. "But with you it was different. It was like, well, I waited sixteen years already 'cause the feds made me, I wanted to prove to you I could wait a few days just 'cause you want me to."

*There he goes again, being thug romantic. I should be mad at some of this shit he's saying, like about taking it and stuff, but I know he doesn't even realize what he's saying is crazy. He's just pouring out his heart. And damn if I'm not touched. Really, really touched.*

Little Joe took a deep breath. "Bottom line, Regina, is that after I fell in love with you, I never fell out. So I'm telling you straight out, Regina, I love you, okay?"

Regina hesitated. She wanted to tell him that she loved him, too, and always had in her own way, but something told her that would be a bad move. So instead, she simply said, "Okay."

Little Joe looked at her, as if waiting for her to say more. Unable to meet his eyes, she turned away again.

"Well, okay," Little Joe said, flicking his cigarette down the sidewalk. "Let me get you home."

They walked silently back to the car. After driving two blocks Little Joe turned and looked at her. "Regina, just so you know. It wasn't no big deal for me to come and help you and Puddin' out tonight, and if some shit had went down, you know I woulda been down with it. And you make sure if you need me, you let me know, 'cause I don't ever want to find out you're in a position to be hurt. I ain't got no problem saying I'd kill a mug over you, girl. And as long as Yvonne, Puddin', and Tamika are your aces, I got their shit backed up, too. I know how important it is to keep your friends safe. So if anyone fucks with y'all, you do just what you did tonight. Come get my ass."

He looked straight ahead again, but when he pulled in front of Regina's brownstone, he turned back to her. "Girl," he said after he turned off the car, "you may not know it now, but you're mines. And you're always gonna be mines." He reached over and brushed her hair out of her eyes. "You don't have to tell me you love me right now, but I know you do. And I'm going to tell you again that I love you, and I always will. You're always gonna be my Satin Doll."

Regina leaned across the seat and kissed Little Joe gently on the lips. "Little Joe, let's go to your place. I'll call Renee a little later and ask her to tell Camille that I had to do overnight research or something. But right now there's nothing I would rather do than see if I can try to make up for these sixteen years we've been apart."

"Umph," Little Joe said as he started the car again. "That's what the fuck I'm talking about. Let's go before your little crazy ass changes your mind."

It took them only a few minutes to reach the huge building complex on 116th and Lenox called Graham Court, where Little Joe lived. Once inside the apartment, they moved straight to the bedroom, which hosted a huge king-size bed with champagne-colored satin bedding and a matching chaise lounge and drapes. A gold area rug lay on the hardwood floor in front of a huge unlit fireplace, and like all the other rooms in the house, a small chandelier hung from the high ceiling. Little Joe used a remote to turn on an expensive-looking stereo system that included a tuner, CD player, reel-to-reel tape recorder, and six-foot speakers that took up almost a whole wall. The sounds of Duke Ellington's "Satin Doll" filled the room.

"I've always liked this song," Little Joe said as he walked back to Regina and pulled her into his arms. "But I didn't start loving it until I met you."

Regina closed her eyes and smiled dreamily as she took in the moment. It was like old times, and it felt good. Better than she had even remembered. His arms were so strong, and the hands that slid beneath her blouse and caressed her braless breasts were so soft. The lips that kissed her neck were so tender. And the man was so confident and experienced.

"You know what I'd like you to do?" Little Joe whispered in her ear.

"What?" Regina asked in a husky voice.

"I want you to dance for me, Gina," he said, nibbling her earlobe. "Dance for your daddy." He stepped back slightly and smiled at her.

Regina smiled back through half-closed eyes, and she began to sway to the music.

"Go ahead, Regina," Little Joe said in a hoarse voice as he sat down on the bed. "You know how to dance for me."

Licking her lips, Regina rubbed her breast with one hand while unbuttoning her blouse with the other, all the time seductively swaying and taking tiny steps back and forth to the music. Once her blouse was undone, she rolled her shoulders back and slid out of one sleeve, then the other, while still on tempo. She took the blouse in one hand and lifted it high in the air before letting it fall to the floor, all the time massaging her bare breasts with one hand until her nipples were hard and erect.

She then raised her arms and raked her hands through her

hair, fluffing it out like a lion's mane as she parted her lips and let her head slightly loll to one side. Her hands slid down into the waistband of her skirt, and she did a slow cha-cha back and forth in front of Little Joe, who was letting out little grunts and groans.

She turned her back to him, reached behind, and was slowly unzipping her skirt when he suddenly reached out and grabbed her. He threw her facedown on the bed, pinning her hands above her head. Before she could even catch her breath, he was literally ripping her skirt and panties off. He was then on her, biting and nibbling the side of her neck and down her shoulder blades as he undid his pants.

It was so fast that it was furious, and Regina moaned in ecstasy as she felt his naked body lower onto hers, his hardness pressing into the small of her back. He used his legs to pry hers open, then while one hand still pinned her arms, he took his other hand and slid it between her buttocks down past her rectum to her vagina, which was overflowing with moisture. They both moaned as he felt her wetness. He used his knees to push her legs even farther apart, and without seeming to take aim, he thrust himself so deep inside her she screamed in both pain and pleasure. She struggled to catch her breath while he pumped inside her furiously, and she valiantly tried to match her movements to his, but she was so close to climax she could barely control herself. He was the one in control, and she knew that was the way he liked it. Always had. She let out another scream as she felt herself climaxing, but just when she reached her peak, he suddenly withdrew.

"No," Regina screamed. "Please! No!"

"Tell me who this pussy belongs to," Little Joe growled in her ear.

"It's yours, Daddy," Regina yelled at the top of her lungs.

"Whose?" he growled again.

"Yours, it's all yours," Regina pleaded.

"Goddamn right it's mine." Little Joe reached under her

stomach and flipped her on her back. "This shit belongs to me!" He thrust himself inside her once again, but this time she was ready and her hips flew up to meet him. Regina's nails clawed into his back and his clawed into hers as they furiously climaxed together.

It was a good five minutes before either of them could once again move or catch their breath. Finally, Little Joe lifted himself off her, then reached over and pushed her sweaty hair away from her face.

"I can't believe I had to wait sixteen years for that," he said with a sigh. "And damn if it wasn't worth it."

# chapter eleven

You seen the *Post* today? Puddin' made it to Page Six."

"Get out of here!" Regina grabbed the newspaper Yvonne handed her and quickly flipped through. Sure enough, there was a smiling Puddin' posing over an unconscious Rob-Cee and holding a bottle of champagne and flashing a victory sign. The caption read "Unidentified woman knocks out gangsta rapper Rob-Cee at listening party. Sources say the unnamed woman, who was Rob-Cee's date for the evening, conked the rapper over the head with a bottle of champagne after he insulted her and her friends."

"Damn," Regina said. She closed the paper and put it down on the table next to her food. "Puddin' just found her fifteen minutes of fame, huh?"

"I wonder why it ran a day late."

"Don't know." Regina shrugged. "The photographer probably got it to the paper late."

"She'd better be glad you came up with the idea of bringing Little Joe to the listening party. Otherwise she'd be six feet under right now," Yvonne said with a little laugh. "Hey, I know I'm a little late, but you could have waited for me before you ordered."

"You're almost twenty minutes late, and I have an appointment in a half hour," Regina said, slicing into her broiled chicken breast.

"Hello, Regina. Long time no see."

Regina looked up at a tall light-skinned man wearing an ill-fitting blue suit. "Robert?" She shot Yvonne a "what the fuck" look before she could stop herself, and immediately hoped Robert hadn't noticed. If he did, he chose to ignore it as he sat down next to Yvonne.

"I came to take Yvonne out to lunch, and she told me she was meeting you, so I asked if I could tag along," he said laconically. "I hope you don't mind."

"Not at all," Regina said quickly. "It's good to see you again." *Boy, does he look bad.* Robert was always thin, but now he looked almost skeletal. His hazel eyes were dull and sunken, his cheeks hollowed, and his skin, which used to have a reddish tint, was now a dull yellow. Even his short wavy hair seemed dreary and dry. He still had a hint of his once good looks, but he was a far cry from the dashingly handsome law student they had all met six years before. Time and drugs had not been kind to Robert.

"It's good to see you, too." Robert reached over and patted Regina's hand. "How long has it been? About three years now? How's little Camille?"

"She's doing fine, thanks. And how are your kids?"

"They're fine, I suppose. My ex won't let me have any contact with them, but that's another story," Robert said with an inappropriate laugh. "Let's just say divorce can be hell."

Regina nodded but said nothing, since she could think of nothing to say. After all, she didn't blame Robert's ex; she wouldn't want a dusthead anywhere near her child, either. And Yvonne was crazy for letting him around her twelve-year-old son, Johnny. "Well, um, how's the job? I heard you're with the Bronx D.A.'s Office."

"It's going fine, thanks," Robert said with a smile as he took Yvonne's hand. "It's different, going from defense attorney to being on a prosecutorial team, but I'm adjusting."

"Good," Regina said, feigning interest. "Do you have any cases yet?"

"He's only been there a week, so he's kind of familiarizing himself with the office," Yvonne responded for him. "But I'm sure he'll be arguing cases soon."

"Well, let me know when you do. I'd love to come to court to show you my support," Regina lied.

"Well, right now I'm assigned to family court. And those are closed hearings," Robert said in an almost embarrassed tone. "But I'm sure I'll work up to Homicide in no time at all. After all, I do have three years' litigation experience."

"I'm sure you will," Regina said, and took another bite of her chicken. "Hey, are you guys going to order or what? I have to split soon."

Yvonne picked up one of the menus the waiter had placed on the table while they were talking. "I think I might just have a salad. Maybe a large Caesar salad. What about you, Robert?"

"I'm starved," Robert said, flipping through the menu. "I'm thinking a steak. Do they have prime rib?"

"I'm sure they do. Maybe I'll have the same," Yvonne said, then closed her menu.

"Okay, babe. Why don't you order for me while I go to the little boys' room." Robert leaned over and kissed Yvonne on the cheek. "I'll be right back."

"Why don't you let this be my treat?" Yvonne said after Robert left. "You got the last one, didn't you?"

"No, Puddin' did," Regina said simply.

"Well, whatever, it's on me this time."

Regina looked at Yvonne but said nothing.

"Oh, all right," Yvonne said as she slammed the menu on

the table. "Don't say shit, okay? I'm treating because Robert hasn't gotten his first paycheck yet. All right, smarty-pants?"

"I didn't say a word."

"Yeah, well, I heard what you were thinking."

Regina shrugged. "It's true he just ordered prime rib on your dime, but you know what Mama Tee always used to say. If you love him, I adore him."

"And you really would if you gave him a chance." Yvonne leaned over the table. "He's really sweet, Gina. And he's treating me like a queen. Fixing me breakfast in bed on the weekends, going food shopping with me . . ."

"With your money."

"Don't start, Regina," Yvonne said in a threatening voice.

"Sorry. Go ahead. You were telling me how great Robert is."

"Well, he just is. And I hope you and Puddin' and Tamika would just give him a chance. If you were around him more, you'd see how great he is."

"Uh-huh, and how does he treat Johnny?" Regina asked in an innocent voice.

Yvonne shifted in her seat. "Well, actually, Johnny's been spending a lot of time with Mama Tee lately. They haven't really been around each other. But when they do see each other, Robert treats him good."

Regina shrugged. "Like I said, if you love him, I adore him."

"Um, hey, baby. Did you order yet?"

Regina looked up to see a wide-eyed Robert standing over the table, shifting from one foot to the other, like he couldn't keep still.

"No, sorry, sweetie. The waiter hasn't come back yet," Yvonne said, and patted the seat next to her.

"Well, um, look. I'm gonna have to take a rain check," Robert said, scratching his neck and looking around. "I, uh, got a phone call from the office while I was in the bathroom. Um, my office. I, uh, gotta get right over there for, um, a meeting."

"Oh. Well, okay," Yvonne said with a crestfallen face. "I'll see you tonight, then, okay?"

"Yeah, baby. I'll try to get home early," Robert said as he continued to scratch and fidget. "Um, come on and walk me outside for a minute."

Yvonne got up without looking at Regina, picked up her pocketbook, and headed to the door with Robert, who left without bothering to tell Regina good-bye.

He was in the bathroom either smoking crack or getting zooted up on angel dust, Regina decided. He wasn't going to keep his job long if he kept going to the office high. But chances were he wasn't going back to the office. He was going to hole up somewhere and finish his high. Damn, Yvonne was really biting off more than she could chew this time.

She reached into her pocketbook, took out her cell phone, and dialed Tamika's number.

"Hey, Mika," she said when her friend answered. "I'm sitting here having lunch with Yvonne, and, girl, we're going to have to have a serious sit-down with girlfriend."

"Gina? Are you home? Can you get over here real quick?" Tamika said in an urgent voice.

"No, I'm on 57th Street at Jimmy's Downtown. I can jump in the car and get to you in like twenty minutes, though."

"Don't worry about it, then. Let me call you right back," Tamika said quickly. "I'm dealing with something right now."

"What's up? You okay?" Regina asked, concerned at the distress in Tamika's usually calm voice.

"I don' know yet. I'll give you a callback in a little bit. I gotta get off the phone now." The line went dead.

Regina snapped her flip phone shut just as Yvonne got back to the table. "Look, girl, I gotta split. There's something wrong at Tamika's, and I'm gonna shoot over there real quick."

"Why? What happened?" Yvonne said as she sat down.

"I don't know, but it sounds serious. So I'm on my way."

Regina picked up her pocketbook and car keys. "You said you're getting the bill, right?"

Yvonne waved for the waiter. "Hold up," she told Regina. "I'm coming with you."

⤳

"Tamika, what's going on? Are you okay?" Regina said as she and Yvonne entered the brownstone and saw Tamika's tearstained face.

"Yes. I mean, no. I mean . . . damn, I don't know what I mean," Tamika all but wailed.

"I can't believe this shit." David's voice boomed from another room.

"Oh my God, did David hit you?" Yvonne said, rushing over to hug Tamika.

"What? Oh come on, Yvonne," Tamika said angrily. "No. Of course, he didn't hit me."

Regina shot Yvonne an angry look, wondering why she would even go there. To Tamika, she said, "Okay, you need to calm down and tell us what the hell is going on."

"You guys aren't going to believe this," Tamika said in a weary voice. "Two thugs came to my door demanding to see Darren. When I told them he wasn't here, they told me that he had their drugs and they wanted it back."

"What!" Regina all but shouted.

"Get the hell out of here," Yvonne said as she sank down in a chair. "Darren?"

"Yeah, Darren." David's towering frame suddenly appeared in the doorway. The six-foot-three man who Regina always thought looked like a teddy bear now looked like an angry grizzly. "Tamika," he thundered, "did you go through the clothes hamper in the bathroom?"

"No, I didn't get to it yet."

David disappeared, and the women could hear him tearing through the bathroom.

"Start from the beginning," Regina said, sitting down next to Tamika.

"Okay," Tamika responded. "These two young thugs came to the door this afternoon and said that Darren had their drugs. They said they had paid him to hold the drugs for them."

Regina nodded. "I know they do that a lot. Get young boys to hold or run for them because if they get caught, they won't get any real time, since they're underage."

"Yeah, but Darren?" Yvonne said skeptically. "That boy isn't into anything but video games. How the hell did he get into drugs?"

Tamika shook her head dismally. "All I can figure is that he was trying to get money to pay for some video station, the Xbox 360, that I refused to buy for him last week. He musta been approached and decided to go for it to raise the money himself."

"Well, where is Darren? What's he saying about all this?" Regina demanded.

"He and Sissy spent the night over at Mama Tee's. I've been trying to get him on the phone all afternoon since this happened, but there's no answer."

Yvonne nodded. "Mama Tee took all the kids to Great Adventure this morning. They probably won't be home until late tonight."

"Regina, you should have seen those guys. They were polite, but they were serious. They said they didn't want any trouble, but they wanted their drugs back. They said they were going to stop by again tomorrow. I called David right after they left, and we've been tearing up the house looking for the drugs ever since."

"Tamika," Yvonne said slowly, "what kind of drugs are they talking about, and how much?"

Tamika started crying again but wiped at her eyes. "Crack. One hundred vials."

"Good Lord," Regina said in a whisper.

"Okay." Yvonne stood up. "You checked his bedroom, I guess. And David got the bathroom covered. Anyone checked the kitchen yet?"

Tamika nodded. "And the living room and den, too."

"Okay, Regina, you take the closets, I'll take Sissy's room."

"I already checked the closets," Tamika said as they all stood up.

"Well, I'll check them again," Regina said, heading for the closet in Darren's room.

This was no time to be neat, Regina decided as she checked shoe boxes and coat pockets, throwing things on the floor after they'd been checked. It wasn't until she moved to the hallway closet and found Darren's favorite jacket that she hit pay dirt.

"I got it," she shouted.

Tamika, Yvonne, and David came running as Regina carefully spilled the stash of little glass crack vials onto the floor.

"Where was it?" Tamika asked.

"In this jacket," Regina said, pointing to the lightweight green jacket.

"I looked in there," David said.

"There's a secret pocket in the lining," Regina said. She picked up one of the vials. "I know because I bought it for him for his birthday last year."

"Will you look at all this shit?" Yvonne picked up another vial. "I wonder how much it's all worth. Did they say, Tamika?"

"No, but I know it's worth a lot." Tamika began scooping the vials up.

"Give me those," David said gruffly.

"What are you going to do with them?" Yvonne asked.

"I'm turning them over to the police."

Regina and Yvonne looked at each other, then at Tamika.

"Um, David, do you think that's a good idea?" Regina asked hesitantly. "I mean, those boys are going to be back here tomorrow for their product."

"And when they do, we'll have the police waiting for them," David said, and hugged Tamika around the shoulders.

"Yeah, but, well . . ." Regina looked at Yvonne for help, but her friend just grimaced and said nothing. "David, you don't know this type. You get them arrested, and that won't be the end of it. The people they work for are going to come after you, if only to save face. They might decide to make an example of you."

"Regina's right," Yvonne broke in. "It might just be better to give them their shit and call it a day."

"Well, I don't see it like that," David said as he hugged Tamika more tightly. "Remember, as a lawyer, I'm an officer of the court. I'm not turning over this poison to these young punks to peddle on the street. And I'm not going to be intimidated, either."

"Oh God." Tamika started crying softly.

"Baby, please don't tell me you think they're right," David said. "You don't really think we should just cave in to these punks."

"No, David," Tamika whimpered. "But I don't want to put Darren, and even Sissy, in any danger. They said as long as I gave them back their stuff, they'd just call it even. Maybe we could—"

"No," David said emphatically. "That's not going to happen. I'm the man of this house, and I'm going to protect my family. And I'm not going to do that by bowing and kowtowing to a bunch of drug dealers. If they come back here, I'll be ready for them. And that's that."

"David," Regina broke in, in a hesitant voice. "There's one more thing you might want to consider. If you go to the police, won't they implicate Darren? I mean, he'll probably get off easy, but . . ."

"But he'll just get a police record," Tamika wailed. "Oh no, David. I don't want my son to have a record."

"Tamika, calm down. If anything, he'll get a juvie record, and I can get it expunged."

"David, I don't want my son to get in the system." Tamika beat him against the chest as she talked. "I've seen what can happen. I'm not going to let it happen to my son. You can't let it happen. You can't."

"Okay, Tamika, okay." David grabbed Tamika's hands and pulled her into a hug. "I won't turn the vials over to the police. But I'm not turning them over to those thugs, either. I'll get rid of the crack. I'll throw it down the toilet or burn it in the fireplace or something. Everything's going to be okay, all right?" He kissed Tamika on the cheek and tried to wipe the tears from her face, but she buried her head in his chest.

"Ladies, thanks for coming over, and thanks for helping out," David said as he cradled Tamika in his arms. "But maybe you should leave now. We'll take care of it from here."

Regina nodded, and she and Yvonne walked back to the living room and gathered their things.

"Morally, David's doing the right thing," Yvonne said as they stepped back into the fresh air.

"Yeah, but I just hope their morals will keep their asses safe," Regina said dismally. "Come on. I'll give you a ride home."

⤙⤚

"Mama Tee, aren't you tired? We've been to seven stores already, and you've only bought one dress." Regina tried to keep the grumble out of her voice, but her feet were hurting and her head was aching, and she knew that her day was far from over. Tamika, Sissy, and Darren were all at Regina's, since the thugs had promised to visit Tamika's house again. Camille and Renee were there, too, so Regina had a full house awaiting her.

When she had promised to take Mama Tee to 125th Street to do some shopping, she thought they'd be finished in an hour, but two hours had already passed, and the seventy-year-old woman still didn't seem ready to go home.

"Hmph. You be too young to be complain so much, mon," Mama Tee said as they strolled out of the children's clothing store. "Look at me. I be old nuff to be you nana and me still be walking straight and strong. De Lawd don't be making women like me He don't. Push me first baby out when I was forty. Still be pushing dem out if me man Sefton ain't die."

"Yes, Mama Tee," Regina said, following the older woman, who was walking at a pace that was unbelievably fast for even a woman of fifty.

"Mon, look at dis," Mama Tee said, pointing at a mannequin in one of the women's clothing stores. "Blumstein's used to be here dis spot. You know dem was de first store on dis street with black dummies in the window."

"You mean black mannequins?"

Mama Tee nodded as she moved down the street with Regina at her heels. "Black dummies and de first black Santy, too. Me and you mama brought you and Yvonne to sit on he lap."

"I remember," Regina lied.

"Course dem only did it 'cause of Adam Clayton Powell, may the Lawd bless his sainted soul." Mama Tee stopped at one of the many vendor tables on the street. "How much you charge me for dis?" she asked, tapping on a hardcover book.

Regina gasped. "Mama Tee, since when did you start reading Zane's books? You're old to be reading this!"

"I charge you twenty dollars for it, auntie," the vendor said in a Nigerian accent. "They sell for twenty-four dollars in the store."

"How you be calling me auntie and den charge me twenty dollars?" Mama Tee asked in an indignant voice. "Mon, you gimme dat book for sixteen dollars or I take me damn money elsewhere."

"Auntie, I got to feed my kids," the vendor protested. "Give me eighteen dollars."

"Mama Tee, do you know what this book is about?" Regina said, snatching the book from the table. "I don't think you want—"

"Me give you seventeen dollars, mon, and not no more," Mama Tee said firmly.

"You robbing me, auntie. You want a bag?" the vendor said, taking the book from Regina's hand.

"Wait. Gimme dis one and dis one, too." Mama Tee picked up two more hardcover books. "Same price."

Regina looked at the titles and shook her head. "Mama Tee, do you know what kind of books Zane writes?" she asked as they continued down the street.

"How you do what de girl be writing 'less you read dem?"

"Yeah, I do, but—"

"Dem good enough for you and not for me?" Mama Tee chuckled.

"Mama Tee, those books are erotica. You don't—"

"Girl, hush now. Me know what kind of books dem be. Done read five of Zane books already. Good books." Mama Tee stopped at another vendor stand, picked up a package of incense, and made a face before throwing it back down. "Me like Zane. If me Sefton ain't die, we be doing dat stuff dat girl be writing, mon. Just 'cause me ting be old don't mean it be dried up. Me still got the juice."

Regina tried to keep a straight face but inwardly laughed. Mama Tee was a mess.

"Blumstein's still were not no good store," Mama Tee said, resuming their earlier conversation as if they had never changed subjects. "Dem ain't hire no colored folks . . ." She paused. "No black folks till Mr. Powell made dey. And dem charge too much money for dey stuff."

Mama Tee stopped in front of another stand, picked up a small plain copper bracelet, and waved it in front of Regina's face. "You got you baby one of dese yet?"

Regina nodded, causing Mama Tee to smile. "You mama trained you right," she said. "Copper bracelets keep a child in good health. Dat and a spoonful of castor oil every day. You be giving dat baby her castor oil?"

"Yes, Mama Tee."

"And her cod-liver oil?"

"Yes, Mama Tee."

"Good girl. Yvonne don't be give the stuff to my grand, but Johnny gets it when he comes stays with his nana." Mama Tee put the copper bracelet back down on the stand.

"You don't want no bracelet, miss?" said the stand vendor, a light-skinned man with shoulder-length dreadlocks.

"No. Don't be needing it," Mama Tee said as she prepared to move away.

"Makes me sick when people be poking around my shit and they ain't intending to buy," the dreadlocked vendor told a teenager standing next to him. "Old fucking hag."

"I beg your pardon, mon?" Mama Tee turned to face the vendor. "What you be calling me?" she asked, fixing him with a stony stare.

"You've got some damn nerve." Regina stepped up close to the man and pointed her finger in his face. "You'd better—"

"If you don't be wanting people to pick up you wares, you don't be putting dey out here to be picked. Every mon be selling on dis street know dat," Mama Tee snapped at him. "And you best learn some respect for you elders."

"This man disrespect you, auntie?"

Regina looked up to see the man from whom Mama Tee had bought her books.

"Called me out me name, de bloody clot." Mama Tee spat on the ground. "De boy got no raising. He need be thrashed." She turned to the book vendor. "Go to it, mon. Thrash him good."

"Miss, I didn't mean no harm," the dreadlocked man said, putting his hands in front of him as if in surrender. "I wasn't even talking about you."

Regina grunted. "Yes, he was. The coward. It's easy enough to talk shit to an old lady, but I see you change your tune when a man steps to you, huh?"

"Tut, tut, tut. Just leave him be," Mama Tee said, waving her hand dismissively. "Dis nancy man not be worth me time. Come on and we go."

"Well, you come and see me next time you come to 125th Street, auntie," the book vendor said, gently patting her on the back. "You know I'll treat you right."

"God bless ye, mon. Me back when me finish me books," Mama Tee said as she started down the street.

"Never did like no light-skin dandies," Mama Tee said when they were almost half a block away. "Just like that damn Robert me Yvonne be spending time with. She be telling me he don't live with her, but every time I be at her place he be there in he undershirt. Me own daughter tink me stupid."

"Well, Mama Tee, I don't think that—"

"Chile, hush you mouth. You girls always be lying for each other, and me done hear enough lies lately," Mama Tee said, not bothering to turn and look at Regina. She stopped at another stand and picked up a pair of cowrie shell earrings. "Yvonne got dese already," she said, putting them back down and moving on, with Regina still trailing behind.

"You put your holes in your baby's ear yet? Her be too young for you putting holes in she ear. She . . ."

⤸

Her feet were hurting so bad by the time Regina finally dropped Mama Tee off that she took her shoes off, threw them in the backseat of the car, and drove herself home in her bare feet. Luckily, she got a parking spot right in front of her brownstone, so she wouldn't have far to walk. In fact, she decided, she didn't even have to put her shoes back on. The rough sidewalk was preferable to trying to squeeze back into her heels.

She saw Tamika running the steps before she got out the car. "Walk me over to my house," Tamika said. "David's still over there by himself, and I'm just worried."

Regina groaned, looked at Tamika, then her shoes in the backseat, and groaned again. "Okay. But you have to give me a foot massage when we get back."

"Gina," Tamika said as they walked the half block to her house, "do you think we're handling this right? Give those guys the drugs back or just turn the matter over to the police?"

Regina hesitated. "Well, like we said yesterday, getting the police involved would have involved Darren, and nobody wants him to get caught up in it. I don't see how else we could handle it. Just give them the product back and let's go on with our lives."

Tamika sighed. "David and I argued all night about it. It goes against everything he believes in, but then, he wasn't raised around here like we were. He doesn't know what people like these are capable of." She opened her door with a key, and they walked in. "David," she called out, "it's me and Regina."

David appeared in the hallway. "Hey. What are you doing over here? I thought we agreed you were going to stay at Regina's until I called and said everything was over with."

Tamika walked over and kissed him. "I know. I just had a funny feeling, so I got Regina to walk over with me. I just wanted to make sure you're okay."

"I'm fine. I was just making myself a sandwich."

Tamika nuzzled up to his chest, and he obligingly put his arms around her in a hug. "Well," Tamika said, "I promise to make you a great big dinner as soon as we're allowed home. How's that?"

David stroked her hair. "Sounds good. How about you make—"

*Buzz.*

David, Tamika, and Regina all froze at the sound of the doorbell. It wasn't until it rang a second time that David pushed Tamika away and walked toward the door. "Ya'll get in the living room," he told them over his shoulder.

"Where's the stuff?" Tamika ran down the hall after him. "Don't let them in. Just give them the stuff through the door and let them leave."

David pushed her away. "Get in the living room," he said roughly. "Now!"

Tamika ran back down the hallway, grabbed Regina, and pulled her into the living room doorway.

"What the hell's going on?" Regina whispered. "David's decided to flip the script?"

Tamika shrugged, then put her finger to her lips, signaling Regina to be quiet so they could hear what was going on.

"Yo, man. We don't want no trouble, either. I came to your house all polite yesterday and me and your lady had a nice little convo, and I'm just following up on our agreement. Now you telling me you ain't giving me my shit?" Regina heard a teenager's voice say.

"If you don't want no trouble, there won't be any trouble," David answered. "I told you we don't have your stuff, and if you come around here bothering my wife or son again, I'm going to handle this in a whole other way. You're lucky we didn't have the police waiting for you today."

Regina and Tamika stepped out in the hallway just in time to see a teenager pull a gun and push David back against the vestibule wall.

"Gina! Quick! Call the police," Tamika said before running toward the front door.

"We're lucky, huh? Motherfucker, you'll be lucky if I don't blow your fucking brains out," the teenager snarled. The voice was different from that of the other teen and twice as frightening. "I was trying to be nice, but hand over my shit before your fucking luck runs out."

Regina pulled her cell phone from her pocket and frantically dialed 911.

"Leave him alone. I'll get you your stuff," Tamika shouted when she reached the men. She tried to pull the teenager's arm away from David, but another teenager grabbed her.

"Get your hands off her," David roared. He tried to get past the teen with the gun, but the boy pushed the gun against his jugular and cocked the trigger.

"Man, ain't nobody trying to hurt the lady," the teenager holding Tamika said. "We ain't come here to hurt nobody. We just want our shit."

"Miss, get a police car out to 219 West 119th Street. Quick. There's a man with a gun and he's holding people hostage." Regina snapped her cell phone shut and walked into the hallway.

"Listen, the police are on the way, but we can settle this real quick," she said in as even a voice as she could manage. "David, just tell me where these young men's stuff is and let me give it to them and then they'll be on their way." She looked at the teenager holding Tamika. "Right?" Regina asked.

The teen nodded. "That's all we wanted. I said it before: we didn't come up here for any kind of shit."

"David," Regina said calmly, "where's their stuff?"

David looked at her from the corner of his eye, since he was unable to move his head because of the gun pressed against his throat. "We don't have it. I flushed it all down the toilet."

"Oh God no," Tamika said before her knees began to buckle. The teenager holding her struggled to keep her on her feet.

"Jerry, man. Let me put a cap in this motherfucker's ass," the teen with the gun said.

"No!" said the now recovered Tamika. "You shoot him, and

you'll all wind up in jail. My husband works for the District Attorney's Office."

"And if you shoot him, you'll be bringing the heat down on you like you don't even know what," Regina added quickly.

"Just tell me how much the stuff is worth, and we'll pay you for it," Tamika pleaded with the one named Jerry. "We don't want any more trouble."

"Hell no," David croaked.

"Shut the fuck up," the teen with the gun said.

"Lady, give us a thou, and we'll call it even," Jerry said angrily. "But hurry up."

"I don't have that much in the house," Tamika said frantically. "But I can write you a check."

"Miss, you really think we're stupid?" Jerry said with disgust. "Come on, y'all, let's get outta here."

The teenager holding the gun against David's throat glared at him angrily, then uncocked the trigger. He pulled the gun away from David's throat, then slammed it against the side of David's head, knocking him to his knees.

"David!" Tamika cried out. She struggled out of Jerry's loosened grip and ran over to her husband, who was trying to stand up. Regina tried to help, but David groggily pushed her away.

"Miss, you know we came to you right when we first came to you," Jerry said as he stood over Tamika and David. "It's not our fault this shit went down like this, but I'm going to tell you it ain't over yet. Not by a long shot."

With that, he walked out the door, followed by the other teenager.

# chapter twelve

Iow do I look, Aunt Gina?" Renee said as she entered the living room, where Regina was flipping through a magazine. "Liz's coming to pick me up for the movies."

Regina looked her niece up and down. Baggy jeans, ball cap, and basketball jersey. Her usual uniform. "You look fine, sweetie," she said with a little laugh.

"What's so funny?"

Regina stood up and gave her niece a hug. "You, silly. You wear the same type of thing every day, and every day you ask me how you look. I just find it kind of funny is all."

Renee smirked, then gave her aunt a kiss on the cheek. "Whatever."

"Whatever yourself." Regina straightened Renee's ball cap. "So how are you doing?"

"I'm fine."

"You sure?" Regina sat back down on the couch and patted the cushion next to her.

"What do you mean?" Renee asked after she sat next to Regina.

"Well, I know it's been hard on you lately. It has to be." Regina put her arm around Renee. "With the way your mother's been acting about your sexuality."

"Yeah. Well . . ." Renee's eyes lowered to the floor, and she paused before continuing a few seconds later. "Well, it's not like I didn't know she was going to take it hard, but I just didn't figure how hard. But it's partly my fault. I was chickenshit for not telling her outright instead of letting her find out by listening in on the phone." Renee shrugged. "But then, I was chickenshit in the way I told you, too. I'm not handling it well, so I don't know why I should expect anyone else to handle it well."

Regina raised her eyebrow. "You're not handling your sexuality well? You're uncomfortable with it?"

Renee shook her head. "No, no. I mean, I'm not handling coming out of the closet well because I don't want to hurt the people I love. Like you and Mom."

Regina sighed. "Well, I'm not hurt. I was surprised, of course, but not hurt. And I really do believe your mom is going to come around. She just needs some time."

"She hangs up on me every time I call, you know."

Regina kissed Renee on the forehead. "She's been doing the same to me. But like I said, she's going to need some time."

Renee sighed, then put her head on her aunt's shoulder for a moment before looking up at the clock on the wall. "Wow! Talking about time, look at the clock. It's almost six. Liz better hurry up, or we're going to miss the movies."

"Six? Oh damn!" Regina jumped up from the couch and hurried over to the stairway. "Camille, will you come on?" she called out. "Aunt Puddin's going to be here in a minute, and you're not even dressed yet. Why don't you just let me help you pick something out?"

"I'm a big girl, Mommy. I can pick out my clothes," Camille called back down. "I'm five years old now."

*Buzzzzz.*

"Oh shoot, that must be Puddin'," Regina grumbled, and went to answer the door. "Camille, will you come on so I can see what you're wearing?"

"Hi, Miss Regina," Liz said brightly as Regina opened the door.

"Come on in," Regina said, stepping aside so the girl could come inside. In contrast to Renee's jersey and baggy jeans, Liz—a tall thin girl with shoulder-length hair—wore a tight black miniskirt and a bright blue polyester button-down blouse. Her makeup was lightly but expertly done: baby-pink lipstick, with just a hint of blush that accentuated her mahogany complexion. *Well,* Regina thought, *I guess I know who plays the boy and who plays the girlie girl in this relationship.*

She watched as the two girls gave each other a quick innocuous embrace, and breathed an inward sigh of relief that they left it at that. Ray-Ray may have been eighteen and able to do what she wanted with whomever she wanted, but Regina wasn't sure she was ready to see her niece kissing a woman. Or even holding hands with one, for that matter.

"Mommy, I'm ready," Camille said as she slowly trudged down the steps wearing a pink party dress and white tights with black patent-leather shoes. A little dressed up to just be going to Yvonne's for dinner, but Regina decided to let it slide. After all, she thought, this was the first time that Camille had been allowed to dress herself.

"You look wonderful, baby," she said, opening her arms so that Camille could rush in. But surprisingly, the young girl walked to her almost in a daze. "Mommy, I'm not feeling so good."

"Oh my God, you're boiling hot, baby," Regina said after she hugged her, then felt her forehead. "Do you have chills or anything?"

"No, but my head hurts. Right here and here." Camille pointed to her forehead and the left side of her head.

"Oh, baby. I guess you've got an ear infection again." Regina kissed her on the cheek. "I've still got some penicillin from last time, and let me give you some Tylenol and get you to bed. We'll get you to the doctor in the morning. I'll call Yvonne and tell her we won't be able to make it tonight. I can't leave my sick baby here all by herself, can I?"

Liz cleared her throat. "Um, Miss Regina, if you want, Renee and I can sit with her while you go out. I heard the DMX movie we were going to see isn't all that, anyway."

"You really wanna, Liz?" Renee asked in surprise. "I mean, I sure don't mind."

"I don't, either. Let's do your aunt a favor," Liz said with a huge smile.

*Uh-huh,* Regina thought. *She's trying to ingratiate herself with the family. Just like any other boyfriend. I mean, girlfriend.* "No, that's okay," she said out loud. "I'll just call Yvonne and say that I won't be able to make it. She'll understand."

"No, she won't, Aunt Gina," Renee said adamantly. "Aunt Yvonne's been calling you all day to make sure you'd be there tonight. And you said yourself that Aunt Puddin' was coming over in a minute."

"Ray-Ray, thanks, but I can't—"

"Mommy, please can't Ray-Ray and Liz stay with me?" Camille tugged on Regina's arm.

"Well, I don't know . . ."

"Please, Mommy?" Camille started whining. "I like it when Ray-Ray babysits me."

"Well, Camille, I don't know." Regina tried to stall to get some time to think. It wasn't that she didn't trust Renee and Liz to be in the house alone, but it really was that she didn't want to leave Renee and Liz in the house by themselves. She didn't think that they would do anything in front of Camille, but, well . . .

Oh God, she was acting just as homophobic as Brenda, she thought, catching herself. Of course, they wouldn't do anything in front of Camille. If Ray-Ray was here with a boy,

Regina would trust her to be levelheaded. She just didn't like the idea of Ray-Ray and Liz sitting on the couch holding hands—or even kissing after they got Camille to sleep. Oh God, she really was acting like a homophobe.

*Buzzz.*

"That must be Puddin'," Regina said, looking at the door. "Okay, if you girls really swear you don't mind, I'd be very grateful if you can watch Camille for me. Chances are she's going to go right to sleep after I give her some medicine."

"And if she doesn't, we can read her a story," Renee said gleefully. "I just bought her a new book, *African Princess*, by Joyce Hansen. We'll just keep her company until she nods off."

*Buzzz.*

Regina picked Camille up in her arms and started carrying her up the stairs. "Okay, let your Aunt Puddin' in and tell her I'll be right down. And thanks again, girls."

∽

"I hope Mama Tee did the cooking. You know that damn Yvonne can't cook for shit," Puddin' grumbled as she and Regina climbed the stairs from the subway station. "I don't know what made her think she should be cooking dinner. And I don't know why you insisted we should go, like I don't have something better to do on a Saturday night."

Regina pulled the scarf from her neck and wrapped it around her head in order to stop it from mussing her newly permed hair, cursing the fact that the car wouldn't start and they had to take the subway. It was only five blocks from the subway to Yvonne's apartment, but her feet were already hurting. The shoes she wore were made for pushing down on an accelerator, not pounding the pavement. Especially after spending the whole subway ride standing up, since they couldn't get seats on the train.

"Well," she said, "I'm pretty sure she just wants to prove

how domesticated Robert is. She's determined to have us like him, you know."

"Yeah, well, whatever," Puddin' grumbled. "Like I said, I just hope that Mama Tee did the cooking. I don't blame Tamika and David for not coming."

"Yeah, well, I wish that was the reason they didn't come." Regina sighed. "I'm really worried about what's going to happen. And David hasn't gone to work since all this crap happened last week."

"Yeah, and I can't believe all this shit that's went down," Puddin' said, and shook her head.

Regina shivered. "Yeah, now, that was some scary shit. I don't know why the hell he couldn't have just given them their shit. That's all they wanted. Now who the hell knows how this shit's going to end up? They probably would have shot David on the spot if Tamika didn't lie and say he worked for the D.A.'s Office." She sighed again. "I just hope those thugs decide to call it a loss and that'll be the end of it."

"Yeah, well, I wouldn't bet on it," Puddin' grunted.

Regina squinted her eyes as she looked up the block. "Oh my God, Puddin', am I seeing things, or is that some guy streaking down the street butt naked?"

"Oh shit, it is," Puddin' said. "I thought that shit went out in the seventies. And looky-looky, the muthafucka got a woodie."

"How the hell can you see that from here?" Regina said as she tugged on Puddin's arm. "Come on, let's cross the street. He's heading this way."

"Naw, I wanna see." Puddin' held her ground and squinted her eyes for a better look.

"Well, you can stand there and see if you want, I'm heading across." Regina pulled her pocketbook farther up her shoulder and prepared to step out into the street.

"Oh shit. Oh fucking shit," Puddin' all but shouted as she

pulled Regina back toward her. "Gina, tell me that's not who I think it is."

"I don't give a shit who it is," Regina said, trying to pull free. "I'm not going to—"

"Gina, maybe I'm blind, but ain't that Yvonne's boyfriend?"

"What?" Regina looked up at the man running toward them full speed. She couldn't be sure, but it did look like Robert with his hair standing on end, a wild look in his eyes, and sure enough, just as Puddin' said, a full erection. "Oh my God. Get the fuck outta here. I do believe that's him. Puddin', let's get the hell outta here."

Regina tried again to cross the street, but Robert barreled into her before she could make her escape.

"Regina, Regina," he shouted as he grabbed her in a bear hug. "I love you. Let's make a baby."

"Get the hell off of me," Regina said, struggling to break free. She looked to Puddin' for help, but her friend was leaning on a building, convulsed with laughter.

"Will you please let me go?" Regina screamed as Robert tried to kiss her on the mouth.

She was so engrossed in trying to get away that she didn't even notice the police car that pulled in front of them until the two officers jumped out, pulled Robert by the scruff of his neck, and threw him across the car.

"Are you okay, miss?" one of the officers asked her as the other pulled out his handcuffs.

Regina was tempted to tell them that she wasn't and let them arrest Robert's ass, but then she thought about Yvonne. Her friend would never forgive her if she just let them haul Robert off to jail.

"I'm fine, I'm fine," she said, looking over at Puddin', who was still doubled over with laughter. "Look, please don't arrest him. This is, uh, my, uh, cousin. He's a little disoriented because of some medicine he's taken. I'm taking him home right now."

"Yeah, yeah, that's good old cousin Robert," Puddin' managed to get out through bouts of laughter. "He just took too much of his antidepressant."

"Well, are you sure?" The officer looked at Regina skeptically.

"Oh yes, believe me. In fact, he's actually an assistant D.A. in the Bronx. I mean, obviously, he doesn't have any ID on him at the moment. But like I said, it's the medicine, and we're going to get him home and calm him down."

"Well," the officer said as he let Robert up from the car, "why don't we just give you all a lift home, then?"

"No, that won't be necessary," Regina assured them. "We're just a couple of buildings down. We'll make it okay. Won't we, Robert?" She turned to him and had to cover her eyes with her hand. In just the few seconds that he had been let free, Robert had run over to a large tree and was kissing and humping it as if he were in bed with a wild woman.

"Leave me alone. I'm going to make a baby with Mother Nature. We're going to start a whole new human race," he shouted as the police pried him away.

Puddin' had actually collapsed on the sidewalk with laughter. "Oh shit," she managed to get out. "He's going to get splinters in that big dick."

"Fuck it," Regina said, throwing up her hands. "What precinct are you guys taking him to? I'll let his girlfriend know, and she can handle it."

❧

"Look, I did what I could," Regina tried to explain to Yvonne, who was seated on the couch seemingly in shock. "They almost let him go—"

"But the bitch started trying to fuck a tree," Puddin' said, shrieking with laughter again. "Talking about he was going to make a baby with Mother Nature."

"Puddin', you watch you damn mouth in dis house," Mama Tee said in her thick Trinidadian accent.

"Sorry, Mama Tee, but if you had been there . . ."

"I still would not be using no such language," Mama Tee huffed.

"Mama, please." Yvonne waved her hand wearily.

"Don't you 'Mama, please' me, you hear me, girl?" Mama Tee raved. "I told you dat man be no damn good. Be smoking that ganja stuff in de bathroom like nobody know what he be doing."

Puddin' snorted and took a seat on the couch next to Yvonne. "Mama Tee, that ain't no reefer that man be smoking. Reefer don't make you act like that. I'm telling you he was downright dusty."

"Say he be what?" Mama Tee asked suspiciously.

"He's smoking angel dust," Puddin' said, ignoring the elbow jab Yvonne gave her. "It's an elephant tranquilizer or something, isn't it, Regina?"

"Um, something like that," Regina said helplessly.

"Oh me Lawd." Mama Tee threw up her hands. "De man be smoking elephant tranquilize in me daughter's bathroom with me grandson right here in de house. Oh me sweet Lawd."

"Mama, Robert doesn't do that," Yvonne said as she gave Puddin' a dirty look. "He's just not been feeling well lately."

"Yeah, well, he looked like he was feeling pretty good tonight." Puddin' chuckled.

"Shut up, Puddin'," Yvonne snapped.

"You shut up," Puddin' retorted. "I'm not the one with a man running down the street humping everything in sight."

"Oh me Lawd." Mama Tee shook her head. "Johnny, get you coat, man. You come stay with you nana tonight."

Yvonne walked her mother and son to the door, then whirled around to face Puddin'. "You know you make me sick, Puddin'. Why'd you have to say all that stuff in front of my mother?"

"Yeah, well, you make me sicker. Bringing that dusty muthafucka around your kid. Do you know how crazy people using angel dust can get? Remember that time we was going to some party in the Bronx, and Ralphie decided we were stupid for walking down the steps from the elevated train because he could just take one step and beat us down? He stepped off the platform and broke both his legs. Stupid bastard coulda killed himself. He was smoking dust that night, you know."

"Not to mention how violent people on dust can get." Regina sat down on the love seat, took off her shoes, and rubbed her feet. "Don't you remember when we were teenagers hearing about that kid on 119th Street who killed his mother, then wrote on the wall in her blood 'I love my mother'?"

Puddin nodded. "Yeah, Fat Freddy. I remember him. He was a sweet kid until he started smoking that shit."

"Look," Yvonne said with a snarl. "Neither of you have any place to talk about who I have in my life. Puddin', you're the biggest coke fiend in Harlem. And you, Regina, you're fucking the biggest dope dealer in the city."

"I may be a coke fiend, but I don't have any children that I'm putting in jeopardy," Puddin' said with a wave of her hand.

"And first off, I don't bring Little Joe anywhere near my daughter," Regina joined in, "and second, he *was* the biggest dealer in the city. He's retired now, and you know it. He's living off his investments."

"Investments made from selling dope," Yvonne retorted.

Regina looked at her friend warily. "Yeah, that's right, investments from selling dope. But be that as it may, he's not selling dope now, and he's certainly not using anything. Especially not something like angel dust, which can make someone violent enough to kill. Dust is the only drug I know that can make a mofo do some shit like that." Regina put her hand on her hip. "And I agree with Puddin', it's fucked-up that you let Robert around Johnny when he's fucking with that shit."

"Well, Robert's not violent," Yvonne said defensively. "And

he musta just had a relapse. This is the first time he's smoked any dust since he's been in New York."

"Oh please." Puddin' sucked her teeth. "Regina told me he got dusty a few days ago when you guys were in the restaurant."

"No, he didn't," Yvonne snapped.

"Oh, so hold up, you knew he was smoking dust when he was in Philly, and you still let him move in here?" Regina said incredulously.

"He admitted he had smoked it a few times," Yvonne said reluctantly. "But he told me he quit, and I believe him."

" 'Cause you wanted to believe him," Puddin' said with a snort. "And after I saw how big his dick is, I can see why. That boy is packing."

Yvonne glared at Puddin', then at Regina. "It has nothing to do with a big dick, okay? And I'd appreciate it if you two would stop ganging up on me in my own house."

"Ain't nobody trying to gang up on your ass." Puddin' waved her hand dismissively. "We're your friends, so we just ain't gonna stand by and let you pull some stupid shit without saying anything."

"What I don't understand is how the hell in this day and age would someone start smoking dust," Regina said. "I mean, Robert? When we first met him, he was barely a social drinker. How the hell did he start on dust?"

"Yeah, I thought that shit played out in the seventies," Puddin' added. She stood up. "Yvonne, what you got to drink?"

"It was after we broke up and I left Philly," Yvonne answered Regina and ignored Puddin'. "He was on the rebound and started messing with some girl from West Philly who got him hooked."

"Oh yeah, so I guess it's your fault for leaving his married ass, huh?" Puddin' said as she walked to the kitchen.

"I didn't say that," Yvonne yelled after her.

"Yeah, if that's the way he put it, then that's what he wanted to make you feel," Regina said angrily. "So you should feel guilty about his habit."

"He doesn't have a habit," Yvonne protested. "I'm telling you this is the first time he's used it since he's moved in here."

"You're in fucking denial," Puddin' said as she emerged from the kitchen holding a bottle of wine and a glass.

"I have to agree with Puddin'," Regina said with a shrug. "And if you're not smart enough to throw his ass out on general principle, you should at least consider it because of Johnny. He doesn't need to be around this shit. I'm glad Camille had a cold and had to stay home with Ray-Ray, or they would have witnessed him trying to make a baby with a damn tree."

"Well, I guess I'd better go try and get him out of jail." Yvonne sighed and got up from the couch.

"Sit your ass back down." Puddin' pulled her back down to the couch. "Chances are they took him to Bellevue Hospital to sleep that shit off. They're not going to release him today. Worry about that shit tomorrow."

"Yeah, she's right." Regina nodded. "You need to sit here and try to figure out your life. Do you really need him in here putting you and Johnny in jeopardy?"

"Yeah, I mean he's got a big dick," Puddin' said, giggling, "but I'm sure if you try hard enough, you can find bigger."

"You are so fucking crass." Yvonne shot Puddin' a dirty look. "We're not together because of the sex. We happen to be in love."

"You love his dick, and he loves his dust," Puddin' said as she took a sip of the wine. "Sounds like a relationship made in heaven."

Regina stood up. "Slow down on that wine, Puddin'. I think I need a drink myself."

# chapter thirteen

That's some crazy shit," Little Joe said as he and Regina sat in Amy Ruth's Restaurant having Sunday brunch. "You would think people woulda learned their lesson from all those people dying from dust back in the seventies and not be fucking with that shit now."

Regina shrugged and took a forkful of her home fries. "All I know is Yvonne is out her damn mind. I just hope she wises up before she gets hurt."

Little Joe nodded. "I'm just saying that angel dust is fucked-up. I never understood why people fucked with that shit. You couldn't pay me to try it."

"You mean there's a drug you actually haven't tried?" Regina teased.

"Shit, there's a lot of drugs I ain't tried," Little Joe said, and took a gulp of his mimosa. "I was hooked on junk for almost eight years, and I had to OD and almost die before I got off that shit."

"You were hooked on heroin?" Regina said. "I didn't know that."

"It was a long time before I knew you. I started using the shit when I was like twelve. Kicked it when I was like twenty. Natty was hooked, too, and we went cold turkey together. I ain't used no drugs since then. Except you know I like to get my drink on," he said, holding his mimosa up as if in salute.

*Wow,* Regina thought. *A former junkie who made a fortune selling junk.* That was unusual. Most former addicts did their best to stay away from the shit because the temptation was too great. Another tribute to Little Joe's self-control.

"I ever told you I tried heroin once?" she asked suddenly.

"Get the fuck outta here." Little Joe almost spilled his drink.

"Yeah, I was about seventeen, and someone had some, so I decided to try it. I didn't shoot up, though. I just snorted it."

"And did you like it?"

"Liked it way too much." Regina shook her head. "Liked it enough to know I shouldn't ever try it again. And anyway, it made me throw up."

"Yeah, it does that to a lot of people the first time. Heroin's a muscle relaxant, you know." Little Joe stared at her intently. "I'm glad you made the right decision, though. It woulda killed me to come out and find you were strung out on smack."

"No, I like myself way too much for that," Regina said simply.

"And I like you way too much myself. I woulda had to come out and kick your ass and then dragged that same pretty ass into detox."

"Aw, don't you say the sweetest things?" Regina smiled as she cut into her sausage. She and Little Joe had been seeing each other for weeks now, though not on a daily basis. More like two or three times a week, but that seemed enough for both of them. She hadn't let Little Joe stay over since that first night, but she'd been back to his big beautiful apartment at Graham Court with its high ceilings and glittering chandeliers a number of times.

He treated her like a queen, or as much as Little Joe knew how to treat someone like a queen. He wasn't the type to pull out chairs or open car doors, but he showered her with affection and made her feel like she was the only woman in the world. She wasn't sure that she was the only woman he was seeing, which was one reason she still insisted that he use condoms, but she had seen no evidence of another woman. It was her robe that hung in his walk-in closet. Her perfume and toiletries in his bathroom. Her picture on his dresser. If he was faking it, he was faking it well. And she was sure as hell enjoying it. The Broadway plays. The trips to Atlantic City. The sweet yet ferocious lovemaking.

"So have you been thinking about that weekend trip to the Bahamas?" Little Joe asked as if he were reading her mind. "We can leave on Friday and be back by Monday morning. Or even Sunday night, if you insist."

"I don't know—," Regina started, but then abruptly stopped. Was that Charles sitting across the room looking at her? It was, she realized. He was at a table not twelve feet away, with a bunch of fat cats in business suits who were laughing it up over something, but Charles seemed oblivious to them as he stared at her. Her own stare made Little Joe turn around to follow her gaze.

"You know him?" Little Joe asked. "Oh, don't tell me. That's the honorable Charles Whitfield, isn't it? Is that why you wanted to come here? To run into him?"

"No," Regina said hurriedly. "I didn't even know he was in town. And I didn't know he even knew about Amy Ruth's."

"Well, it certainly looks like he's in town, doesn't it?" Little Joe turned around to face her. "You wanna leave?"

"Yeah, maybe we should," Regina said, wiping her mouth with her napkin before dropping it on the table and gathering up her pocketbook. "I don't think he's going to say anything to us, but I don't want to make him feel uncomfortable. It might be kinda hard on him—"

"Hey, Regina, how are you doing? Good to see you."

Regina looked up to see a smile on Charles's lips that some-how didn't reach his eyes.

"Oh, I'm fine," she said with a calmness she didn't feel. "I didn't know you were in town."

"I just flew in this morning. I was going to give you and Camille a call after I was through with brunch. By the way"— Charles crossed his arms—"where is Camille?"

"Ray-Ray took her to the zoo." Regina shifted in her chair.

"What time will they be back? I'd like to spend some time with my daughter before I fly back to Washington tonight," Charles said, tapping his foot.

"Oh, is Congress in session?" Little Joe asked casually, then took a sip of his drink.

"Actually, no," Charles said, turning his attention, though not his body, toward Little Joe. "But I have a couple of bills that will be coming up when it does go in session, and I need to get a head start. And you are?"

"Joseph Blayton." Little Joe extended his hand, which Charles shook tersely. "Good to meet you."

"The pleasure is mine, I'm sure," Charles said with sarcasm dripping from his voice.

Little Joe rose slowly from the table. "Well, I need a quick trip to the men's room. I'll be back shortly, Regina. Good meeting you, Congressman."

"Well," Regina said after Little Joe departed, "what brings you on a one-day trip to New York?" She tried to keep her voice light, but her stomach was doing flip-flops.

"Just schmoozing some of the local politicos about that pos-sible senatorial bid," Charles answered. "And what a surprise running into you. Having a nice brunch with your latest, I sup-pose?"

Regina pursed her lips for a moment before responding. "Charles, we've been divorced how long now? Four years? I really don't think I need to answer to you because I'm out eating with a friend."

"No, of course not," Charles said after a brief pause. "You didn't say what time Ray-Ray would be bringing Camille home."

"Probably four or five."

"Good, maybe I can take them both out to dinner and catch a late flight to D.C. You're free to join us, of course." He paused again. "That's if you're free."

"I'll have to let you know," Regina said lightly.

"Of course. I don't want to put you out of—"

"Don't worry. I won't let you," Regina said, cutting him off just as Little Joe arrived back at the table.

"Mr. Congressman, I see you're still here," Little Joe said before taking his seat.

"I was just going back to my table," Charles said curtly. "It was good meeting you. I'll talk to you later, Regina." He walked stiffly back to the three men at his table.

"I hope that wasn't too painful," Little Joe said, waving for a waitress to bring him another mimosa.

"No, it was fine." Regina picked up her fork and started playing with her food. "I'd like to go ahead and leave now, if you don't mind."

"Okay. I'm not finished eating, but we can go." Little Joe called the waitress back to cancel his drink order and ask for the check.

As they exited the restaurant, Regina noticed one of the men at Charles's table look at Little Joe intently, then lean over and whisper something in Charles's ear. *This can't be good,* she thought.

Sure enough, she hadn't even fastened her seat belt in Little Joe's BMW before her cell phone started ringing. She flipped open the phone and saw that, as she suspected, it was Charles's cell phone number. She flipped it closed without answering it. If Little Joe noticed, and she was sure he had, he decided to say nothing. She leaned her head back against the seat and closed her eyes, saying nothing during the entire ride home, ignoring her cell phone, which kept ringing on and off.

They had just turned the corner to her house when she saw fire engines and smoke coming from a house a little farther down the block.

"Oh shit." She bolted upright in her seat. "That's Tamika's house."

"Get the fuck outta here." Little Joe sped down the block and parked directly behind the fire engine. Regina jumped out before he could even take the key out of the ignition.

"Tamika," she said as she ran up to her friend, who was standing on the sidewalk holding Sissy and Darren in her arms. "What happened? Are you okay? Oh my God, where's David?"

"We're okay," Tamika said, trying to keep the panic out of her voice. "David's okay, too. He's over there talking to the fire chief."

"What happened?" Regina said as Little Joe rushed over to her side.

"They firebombed us," Tamika said angrily. "Those mother . . ." She looked down at her frightened children. "Little Joe, would you mind if my kids sit in your car for a while?"

"Sure, no problem," he said, though he made no attempt to move. "The doors are open," he told Darren.

"Now, what motherfuckers did this?" he asked Tamika after the kids were in the car.

"You didn't tell him, Regina?" Tamika said wearily.

Regina shook her head.

"Darren was holding crack for some local dealers, and he ran off with their stuff because he got scared," Tamika said. "They knocked on my door asking for their stuff, but it was the first I'd heard about it. We found it later, but David flushed it down the toilet—"

"Stupid move," Regina muttered.

Tamika ignored her. "Anyway, when they came back the

next time, they got into it with David, and later he had them arrested—not for the drugs, but for harassment. But they musta made their bail. I'm guessing this is their retribution. Throwing a Molotov cocktail through my living room window."

Little Joe stood with his arms crossed over his chest as she talked, and when she finished, he asked, "Who's David?"

"Her husband," Regina said. "He's a lawyer."

"And what's the name of these punk dealers?" he asked Tamika.

"Jerry something or other and—" She caught herself. "Look, Little Joe, it doesn't matter," she said hurriedly. "I don't want you to get involved."

Little Joe uncrossed his arms and shrugged. "Didn't say I was gonna get involved, sweets. Your husband's a lawyer, huh? Let's see if he can take care of it the legal way."

Before anyone could answer, David strode up to Tamika. His face was grim, and his eyes were red, Regina assumed from the smoke.

"Baby, the fire chief wants to know if we have fire insurance," he said as he gently massaged the back of Tamika's neck. "We do, right?"

"Yes, of course, we do, David," Tamika answered. "You know we do."

"Yeah, I was pretty sure, but I'm just a bit, you know, a little scattered right now, so I just wanted to make sure," he said with a sigh. "Hey, girl," he said, giving Regina a quick hug. "Thanks for coming over. Tamika could use a little support right now. She's a bit shaken up."

"Looks like you need some support right now, too, Dave," Regina said gently. "You going to be okay?"

"Yeah, yeah, I'm fine," David said absentmindedly as his cell phone began to ring.

"Hello? . . . Yvonne, didn't I say I'd get back to you on that? I'm dealing with my own stuff here . . . Well, Robert's problems aren't my problems . . . Yvonne, please, I don't want to hang up on you, but I'm going to have to if you don't stop . . . Look, Yvonne . . . Damn it, my house was just set on fire. Tamika and I have our own problems . . . All right. I'll see what I can spare. But I'm not footing the whole thing. Maybe I can spare a few hundred . . . That's right, just a few hundred. And I'm warning you not to push it . . . Hell no, I'm not going to represent him. Y'all got that crap. Like I been trying to tell you, I got my own situation here I'm trying to deal with . . . Yeah, I promise I'll call you back as soon as I talk to Tamika and we can figure out what we can spare . . . No, sorry, but I'm not going to keep this from Tamika. In fact, I'm talking in front of her right now . . . Yeah, well, good-bye, Yvonne. I'm hanging up."

"Don't tell me she's harassing you to loan her money to bail out Robert, huh?" Regina shook her head in disgust. "She called me this morning. Bail's only set at fifteen hundred, but she's broke and I refused to help her get his ass out. Just on G.P."

"She's already called me three times. I'm more than tempted to just tell her she's on her own. I don't care how long I've known Robert, I didn't sign on for this crap," David said in a disgusted voice. "Especially right now." He gave Tamika's arm a quick squeeze and turned to walk away, but then turned back.

"Hey, man," he said, extending his hand to Little Joe, "I'm sorry to be rude. I'm David Corbett. Tamika's husband."

"Joe Blayton," Little Joe said as he shook his hand. "I'm sorry to meet you under these circumstances."

"Mr. Blayton is, uh, a friend of mine," Regina stammered. *Damn,* she thought. She'd been hoping that she wouldn't have to make introductions. It was bad enough that Little Joe had to meet Charles this afternoon; now he had to meet Charles's best friend, too? "He was just giving me a ride home when we saw what was going on."

"The kids are sitting in his car," Tamika said, pointing to Little Joe's BMW, "so they can get a little peace from all this hullabaloo."

"Good looking out, man. Thanks." David gave Little Joe a pat on the back, then went back to talk to the fire chief.

Little Joe looked at his Rolex. "Look, I gotta shove off, unless there's something you think I can do around here."

Regina and Tamika both shook their heads.

"Okay, then. I got an appointment I got to make." He gave Tamika a quick hug, then turned to Regina. "How about dinner tonight? You gonna be free?"

Regina looked at Tamika and shook her head. "No, I'm gonna stick around and make sure everything is okay. In fact, Tamika, why don't you and the family stay with me for a while until everything settles down? At least until you can repair the damage to your house."

Tamika sighed. "No, that's okay. The house is livable. Only the kitchen was really destroyed. Some smoke damage to the rest, but like I said, livable. I'm going to get in there as soon as the fire chief clears the scene."

"Then I'll stick around and help you, Mika." Regina hugged her friend.

"Well, then, I'll talk to you later, Regina." Little Joe kissed her on the cheek. "Tamika, I hope everything works out. Regina, come walk me to the car so you can get the kids."

"So," he said as they headed toward the car. "Any reason you didn't introduce me to Mr. Lawyer back there?"

"No," Regina said slowly. "It's just that with everything going on . . ."

"Or to your husband back at the restaurant?"

Regina looked down at the ground as she thought about what she could say in her defense.

"Don't bother, I got it," Little Joe snapped. He opened the car door. "Okay, kiddies, go on back to your mommy. I'll see you later." After they scrambled out, he got in and pulled off without looking back at Regina.

Regina's shoulders slumped as she escorted the children back to Tamika. She had a lot of explaining to Little Joe to do, and she had no idea how she was going to pull it off. Especially since she wasn't exactly sure why she hadn't made the introductions.

"You okay, Gina?" Tamika said after she hugged her children, then sent them across the street to sit on the stoop of one of her neighbors' houses. "You look like your house just burnt down."

Regina shrugged. "It looks like my little house of cards is certainly tumbling down."

"Trouble with Little Joe?"

"Nothing I can't handle. By the way, I didn't tell Little Joe about those punks for the same reason you just realized you shouldn't have," Regina said, shaking her head. "I didn't think you wanted him involved, and Little Joe doesn't know how *not* to get involved when it comes to his friends. And you have to remember," she continued, "even though we're grown women now, he really still thinks of all of us as fifteen- or sixteen-year-olds who need protection."

Tamika sucked her teeth. "I can't believe I messed up like that. At least I caught myself before I gave out those names."

"You gave him the name of one of them."

"Yeah, well, not his last name."

Regina looked at Tamika as if she had lost her mind. "Mika, come on now. You know you don't need somebody's last name to track them in the street."

Tamika crossed her arms, then shrugged. "Well, I just kinda said his name kinda quicklike, so maybe Little Joe won't even remember."

Regina looked up when she heard a car screech to a halt halfway down the block. To her shock, Charles emerged, a stern look on his face, and strode toward them. For a moment she thought he had hunted her down because he was upset about her not answering his calls, then felt silly when she realized that his best friend, David, must have called him and told him what had happened.

"Tamika," Charles said, pulling her into a hug and ignoring Regina. "Are you okay? Is everyone all right?"

"Yeah, we were all in the living room watching television when it happened. No one was hurt. Just scared as all hell."

"Good," he said, releasing her. "Where's David?"

"I think he's still talking to the fire chief." She pointed in the direction of the fire engine.

"Okay. Let me go talk to him real quick," Charles said before striding off.

"Um, was it my imagination, or did Charles just dis the hell outta you?" Tamika asked timidly.

"Yeah, he did." Regina gave a sigh. "He saw me and Little Joe at Amy Ruth's a little bit ago, which was bad enough for his ego, but then to make it worse, as we were leaving, I think someone at his table told him about Little Joe's past."

"Uh-oh." Tamika chuckled. "The shit is about to hit the fan. Speaking of which, here come David and Charles now."

David gave Tamika a distracted hug. "Mika, they're getting ready to pull off. They said it's all right for us to go back in the house. But why don't we see if the kids can stay with Mama Tee tonight while we—"

"They can stay with me," Regina cut in. "Ray-Ray, Camille, and I aren't doing anything tonight. We'd love to have them."

*Oh shit,* she thought almost as soon as she finished talking. Just that fast she had forgotten that Charles had wanted to take Camille and Ray-Ray out for an early dinner. She looked at him, and at first he returned her look with an accusing glare, but then said, "Yeah, I can buy pizza and ice cream, and we can have a little party to try and get their minds off of everything. That's if Regina doesn't have other plans."

"I said I don't," Regina said huffily.

"Just checking," Charles retorted. "I wouldn't want you to have to change your plans on my behalf."

"Didn't I say I don't have plans, Charles?" Regina snapped. "How about we just drop it? We'll be home, and if you want to bring over pizza and ice cream, that'll be fine. If not, that's fine, too."

"Excuse me," David broke in, "I don't mean to interrupt whatever shit you two are going through, but I'd say right now Tamika and I are going through some bigger shit. So get a grip, okay?"

A guilty look spread across both Regina's and Charles's faces.

"Look, I'm sorry," Regina said. "We'd love to have the kids over." She turned to Charles. "And thanks, in advance, for the pizza and ice cream. You're right. It will be like a little party."

"Yeah, man." Charles slapped David on the back. "And like I told you before, you just let me know what I can do, and you know you got it."

The two men exchanged pounds, then gave each other a quick hug.

"Thanks, man," David said as they broke free. "It's good to have friends like you and Regina. And I'm sorry for snapping at you like that."

"No prob, man. It was our bad. And I'll try and get in touch with Robert to let him know what happened, not that he'll be much help. But just so he knows, since he's right here in the city."

"Um, Charles?" Regina tugged his arm. "Robert's in jail. Yvonne's trying to raise bail money for him now. I'm surprised she hasn't called you yet."

"Robert's in jail?" Charles's head swung from David to Regina. "What happened?"

"Oh God, that's a long story. I'll tell you over a slice with pepperoni," Regina said with a sigh as they walked up the street toward her house. "I promise you'll find it interesting, though."

"Oh my God, Aunt Gina! What happened?" Regina looked up to see Renee and Camille running toward her, with Liz trailing a little behind. "Is that Aunt Tamika's house with the fire engine in front of it?"

"Daddy!" Camille yelled, and jumped into Charles's arms.

"Hey, little girl!" he said, kissing her and twirling around.

"Daddy," Camille said, looking over his shoulder, "what happened to Aunt Tamika and Uncle David's house?"

"That *is* Aunt Tamika's house," Renee exclaimed as Liz finally caught up to them. "What happened? Is everyone okay?"

"They're fine, Ray-Ray." Regina put her arm around her niece and turned her around so they could all go back to her house. "There was a little accident. But I'll explain it to you later, okay?"

"Hey, you too big to give your Uncle Charles a hug and a kiss?" Charles playfully slapped Renee on the head. He gently put Camille down.

"I'm sorry, Uncle Charles." Grinning, Renee stood on her tiptoes to hug him around the neck. "I didn't know you were in town."

"Just got in today." He kissed her on the cheek. "And who's your little friend here?" he said, nodding toward Liz.

"Oh, this is my girlfriend, Liz Boyce," she answered. "Liz, this is my Uncle Charles. Camille's father."

Regina smiled to herself at the ambiguity of the word "girlfriend." She hadn't told Charles about the sexuality announcement.

"Good to meet you, Liz." Charles extended his hand, and the girl shook it with a smile.

"Hey, why don't you girls run up in front of us so you can start straightening up the house? Sissy and Darren are coming over, and we're going to have a little mini-party, okay?"

Renee, Camille, and Liz hurried ahead.

"I'm glad Ray-Ray's hanging out with a girl who knows how to dress like a girl," Charles said to Regina in a whisper. "Maybe she'll finally stop wearing all these sweat suits and actually get into a skirt. Although maybe not as short as Liz's."

Regina smiled and tucked her hand through Charles's arm. "Charles, it seems the Robert story isn't the only one I need to explain to you this afternoon. But like I said to you before, you'll find it all very interesting."

# chapter fourteen

Well, you look like shit warmed over," Regina said after opening the door for Tamika the following morning.

"Thanks," Tamika croaked in a hoarse voice. "Just so you know, I feel a helluva lot worse than I look." Her locks were pulled back into a ponytail, which usually made her look younger than her thirty-one years, but now only served to accentuate a haggard face. There were dark bags under her bloodshot eyes, and her shoulders sagged as she shuffled past Regina and into the living room.

Camille, who was sitting cross-legged on the hardwood floor, was the first one to notice her. "Hey, Aunt Mika. You gonna play 'Nopoly with us?"

"Monopoly," Renee corrected her. "And we're not playing until everyone finishes their food. Hi, Aunt Tamika."

"Mommy!" Sissy jumped up from the floor and ran over to her mother, almost knocking her down. "I thought those guys mighta come back and killed you and Daddy."

"Oh, shut up, stupid." Darren stood in the corner of the

room, hands in his pockets, alternately glaring at his little sister and looking down at the floor.

Tamika managed a weak smile and put her hands out toward her son. "Don't call your sister stupid, Darren. Now, come give Mommy a hug."

"I don't need a hug," Darren muttered.

Tamika walked over and tried to pull him into her arms. "Well, maybe *I* do. You know I miss you and your sister when you spend the night out." She kissed him on the cheek, though he stood immobile, his hands still in his pockets. "You okay, baby?" she asked gently.

He nodded but chewed his lips as if trying not to cry.

"Okay," she said, stepping away from him. "Looks like you kids are in the middle of breakfast, huh?" she said as she looked at the plastic plates.

"Come on in the kitchen and get some coffee," Regina said to Tamika, leading the way.

"I can't believe you cooked pancakes and sausage for all these kids," Tamika said, sitting down at Regina's kitchen table. "Why didn't you just give them all a bowl of cereal and call it a day?"

"I would have," Regina said. She retrieved a container of orange juice from the refrigerator. "You can thank Liz here. She was up at the break of dawn cooking and baking. You have to taste her biscuits. Homemade, I might add. No help from the Pillsbury Doughboy."

"It was nothing, Miss Regina," Liz said as she stood over the sink washing dishes. "I really love to cook. And since it's only me and Frank at home, I don't really get a chance to cook for a lot of people."

"Frank?" Regina asked with a raised eyebrow.

"My father. I've always called him Frank."

"Liz, why don't you take a break and sit down with us for a moment?" Regina said.

"Sure, as soon as I finish. It won't be but a minute."

Regina looked at the girl and shook her head. Here it was not even 10 a.m., and Liz was perfectly made up, her hair pulled into a stylish bun, with just a few tendrils escaping to frame her face. She wore the black skintight jeans she had changed into the night before, but this morning it was topped off by one of Renee's oversize sweatshirts. But instead of looking boyish, she looked like a ballet dancer.

"Mommy, can I have some more orange juice?" Camille's voice rang out from the living room.

"I'll get that, Miss Regina," Liz said. She grabbed a glass and the orange juice from the table.

"Did she spend the night?" Tamika whispered after Liz left.

Regina nodded. "In the guest room, of course."

"Well, she seems like a really nice girl," Tamika said, picking at her toast. "Ray-Ray could have done a lot worse."

"Yeah," Regina said dryly. "She'll make a great wife."

"Gina," Tamika said softly, "are you having a problem with their, um, their relationship?"

"I'm trying not to," Regina said with a shrug. "I mean, you know I've never had a problem with people's sexuality, but . . ." She stopped speaking when Liz reentered the kitchen.

"Do you want some more toast, Miss Tamika?" Liz asked on the way back to the sink. "Or are you sure you don't want me to make you some bacon or sausage?"

"No, honey, I'm fine," Tamika said, and took a sip of her coffee. "So you said it's just you and your father at home?"

"Uh-huh." Liz nodded. "My mother died in an automobile accident when I was two, and I lived with my grandmother for a while, but she had a stroke when I was six, and I went to live with Frank. It's just been me and him ever since."

Regina's hand flew to her mouth. "Oh, I'm sorry. I didn't know your mother was dead. You poor thing."

Liz shrugged. "Such is life, huh? But, you know, you have to do the best you can with what you have, right?"

"I guess," Regina said weakly as Renee entered the kitchen.

"Liz? We're going to play a game of Monopoly. You want in?" Renee asked.

"Sure," Liz said quickly, then looked at Regina and Tamika.

"Go ahead. I need to talk to Tamika about a bunch of stuff, anyway," Regina said with a wave of her hand.

"Poor kid," Tamika said after Liz and Renee left the kitchen. "First her mother dying and then her grandmother."

"Yeah, and she's such a sweet girl," Regina said. "Damn, now I feel bad for trying so hard not to like her. Especially since she's always gone out of her way to be helpful." She sighed. "Maybe I'm just a bitch. I don't know, maybe I'm just tired. I didn't really get any sleep last night."

"Worrying about Ray-Ray sneaking into the guest room with Liz, or worrying about Little Joe and Charles?" Tamika asked with a grin.

"Both, and you don't have to be so damn smug about it, you know." Regina cut her eyes at her friend. "But enough about me and little minor problems. What's going on with the house?"

"Well, the kitchen has to be redone, and we're going to have to paint all of downstairs, but the upstairs was pretty much spared except for some minor smoke damage. David and I were up most of the night trying to put things together." Tamika picked at the toast in front of her as she spoke. "David called a contractor. That is, after Yvonne came over at seven this morning to pick up money for Robert's bail."

"How much did she get from you guys?"

"Five hundred. Not that we can really afford it right now, but that girl really knows how to beg," Tamika said. "It's not like it's going to break us, but this sure isn't the time to be loaning out money."

"Yeah, she finally begged three hundred out of me. She walked over here right after she came from your house," Regina said. "And I told her ass off about bugging you guys right now, but you know how that girl is when she's on a mission."

"Yeah, I know. She's always been like that. But I've never seen her like this about any man but Robert. I can't understand it. He must have some kind of a spell over her."

"Well, I don't know if he has a spell, but I got to tell you he's probably laying some serious pipe on her. He certainly has the equipment," Regina said with a giggle. "Did I tell you his johnson is like ten inches? And skinny as he's gotten, it doesn't look like his dick has lost any weight."

"Get out." Tamika started laughing. "Girl, I wish I had been there that night. I would have been right there with Puddin' rolling on the sidewalk cracking up."

"Girl, it was a mess." Regina shook her head. "That was the funniest shit I've ever seen. Even when they handcuffed him and threw him in the back of the police car, he laid down on the seat and started humping that. I guess he wanted to make little baby patrol cars or something."

"Hmph, that man is really messed up. And it's so hard to believe. Remember when we first met Robert, Charles, and David at that club that night? It was Robert that was the most suave and sophisticated," Tamika said.

"And the smoothest talker. David was all shy, and Charles was acting like a sarcastic asshole, but old Robert was laying his rap down like he didn't care. He had Yvonne's nose open that first night."

"And ever since—" Tamika started.

"Mom, can me and Sissy go home now?" Darren interrupted them. He walked over to his mother, his shoulders sagging and his head bowed down almost to his chest. "We really want to go home."

"No, I don't, Mommy," Sissy called from the living room. "I'm beating Ray-Ray and Liz at Monopoly."

"She's not beating me, though," Camille's voice rang out.

"That's 'cause she's cheating!" Sissy charged.

"Well, she can stay, but I really do want to go home." Darren lifted his head up, revealing red swollen eyes. "Please?"

"Darren, baby, are you okay?" Tamika tugged him close to her.

"I'm fine," Darren said as he pulled away. "I just wanna go home."

Tamika looked at her son a minute before saying anything. "Okay, baby, we'll be going home in a minute. Go get your stuff ready."

"He's been crying all night," Regina said after he left. "He wouldn't say anything to anyone, and he didn't want any pizza or ice cream. He barely touched his breakfast this morning."

"He blames himself for what happened," Tamika said, her eyes suddenly brimming with tears.

"Well . . ."

"Yeah, I know ultimately it is his fault, and he knows he did wrong, and he's really sorry. He feels so damn guilty I'm almost afraid he's going to hurt himself. No twelve-year-old kid needs to be going through all this," Tamika said defensively. "And I feel so helpless, because I don't know how to make it stop at this point. I even suggested to David that we sell the house or rent it out and just move, but he won't even discuss it."

"Damn. I hate for you to have to move over this shit. Can't David get them locked up?"

"We can't prove it was them that did it. Mrs. Evans said she saw a blue car drive up to the house, then someone get out the backseat and throw something through the window before the fire started, but she didn't get a good look." Tamika took a deep breath. "And even if she did, she wouldn't admit it in court. She'd be afraid she'd wind up in the same spot we're in now."

*Buzzz.*

"That must be Puddin'," Regina said, getting up from the table.

Tamika looked at her watch. "Puddin'? It's not even eleven in the morning. She doesn't usually get up until like four or something. Why's she coming over here so early?"

"For you, sweetie. When I called her and told her what happened yesterday, she felt so bad about not being there for you that I actually got her to agree to come over so we could help you put everything back together," Regina said before she headed out the kitchen.

"I'll get the door," Renee called out before Regina got far.

"Of course," Regina said to Tamika as she returned to the table, "we didn't remember what a dynamo you are, putting everything back in order in just one day."

Tamika grinned. "Well, you guys can help me paint the—"

"Regina, you'd better get the fuck out here," Puddin' interrupted as she strode into the kitchen. "Looks like we got another fucking crisis on our hands."

"Oh my God." Tamika jumped up. "Are those guys back? Is my house okay? Where's Darren and Sissy?"

"What guys?" Puddin' said impatiently. "Oh. Yeah, no. It's not that. It's just a whole bunch of shopping bags full of clothes on your stoop, and Ray-Ray started crying her eyes out as soon as she saw them."

"What?" Regina walked toward the door with Tamika and Puddin' close behind. "That fucking Brenda," she said when she reached the stoop. There were six or seven brown paper shopping bags, one of them spilling out a smashed Sony Walkman and MP3 player, along with a number of CDs—all snapped in two. Another four or five small plastic shopping bags overflowed with shredded jeans and sweatpants. Ripped sneakers were strewn on the steps and the sidewalk. And Renee sat in the middle of it all blubbering, with Liz sitting with her arm around her, trying to comfort her.

Puddin' pointed to Liz. "Who the hell is she, and where did she come from?"

"That's Liz, Ray-Ray's girlfriend. She spent the night," Regina answered. "In the guest room." She walked over to Renee. "Come on, sweetie." She pulled the girl up from the step and into her arms. "Don't let this get you down. You know how your mother is. She's just really angry right now, but you know she'll get over it."

"I don't care if she ever gets over it. I hate her," Renee wailed into Regina's shoulder.

"Don't say that, Ray-Ray, she's still your mother," Regina said as she patted her on the back. "She's just having a very hard time adjusting to your lifestyle. It came as a shock to her, and you know Brenda doesn't handle surprises well."

"Yeah, Ray," Liz said, standing behind them. "It took Frank a while to get used to it, too."

"Yeah, but your father loves you," Ray-Ray said, turning to look at her through red eyes. "My mother hates me."

"She does not," Tamika said. She picked up two of the shopping bags and dropped them into the large metal trash cans next to the stoop. "She loves you very much."

"All this because Ray-Ray likes girls?" Puddin' said, taking a seat on the steps. "Damn."

"If she loves me, then why has she been hanging up on me every time I try to call for the past week and a half?"

"Because she's a bitch. But that doesn't mean she doesn't love you," Puddin' said while taking a good long look at Liz, who shifted from one foot to the other under her stare. "So your name is Liz, huh?" she finally asked the girl. "And you're Ray-Ray's friend?"

"Yes, ma'am." Liz tried to match Puddin's stare but failed, her gaze dropping to the sidewalk.

"And who's this Frank?" Puddin' demanded.

"Um, my father."

"Oh, you call your father by his first name, huh?" Puddin' snorted.

"Puddin'," Regina said in a warning tone.

"Mommy, what's all this stuff on the steps?" Camille called from the vestibule.

"Mille, go on back in the house with Darren and Sissy. I'll

explain when I get inside," Regina answered, still hugging Renee.

"I'm sorry, I didn't make introductions," Renee sniffed. "Liz, this is my Aunt Puddin'. And Aunt Puddin', this is my friend Liz Boyce, so stop being mean, Aunt Puddin'."

"How are you, Miss Puddin'?" Liz extended a hand to Puddin'. "It's good to meet you. Ray's told me so much about you."

"Who's Ray?" Puddin' said, ignoring the girl's hand. "Your grandfather?"

"Um, I mean, Renee," Liz stammered.

"Well, since you know her name is Renee, you should call her Renee," Puddin' said. She stood up and wiped off the seat of her jeans. "Or since you're her friend, maybe you can call her Ray-Ray like her other friends do. But don't call her Ray, that's a boy's name. And Ray-Ray's not a boy."

"Oh come on, Aunt Puddin'," Renee said with a smile as she walked over and hugged her. "Stop being like that." Renee looked at Liz. "She always tries to make people believe she's mean, but she's not really a hater like that. Are you, Aunt Puddin'?" Renee stood on tiptoes and gave Puddin' a kiss.

"Look, don't try to—"

"Are you, Aunt Puddin'?" Renee said again, and started to tickle Puddin' under the arms.

"Stop, Ray-Ray," Puddin' said. She suppressed a giggle as she tried to back up, but Renee stayed on her.

Regina lightly elbowed Liz in the side before shouting, "Get her, Ray-Ray."

"Ray-Ray, stop. I swear I'm gonna kick your ass." Puddin' backed up against the cement stoop pedestal while overcome with laughter.

"No, you won't," Renee said, then finally stopped and gave Puddin' another hug. "You love me too much. And so does Liz. So be nice, okay?"

"Hmph." Puddin' stood up and straightened her clothes and hair. "I wasn't being not nice."

Renee started helping Tamika, Regina, and Liz throw the rest of her tattered belongings in the trash cans. "I'm sorry I said what I said about my mother, but this . . ." She gave a little sigh as she put the last of the bags in the trash. "Well, you gotta see this hurts. I really thought she woulda let up by now."

"You know," Tamika said as they walked back up the steps, "I thought Buddhists were supposed to be more, well, enlightened and compassionate. I wouldn't think they would go crazy about homosexuality."

"Didn't Aunt Gina tell you?" Renee asked as they walked into the house. "My mother's Christian again. She's a member of the Church of the Unified Reformers."

"What's that?" Tamika asked.

"Basically—" Regina started.

"A cult," Renee finished for her.

"Yeah, well, just be careful if she offers you any Kool-Aid," Puddin' said with a snort.

"You okay now, Ray-Ray?" Regina asked, putting her arm around her niece.

Renee shrugged. "I'm fine. A little bummed, but fine."

"Well, then, I have an idea," Puddin' said suddenly. "Why don't you come hang out with your Aunt Puddin' for the day? We can go to the movies or even Atlantic City. Yeah, how about we take a trip to Atlantic City? Gina, you'll let me borrow your car, right?"

"Puddin', I thought you were supposed to be helping Tamika out today," Regina said with a smirk.

"She's got *you* to help her out. *I* gotta take care of our little girl," Puddin' shot back. "So can we take the car?"

"Ooh, that would be so great." Renee almost jumped up and down in glee.

"Yeah." Regina made a face, then got her car keys from the coffee table and threw them to Puddin'. "But damn it, don't you go around killing grandfathers in my car."

"Killing who?" Liz looked from Regina to Puddin'.

"I'll explain it to you while we're on the way," Renee said, pulling her up the stairs. "Come on, let's go get ready."

"Hey," Puddin' called after them, "I thought it was going to be—"

"We'll be ready in a minute," Renee shouted over her shoulder. "Promise we won't keep you waiting."

"Puddin', we're just going to have to face it. They're a couple." Regina grabbed her friend around the waist and pulled her into the kitchen. "Now, let's go over this thing about not hitting grandfathers in my car—"

*Ring.*

Regina picked up the telephone that hung on the kitchen wall. "Hello."

"Hey," a dry voice on the other end replied.

"Oh," Regina said, recognizing the voice. "Hey, Charles."

"Hey."

"Did you make your flight okay? Are you in D.C. now?" Regina asked as she twirled the telephone cord around her fingers and avoided looking at the women in the kitchen.

"Yeah to both," Charles said curtly. "But that's not why I'm calling. I want to talk to you about your friend. I didn't want to bring it up last night in front of the kids, but I just need to know if you've lost your freaking mind."

Regina sighed. "I have company right now, Charles. Can you call me back later so we can talk?"

"No, because I'm not giving you the opportunity to check your caller ID and not take my calls the way you did yesterday after you left the restaurant," Charles said coldly.

"Well, then, let me run upstairs so I can take this call in my bedroom, because—"

"Don't bother. I'm not going to keep you but a minute. I just want an answer to my question. What the hell is wrong with you bringing a gangsta like Joseph Blayton around my daughter?"

Regina looked around to see if Puddin' or Tamika was listening to the conversation, but they seemed engrossed in their own discussion. "Look, I'm not in the mood to argue at the moment," she said in a low voice. "But let me just say that number one, no matter what you might have heard, he's not a thug, and number two, he doesn't have anything to do with your daughter. I don't bring him around here."

"Well, the way I heard it, Joseph Blayton—or Little Joe, as everyone seems to call him—is one of the biggest heroin dealers in New York," Charles snarled.

"Was," Regina corrected him. "And that was only alleged, never proven. And again, I'm not going to argue about this. Little Joe is a very old friend of mine, and I'm not going to drop him simply because you don't approve."

"Don't give me that 'alleged' crap, Regina. I've been on the Internet and looked up old news clippings on this punk. They may not have made a good case against him, but there's no doubt about his activities." Charles was all but shouting into the telephone. "And this is not about my approval. After all, like you keep reminding me, I don't have any more claim to you. I don't give a shit about what you do. I'm worried about you having people like that around my daughter. If you want to hang out with lowlifes like Blayton, then you—"

"It was nice talking to you, Charles. Give me a call when you get back from D.C., won't you?" Regina said pleasantly before hanging up. She turned back to her women in the kitchen. "Now, as I was saying—," she began.

*Ring.*

Regina cut her eyes at the telephone and considered not answering, but then suddenly picked up and brought the receiver to her ear. "Hello," she said brusquely.

"Hey you," the voice on the other end said.

"Hey you back." Regina looked over at Puddin' and Tamika, who were settling in at the kitchen table. "Hold on for a minute while I change phones, okay?"

"Nah, don't do that. I'm only gonna be on for a minute," Little Joe replied. "I just wanna make sure Tamika and her family's okay."

"They're all fine. In fact, Tamika's over here right now." Regina took her mouth away from the phone. "Hey, guys," she called to Tamika and Puddin', "Little Joe says hello."

"Tell him hello back," Tamika responded with a wave.

"Tamika and Puddin' say hello," Regina told Joe.

"Thanks for putting words into my mouth," Little Joe said in a sarcasm-filled voice. "And for the record, I still don't appreciate that shit you pulled yesterday."

Regina fingered the telephone cord. "Um, let me hurry up and change phones real quick so we can talk."

"Nah. I'm getting off," Little Joe said laconically. "I'm flying to Beverly Hills tonight. I should be back in a couple of days."

"Really?" Regina couldn't keep the surprise out of her voice. "What are you going out there for?"

"Remember that movie producer guy that was at that club party a little while back?"

"Oh yeah, what's his name . . ."

"Tecumseh Joseph. Yeah. Well, he talked me into flying out there for a little sit-down to discuss possibilities. Sent me two first-class tickets."

"Two?" Regina chewed her lip, knowing what was coming next. Of course, Little Joe wanted her to go, but she couldn't abandon Tamika right now, and anyway, she couldn't just drop everything on a moment's notice and fly across the country. But damn, she thought, she'd never been to Beverly Hills. It would be nice—

"Yeah, two. I'm gonna take one of my boys, since it's pretty obvious you and I need to take a break from each other so you can get your head straight and decide what the fuck you wanna do."

"Oh," was all Regina could think to say. "Well, I hope you have a good time and everything."

"Yeah."

"Okay, and, um . . . look, I'm really sorry about yesterday," Regina said slowly. "Make sure you call me when you get back so we can really talk, okay?"

"Yeah, okay. Talk to you then."

Regina quietly hung up and went and sat at the kitchen table with Tamika and Puddin'. "So, anyway . . . as I was saying, Puddin'—"

Puddin' cut her off with a wicked grin. "So you hung up on Charles, and then Little Joe hung up on you, huh? That's fucked-up."

Regina's mouth dropped in surprise. "What?"

"Oh come on." Puddin' sucked her teeth. "I didn't hear everything, but I heard enough to figure that shit out."

"Eavesdropping skank," Regina muttered.

"So what's going on? Are they demanding that you choose between them?" Tamika asked before Puddin' could respond to the insult.

"They're just trying to drive me nuts, and doing a good job of it, I might add," Regina said with a sigh. "All this serious stuff going on, Tamika . . . with you and your family, Yvonne and Robert, and Brenda and Ray-Ray, and then I have to get shit from them. Charles is blowing a gasket because he thinks I'm bringing Little Joe, who he calls a gangsta, around Camille. Which"—she looked pointedly at Tamika—"you know I'm not."

Tamika nodded sympathetically.

"And Little Joe is busy telling me off because he thinks I'm ashamed of him since I didn't introduce him to Charles or David," Regina continued.

"Well, are you?" Puddin' asked in a flippant tone.

"Am I what?"

"Are you ashamed of Little Joe?"

"No, of course not," Regina said in a defensive tone. "I've never been ashamed of him."

"Well, why didn't you make the introductions, then?" Tamika asked in a puzzled voice.

"How the hell do I know?" Regina waved her hand dismissively. "Like I said, there's just been so much crap going on that I don't even know what I'm doing or not doing or why or why not. Ya know?"

Tamika shrugged but gave Puddin' a knowing look, which she had to realize Regina couldn't miss but would decide to ignore.

# chapter fifteen

"Aunt Gina, wake up! Tamika's downstairs and she said it's an emergency!"

"What? What?" Regina said sleepily as she turned over in the bed to face her niece. The words suddenly registered, and Regina jumped up from the bed. "What!?"

She pushed past Renee and ran down the stairs in her nightgown. "Tamika, oh my God. What's wrong? What happened? Are you okay?"

"It's not me," Tamika said, rushing to the bottom of the stairs to meet Regina. "It's Yvonne. We gotta get over there quick. I've been trying to call you, but the phone kept going straight to voice mail."

"I think you accidentally knocked the phone in your bedroom off the hook," Renee told Regina as she ran down the stairs toward them. "I just put it back on."

"Mrs. Evans across the street is watching the kids, and David's outside in the car waiting for us. Hurry up and get some clothes on."

"But what happened?" Regina was still dazed from waking up in a shock.

"Robert just beat the crap out of Yvonne," Tamika said in a rush. "She sounds real bad off, but she won't go to the hospital. We gotta get there quick."

"Right, right." Regina nodded. "Ray-Ray, can you and Liz watch Camille until I get back?"

"Aunt Gina . . ."

"Right, right, right," Regina said as she started running up the stairs. "I forgot. She's spending the weekend with Charles. Sorry."

"Hurry up!" Tamika shouted

"I'm hurrying. I'm hurrying."

⌒

"What the fuck? Oh my God," Regina cried when Yvonne opened the door. Both of the woman's eyes were swollen almost shut, there was a massive gash across her forehead, and her cheeks were so badly bruised that they looked black. Her hair was matted with blood, and when Yvonne opened her bloody, puffy lips to talk, they revealed a gap where three of her top teeth should have been.

"He . . . he . . ." Yvonne leaned against the door, then fell into Regina's arms, crying hysterically. "He beat me. He just went crazy. I thought he was going to kill me. He kept hitting and kicking me until I passed out. Thank God, Johnny's over at Mama's house. He might have hurt him, too."

David gently pried Yvonne out of Regina's arms, picked her up, and carried her to the couch. The room looked like it had been hit by a cyclone. All of Yvonne's new furniture and statues were smashed, and the rug was littered with shattered glass. The curtains had been pulled down from the rods, one of the windows was broken, and the television screen had been kicked in.

"How . . . why . . . what set him off?" Regina asked in bewilderment as she started trying to right some of the chairs.

"Because it took me so long to get him out of jail." Yvonne put her hand on her forehead, then grimaced in pain. "I told him it took me time to raise all of the bail money, but he said I left him in there to punish him. And of course"—she started crying—"and of course, he was high, so that didn't help matters any."

"Tamika," David said, "call 911 and get an ambulance over here quick."

"No, I don't want to go to the hospital," Yvonne said as she struggled to sit up.

"Honey, look, that doesn't make sense. You've got to see a doctor," Regina said, stroking Yvonne's matted hair. "You might have some internal injuries or something."

"No, I can't go." Yvonne covered her face with her hands. "I'm okay. I just need to get some rest. I'll be better in the morning."

"Better in the morning?" Regina reached inside her pocketbook and pulled out a makeup compact, which she snapped open. "Take a look in the mirror and tell me that some rest is going to make all this better."

"No!" Yvonne pushed the compact away without looking. "I can't go."

"Why not, sweetie?" Tamika said as she sat down next to Yvonne.

"Because I can't!" Yvonne said through her tears. When she looked up and noticed David pushing the buttons on his cell phone, she suddenly reached out and knocked the phone from his hands. "Don't call an ambulance," she screamed. "I can't go!"

Regina jumped to her feet. "What the fuck is wrong with you, Yvonne? We gotta get your ass to the hospital. And we're gonna get you there even if we have to tie you up and throw you in Tamika's car."

"You don't understand." Yvonne pulled her battered body from the couch and slowly walked over to the love seat and sat back down. "I'd be too embarrassed."

Tamika walked over to her and knelt down. "Yvonne, there's no reason to be embarrassed, girl."

"Like I said, you don't understand." Yvonne wiped her eyes. "I'd be embarrassed because I've been to the hospital twice in the last month already."

"What?" Regina almost shouted.

"That crazy bastard," David growled as he slammed his fist into the back of the couch. "I'm going to kill him when I see him."

"But . . . I mean, we've never seen any bruises on you," Tamika said in a puzzled tone.

"One time he knocked me down and kicked me in my stomach and kidneys, and I had to go to the hospital because I started urinating blood," Yvonne said through her sniffles. "Another time he punched me in the chest and bruised one of my ribs."

"Oh, Yvonne," Regina said sadly. "I feel so bad. Here we are your best friends, and we didn't even realize what's been going on."

"No one did," Yvonne sobbed. "I think Mama suspects. I'm sure that's why she's been insisting on Johnny staying with her all the time lately.

"Both times they asked me at the hospital if I was experiencing domestic abuse, and both times I told them no, that I was horseplaying around some kids. I know they didn't believe me, but . . ." Yvonne shrugged. "But how can I go back looking like this?"

"But, Yvonne—" David started.

"No!" Yvonne shouted. "I'm not. Do you know what it feels like? I'm supposed to be this intelligent, professional woman, and I have to admit to those people that I've not only been beat up by my boyfriend three times, but I've been too stupid to press charges, or even to leave him. I'm not going to do it."

David rubbed his chin for a moment, then wearily sat down next to her. "Yvonne, you don't know how bad I'm feeling right now. To know that someone I've known since high school could do this to you. I mean, man." He shook his head. "And I know you're confused right now, and hurting inside and out, but you can't just sit here and let him make you a victim." David put his arm around her and pulled her close. "You know what I would do if someone did this to one of my sisters? I'd kick their funky ass. And that's exactly what I'm going to do to Robert as soon as I see him. But first, if it were my sister, I'd tell her that she'd have to get over her feelings of embarrassment and go to the hospital. Because her health is important. Not just for her, but for her kids. That's what I'd tell her. And that's what I'm telling you." He gave her arm a little squeeze. "Because you're like a sister to me. And I love you, Yvonne. And I need you to be okay. And your friends need you to be okay. And most importantly, your son needs you to be okay. So let's get to the hospital so we know that you're really okay." He gently kissed her on top of her head. "Okay?"

Yvonne looked at Regina and Tamika, then back at David. "Okay," she finally said with a nod.

"Holy fuck!"

Everyone looked up to see Puddin' standing in the doorway, her mouth gaping as she looked over the living room. She slowly walked to the center of the room and did a silent slow turn. When she finally faced the love seat and got a good look at Yvonne, she almost fell backward. "Fuck, fuck, fuck," she screamed as she ran over and grabbed Yvonne to her chest. "Oh my God. What the fuck. Oh my God, what the fuck."

"Puddin', you're hurting her," Regina cried as Yvonne struggled to break free.

"That motherfucker did this to you?" Tears filling Puddin's

eyes, she let go of Yvonne and stood up. "Where is he? I'm going to fucking kill him. Where the fuck is he?"

"I don't know. He left after I passed out," Yvonne said as Tamika helped her back into a sitting position on the love seat.

"He knocked you unconscious?" Puddin' peered at her. "Oh shit, he knocked your fucking teeth out? Your fucking teeth?"

Puddin' covered her mouth with her hands as tears streamed down her face and her body began to shake. "I'm going to kill him," she said softly. "I'm going to go get a gun, I'm going to hunt him down, and I'm going to fucking kill him."

"Puddin', calm down," David said.

"Don't you fucking tell me to calm down," Puddin' screamed, and advanced toward him with her fists balled. "Your fucking friend almost killed my girl, so don't fucking tell me to calm down."

David put his hands up in front of his chest in a form of surrender and backed up. Regina jumped between them, grabbed Puddin', and propelled her backward toward the couch and pushed her down.

"We're all fucked-up about this, but you gotta cool out. David's going to drive us all to the hospital now, and then Yvonne's pressing charges against Robert. The police are going to take care of his ass."

"Fuck the police, I'm going to shove my foot straight up his ass as soon as I catch up with him," Puddin' said, snatching up her pocketbook from the floor.

"You know," David told Regina and Tamika, "Robert better hope that the police or I get to him before Puddin' does, because I swear, as big as I am, I wouldn't want to tangle with that girl."

"Bigger men than you have found the truth in that statement," Regina said. "The stories I could tell."

"Damn, it's three o'clock already. We spent three hours in the hospital. I still wish Yvonne had let them keep her overnight," Regina told Puddin' in the back of a taxicab. "But at least she has sense enough not to go back to her apartment. There's no telling if that maniac is going to show back up. I'm glad she let David and Tamika take her to Mama Tee's."

"I just don't see why we couldn't have gone along," Puddin' grumbled.

"Because Mama Tee's going to be upset enough when she sees Yvonne. She's not going to need you adding fuel to her fire, and you don't know how to stop throwing gasoline."

The taxi pulled into her block, and Regina told the driver, "Right here." She wearily grabbed her purse and paid the fare showing on the meter. "Okay, you have enough money to get you back uptown, Puddin'?"

"Regina," Puddin' said urgently, "your front door is wide open."

"What?" Regina jumped out the cab and ran up the brownstone steps with Puddin' on her heels.

In the vestibule Regina reached into the umbrella stand and pulled out the baseball bat she kept hidden there. "Ray-Ray? Liz?" she called out as she cautiously entered the house.

There was no verbal answer, but she could hear a series of grunts and moans coming from the living room. She threw open the door and gasped. Liz lay either unconscious or dead on the floor, and a few feet away, also on the floor, was a semi-conscious Renee, with a crazed bare-chested Robert tugging at her panties. The man seemed oblivious to them as he grunted and smacked his lips while alternately looking down at the moaning Renee and up at the ceiling.

Regina swung the bat with all her might, aiming for his head just as Puddin' screamed, "You motherfucker, get off her!" and charged.

The bat only grazed his head, but between it and Puddin's full-body tackle, he was knocked off Renee and landed on his stomach on the floor with a thud. Unfortunately, he was down but not out. He jumped to his feet and punched Puddin' square in the jaw, knocking her almost clear across the room, but she was up and charging him again in less than a second, this time with a switchblade she had slipped from her back pocket. Regina ran up to him from behind and caught him between the shoulder blades with the bat, sending him tumbling toward Puddin', who slashed him across the face from chin to ear.

Miraculously, he seemed oblivious to the blows and the cuts. He yelled and pounced on Puddin', who caught him across the chest, then across the throat with the switchblade, somehow missing his windpipe.

"Puddin', duck so I don't get you," Regina screamed as she swung the bat again. This time she managed to get a clean shot at his head with what she thought was enough force to crack his skull, but instead of falling to the ground, he simply turned to her with a wide-eyed look, as if noticing for the first time she was there. Regina reared back to swing again, but before she could, Puddin' stabbed him in the back, and Robert bowled into her, knocking her to the floor. Even with the blade in his back, Robert scrambled up and dashed out the door, with Puddin' in hot pursuit.

Regina ran over to Renee, who was by now completely out cold, and knelt down and cradled her in her arms. "Oh, baby. My baby," she cried as she looked at the teenager. Both her eyes were black, her upper lip busted, her entire face already beginning to swell. It looked as if her jaw was fractured, and the way her arm fell to one side, it looked as if it might be, too. Regina realized she should put the girl down and not move her for fear of aggravating her injuries. She grabbed the telephone and called 911, at the same time checking Liz. She sighed with relief when she saw the girl was breathing. There was a large bump and bruise on her forehead, but no other sign of injury. Robert probably knocked her out with one blow. Renee, of course, was a fighter, and it would have taken a lot more to bring her down.

"The fucking bastard got away," Puddin' said as she walked in the door breathless. "He got a busted head and a knife in his back, and he still managed to do a three-fucking-minute mile down Lenox Avenue. That fucking angel dust is a mother-fucker."

"Don't touch her," Regina warned as Puddin' approached Renee. "She might have a fractured spine or something. The ambulance is on the way. Tamika and David will be here in a minute, too. I just got him on his cell phone."

Puddin' nodded and sat down on the floor beside the motionless teenager and began to sob, not bothering to cover her face. For the first time, Regina realized she herself hadn't shed a tear. She must be in shock, she decided.

*Ring.*

Regina picked up the telephone, thinking it was Charles, since she had left an urgent voice mail message for him to call her back.

"Hey you."

"Little Joe?" Regina's voice cracked as she spoke his name.

"Regina? What's wrong? Did something happen to Tamika?" The concern in Little Joe's voice touched off something in Regina, and she began to sob along with Puddin'.

"No. It's Ray-Ray," she cried into the telephone. "Yvonne's boyfriend came in while I wasn't here and beat her up and tried to rape her."

"What? Fuck!" Little Joe yelled into the phone. "Is she okay? That sorry motherfucker."

"No." Regina sat down on the couch and continued to talk between sobs. "She's unconscious, and it looks like she's hurt really bad. The ambulance is on the way."

"Where is he now? Did the police catch him?"

"Puddin' and I walked in the door while he was trying to pull down her panties. We managed to chase him out of here,"

Regina said, wiping her eyes. "Oh, Little Joe, she looks real bad. I'm so afraid." She started sobbing again.

"Oh God, Regina. Fuck. I'm still in Los Angeles. Otherwise I'd be there in a second." Regina could hear the anger and frustration in Little Joe's voice. "Why the fuck did I come out here?"

"I gotta hang up, the ambulance is here," Regina said as she heard the sirens come up the street.

"All right. Call me from the hospital and let me know if she's okay. Don't forget, because I'm not going to go to bed until I hear something. And I'll see if I can get a flight outta here in the morning. I promise."

"Okay," Regina said. Then for the first time in her life, she hung up before Little Joe did.

# chapter sixteen

Regina, I got here as soon as I could. Are they going to be okay?"

Regina stood up and gave Yvonne a weak hug. "Renee's liver is damaged. They have her in the operating room now. We're waiting for one of the doctors to come out and tell us what's going on."

"Oh my God!" Yvonne's knees buckled, and David rushed to sit her down next to Tamika. "Oh my God!"

"You shouldn't have come, Yvonne. You're in bad enough shape yourself," Tamika said gently.

Yvonne shook her head dismally. "How could I not? It's all my fault. I knew Robert was dangerous, and if I had just pressed charges and gotten him locked up the first time he hit me, none of this would have happened."

"Don't blame yourself, Yvonne." Regina sighed. "The good news is that it looks like Liz is going to be okay. She's regained consciousness, and they did X-rays and MRIs and everything. They want to keep her overnight for observation, though."

Yvonne looked around the waiting room. "You still haven't been able to reach Brenda?" she asked.

Tamika shook her head. "She doesn't have a cell phone, and we've left a half dozen messages on her answering machine at home, but she hasn't gotten back to anybody yet."

Puddin', who was sitting in one of the chairs with her arms crossed, looked up and said, "She's probably out somewhere praying to Satan or whoever the fuck it is she's worshipping this week."

"Puddin' . . . ," Tamika started, but Puddin' just sucked her teeth and looked away.

"If she hadn't thrown Renee out in the first place, she wouldn'ta been at Regina's house, and none of this shit woulda happened to her," Puddin' said dryly.

Regina looked up as a nurse walked by. "Excuse me, Nurse. Can anyone tell us exactly what's going on? They said the operation was only going to take an hour, but it's been almost two hours already, and no one's telling us anything. Have there been any complications?"

"I'm sorry, miss, but like I told you the last time you asked, I'm sure one of the doctors will be out shortly to give you an update," the nurse said with a pretty smile. "But I'm sure everything is going fine."

David stood up. "Nurse . . ." He paused as he looked at her name tag. "Nurse Jordan . . ."

"Jordan's my first name, sir." The nurse turned her pretty smile toward him. "My last name's Garrett."

"Okay, Nurse Garrett," David said impatiently. "You said the exact same thing a half hour ago, and I want to—"

"I'm sure the doctor will be out shortly," the nurse said brightly.

Regina curled her lip, readying herself to curse the nurse out when she heard a commotion in the corridor. There was a grim-faced Charles striding toward them, flanked by two nervous-looking men wearing business suits.

"Charles!" Regina rushed to him and was pulled into a one-arm embrace. "Thank God you're here. But how did you get here so fast from Philadelphia? I only reached you an hour ago."

"By helicopter. There's a landing pad on the roof of the hospital." Charles stroked Regina's hair and looked over her head at David. "What's the news?"

"Well, that's what we've been trying to find out," David replied. "The nurse here's been giving us the runaround."

"Oh, I'm really sorry you feel that way," the nurse said with her ever-present smile. "I was just trying to explain to the ladies and the gentleman that they're going to have to wait until one of the doctors comes out from the operating room."

"Nurse," Charles said as he continued to hold Regina, "I'm a United States congressman, and I would advise you to go into that operating room and either come back with a report or send somebody out who can."

Regina couldn't resist turning in Charles's arms so she could face the nurse and see her reaction. The smile had frozen on her face as she looked from Charles to the nervous-looking men behind him.

One of them cleared his throat and said, "Nurse Garrett, please go in right away and have one of the doctors come out and tell Congressman Whitfield and his family what's going on."

"Yes, sir, Dr. Rosenthal," the nurse said, and hurried away.

Dr. Rosenthal extended his hand toward Regina. "I'm Dr. Rosenthal, Miss . . ."

"Mrs. Whitfield," Charles answered for her.

Normally, Regina would have corrected Charles, since she had reverted to her maiden name after the divorce, but this time she smiled and kept silent.

"Mrs. Whitfield, of course," Dr. Rosenthal said. "I'm the hospital administrator, and I want to apologize for my staff. You and your family should have been given regular updates.

And, Mr. Congressman," he said, turning back to Charles, "if you had just radioed us earlier, we would have had the update waiting for you on arrival."

"I had no reason to believe that my family hadn't already been updated, Doctor," Charles said wryly.

"Of course," Dr. Rosenthal said smoothly. "Why don't we all go down the hall to my office, where you'll be more comfortable? I'll leave word for the doctor to meet us there."

Tamika shook her head. "I think we'd better wait here. Frank Boyce, Liz's father, won't know where to find us."

"We'll be fine right here," Charles agreed.

They all watched a doctor in surgical scrubs hurrying toward them. "Congressman Whitfield, it's good to meet you, sir. I'm Dr. Stone," he said when he reached them. "I understand you'd like to know your niece's status."

Charles nodded toward Regina. "Actually, she's Mrs. Whitfield's niece, but go ahead. They've been waiting long enough," he said brusquely.

"Yes, sir," Dr. Stone said quickly. "The patient, Miss Harris, has sustained damage to her liver and spleen probably all due to blows to her back and stomach—"

"Oh no." Regina's legs grew weak, and she sagged against Charles.

"Please don't worry, Mrs. Whitfield," the doctor said quickly. "All of the damage was minor, and chances are she'll recover fast. We're stitching her up right now. But in addition, Miss Harris has sustained a fracture to her left arm, right leg, and also a scratched retina in her right eye." He cleared his throat. "We're going to have an ophthalmologist look at her, but there's no reason, at this point, to believe she'll have any permanent loss of vision."

Charles helped Regina to a chair, then turned back toward the doctor. "When will we be able to see her?"

"As I said, she's being stitched up right now, and her casts have already been set, but we should have her wheeled into the recovery room within the next half hour or so."

Dr. Rosenthal stepped up. "Normally, we discourage visitors in the recovery room, but I'd be glad to make an exception in this case. Perhaps if we can keep the visitors to, say, two at a time? Staying no more than five or ten minutes each?"

"Actually, she won't be awake for another few hours," Dr. Stone said.

"Well, we'd like to be able to look in on her, anyway," Charles said.

"Excuse me," Nurse Garrett said with her perfect smile back in place. "Are all of you family members?"

"Nurse, we'll handle this," Dr. Rosenthal said brusquely. "We'll be glad to accommodate all of you, Congressman Whitfield."

"Who the hell are you people, and what did you do to my daughter?"

The loud, slurred words startled everyone. Regina turned to see a short, portly, balding man staggering toward them. The smell of cheap wine was almost as loud as his voice, and his eyes were glazed, though he kept blinking them as if trying to focus. He lurched toward David, swinging and missing, and would have fallen over if David hadn't caught him and placed him on a chair. After a few seconds the man tried to get up but fell flat down on his backside.

Puddin', who had been sitting quietly in one of the chairs up until this point, nudged him with her foot. "Let me guess. Liz's father, huh?" She snorted, then crossed her arms, closed her eyes, and leaned back in her seat so that her head rested on the wall. "What a fucking piece of work."

"Nurse," Dr. Rosenthal said. "Get hospital security up here *now*. And call the police."

"No, that's okay," Regina said, helping David get the man to his feet. "I'm sorry, sir," she said when they had him back in the chair. "Are you Mr. Boyce? I'm Regina Harris . . . um, Regina Whitfield. I'm Renee's aunt."

"Well, I'm Liz's father," Boyce said as he tried to regain his feet. "And the folks here told me you put my little girl in the hospital."

"Sir," David said gently, helping him back down into the chair, "we brought Liz here in an ambulance, but we're not the ones responsible for her being here."

"Well, then, who is?" Mr. Boyce said belligerently. "Who knocked her out?"

Yvonne hung her head but said nothing.

"Congressman Whitfield," Dr. Rosenthal said, "I really suggest that we move your family upstairs and let security—"

"Who's a congressman?" Mr. Boyce said as he tried to straighten up again. He peered at Charles through bloodshot eyes. "Yeah, I seen you on TV. You the one they be talking about saved them hostages or something, right? Well, do you know who did this to my Liz, then? Or don't nobody care about her?"

"Mr. Boyce, we know who did it, and the police are out searching for him now," David said. "I'm sure he'll be locked up soon, if he isn't in custody already."

"Well, he better be," Mr. Boyce said while trying to straighten his clothes. "And if he raped her, then I'm going to kill him and then sue every-fucking-body in here."

"The doctor's checked, and there's no indication that your daughter's been sexually violated, Mr. Boyce," Tamika said soothingly.

"Well," Mr. Boyce said defiantly, "I'm just saying—"

"Mr. Boyce," Dr. Rosenthal said, "I can assure you we checked your daughter out thoroughly, and she was not raped."

Mr. Boyce glared at him with his bloodshot eyes. "You'd better get that attitude out your voice, and I hope you checked my Liz as good as you done checked these people's little girl. Just 'cause she ain't got no politicians in her family doesn't mean she ain't supposed to get top-notch treatment. She's just as good as anybody else." He paused and looked as if he were going to say something else, but then covered his face with his hands and started sobbing. Finally, he recovered some composure. "Liz is my little girl. She's all I got. She'd better be okay. She just better."

"Shit!" Puddin' shot him a look of disgust and got up to walk away, then suddenly turned back to him. "Look," she said, bending down, "Liz is going to be fine. She's fine right now. Isn't she, Doctor?" she said, looking up at Dr. Rosenthal.

The man nodded.

"See?" Puddin' told Mr. Boyce. Tears were now evident in her own voice. "So come on, stop crying. 'Cause you're going to start us all crying again, and we've already done enough of that shit. Come on. Wipe your face"—she looked around—"wipe your face on your sleeve or something."

Regina walked over to Dr. Rosenthal and said in a low voice, "Do you think it might be possible to find a room where Mr. Boyce might—"

"Sleep it off?" Dr. Rosenthal said abruptly.

"Where Mr. Boyce might get some rest." Regina shot him a withering look. "And I agree with Mr. Boyce. Get that attitude out your voice, or you'll see just how bad my attitude can be."

∽

It was so painful looking at Renee that Regina found herself averting her eyes from her niece's bruised and battered face, which was so puffed up her features were almost unrecognizable. The girl still hadn't recovered consciousness and lay in bed in traction, her arm and leg suspended, her right eye covered by a bandage, and her right arm hooked up to an intravenous line.

"Oh God, she looks so helpless," Regina said, turning to Charles. "No one deserves to be hurt like this."

Charles nodded, his own face pinched and ashen as he looked at Regina, tears in his eyes. "I can't believe Robert did this. I can't believe he's really become such a monster."

David and Tamika stood near the door of the recovery room, holding each other, while Puddin' sat in a chair rocking back and forth, her mouth set in a grim line.

"Is she going to make it?"

Regina looked up to see Brenda standing in the doorway almost motionless, her face drained of blood.

"Is my baby going to make it?" Brenda repeated.

"She's going to be fine," Regina said. She walked over and put her arm around her sister. "It looks bad now, but you know Renee's a fighter. You know she's going to pull through. I promise."

"You promise?" Brenda said numbly. She sat down in a chair next to her daughter's head and stroked her matted hair. "You promise?" she whispered.

Tears filled Regina's eyes as she looked at her sister. "Yeah," she said, rubbing Brenda's back. "I promise."

The doctors had said that it might be hours before Renee regained consciousness, and now Regina wished they had all listened and waited in the lounge rather than in the recovery room. The whole scene seemed so eerie and unreal.

Regina looked down at her pocketbook when she felt it vibrating and realized it was her cell phone. She dug it out and looked at the number before answering.

"Hey," she said, and walked out of the recovery room.

"Girl, I thought you were supposed to be calling me back," Little Joe growled over the telephone. "Is she going to be okay?"

"Oh man," Regina said, rubbing her temples. "The doctors say she's going to be okay, but if you saw her, you'd have to wonder."

"That bad, huh?"

"Yeah, that bad." Regina sat down in a chair in the hallway.

"Little Joe, Robert simply can't get away with this shit—beating up a kid and then trying to rape her. He just can't. Someone needs to catch him, cut off his dick, and shove it up his fucking mouth."

"Yeah, that sounds about right," Little Joe said in agreement. "But no one even knows where he is, huh?"

"No. I think every cop in the city is looking for him, though. And did I tell you he beat the shit out of Yvonne earlier this evening? We had to take her to the hospital, but they just treated and released her."

"Damn, that muthafucka is off the hook, huh? But don't worry, the cops'll find him soon enough," Little Joe said soothingly. "So okay, how are you doing, Gina? You hanging in there?"

Regina let out a deep breath. "I'm trying to be okay. I really am. But I'm having a hard time holding it together. Brenda's with Renee now, and she's having a harder time than me. I need to get back in there and make sure she's okay. When will you be back in town?"

"Damn, baby. The earliest flight I can get outta here is at seven a.m. tomorrow, which won't put me in New York until about two p.m. Can you hang in there until then?"

"Get here as soon as you can, will you?" Regina said tenderly. "It'll be good to be with you, Little Joe."

"Same here, babe. Same here."

Regina had just snapped her telephone shut when Charles walked out of the recovery room. "Everything okay, Gina? I turned around and you had just disappeared."

Regina stood up, hoping the guilty look on her face wouldn't be too noticeable. "Yeah, I just came out here to get some air. It's so damn depressing in there."

"Ain't that the truth?" Charles said with a sigh. "Brenda's in there crying, Tamika and David look like they're about to fall apart any minute, and Puddin's almost catatonic. I'm glad Yvonne decided to go home rather than join this motley crew."

He walked over to Regina and kissed her on the cheek. "Come with me to get a candy bar or something. The doctor told me he's got Renee so heavily sedated she won't be awake for quite some time."

Regina slipped her arm around his waist so naturally that she had to wonder about her own sense of morality. Here she had just gotten off the telephone with her lover, and now she was seeking comfort from her former husband. The thought made her shudder, and she pulled her arm away. "No, I'd better get in there and make sure Brenda's okay. I'll see you when you get back."

Charles shrugged and put his arm around her waist just as she had done to him a few seconds before. "I really don't need a candy bar. I was using it as an excuse to come out here and make sure you were okay." He kissed her on the forehead. "Come on," he said, leading her back to the recovery room.

"You know, sometimes I wonder what I'd do without you." Regina gave Charles a weak smile. "It seems like you're always here when I need you."

"That's my job, baby." Charles gave her waist a squeeze. "Oops. I'm not supposed to call you baby, right?"

"Right." Regina smiled inwardly. Her last telephone conversation with Charles earlier that day in the kitchen was the first time since the divorce that he hadn't used the endearment and given her the opportunity for her one-word comeback. It felt good to use it again.

"You know, Gina, if there's one thing I can always count on with you, it's reminding me of my place. I guess I should thank you for that." Charles leaned down and kissed the top of her head before opening the door to the recovery room.

"Has she come to yet?" Regina asked as she walked over to Renee's bedside.

Brenda shook her head, then looked up at Regina. "But she will, right? She has to, right? The Lord wouldn't take my baby away, would He?"

"He wouldn't," Regina said, bending down to kiss her sister.

It was almost two hours later when Puddin' suddenly said in an excited voice, "I think her eyes just winced. At least the one that isn't bandaged up." Puddin' moved in for a closer look. "See? She did it again."

"Oh, thank you, Jesus!" Brenda jumped to her feet, her hands clasped. She leaned down and spoke close to Renee's ear. "Ray-Ray. Baby, can you hear me? It's your mother. It's me, baby. I'm here for you."

Tamika, David, and Charles crowded around, and they all heard Renee begin to softly moan.

"Ray-Ray, sweetie," Regina said, and gently stroked Renee's hand. "Your Aunt Gina's here, too. And your Aunt Tamika, your Uncle David, and your Uncle Charles."

"Uncle Charles?" Renee said in an almost inaudible whisper through her wired jaw.

"Hey, Ray-Ray. I'm right here." Charles's voice was low but excited. "I flew from Philadelphia in a helicopter to be right here with you."

Renee slowly opened her eye and blinked a few times. "In a helicopter?" she asked in a slurred voice. She tried to turn her head to look at him but winced in pain. "Where am I?"

Tamika whispered to David to get a nurse, and he quickly left.

"You're in a hospital, baby," Brenda answered. "You had an accident, and your Aunt Regina brought you to the hospital. But the doctors said you'll be okay."

"Your Aunt Regina and your Aunt Puddin'," Puddin' interjected. "You know we had to look out for our girl."

"And I got here as soon as I heard," Brenda added.

"An accident?" Renee blinked her eye rapidly as if trying to wake up. "What happened?"

"It was nothing, sweetie. You'll be fine," Regina answered as she massaged Renee's hand. "Everything's all right."

Renee closed her eye, and Regina thought the girl had fallen asleep, but she reopened it in a few minutes and tears trickled down her cheeks.

"It was Uncle Robert," she said in a louder, hoarse voice. "He rang the bell and I let him in and then he just went crazy."

"It's okay, Ray-Ray," Tamika said. "Get some rest, and we'll talk about it later."

"No!" Renee shouted, and tried to rise up from the bed, but she fell back and started sobbing. "Where's Liz? He hurt Liz. Where is she?"

"Renee, calm down, sweetie," Regina said urgently. "Liz is okay."

"Mom, my head hurts so bad." Renee sobbed. "Mom, I hurt all over. And I can't move my arm or my leg. Mom!"

"It's okay, baby. Your arm and leg are in a cast. But they'll be okay, and you'll be able to move them soon. Everything is okay," Brenda said frantically.

"Miss Harris, good to see you awake. You say you're in pain?"

The words were spoken with a Jamaican accent, and Regina turned around to see a middle-aged nurse walking toward the bed with a medical chart in her hand.

"She said she hurts bad," Brenda said, turning toward the woman, who ignored her and continued to address Renee.

"You're in pain, dear?" the nurse asked as she leaned over Renee.

"I just said she was," Brenda said indignantly. "And I'm her mother."

"And that's very nice for you, I'm sure, but I was asking the patient," the nurse said, checking Renee's vital signs. "Now, dear, tell me, are you in pain?"

"Yes, but I want to know where Liz is," Renee said. "She's my friend. And she was hurt, too."

"I don't know where Liz is, but I can find out for you," the nurse said soothingly. "But right now I'm going to increase your morphine dosage so you can be more comfortable. I'll be right back."

"I don't want morphine," Renee said in a hoarse voice as the nurse disappeared. "I want to see Liz."

"She's here in the hospital, too, and she's okay. She's resting, and you should be, too," Regina said, massaging Renee's hand ever harder. "You have to calm yourself."

"I am calm," Renee protested, her one good eye blinking rapidly. "But I wanna see Liz. I wanna make sure she's okay. Uncle Robert smashed her head into the wall. And I wanna make sure she's okay."

"Ahem. Congressman Whitfield." Regina looked up to see Dr. Rosenthal addressing Charles. "I hate to ask you and your family to leave the room, but we did say you would only be able to stay a few minutes, and you seem to be getting the patient overly excited. If you would just step back into the waiting room while we tend to—"

"Mom! Aunt Gina! Tell him I want to see Liz," Renee said urgently.

"Don't worry," Brenda said. "I'll tell them."

"I'm right here!" Liz's voice rang out from the doorway. "I'm right here, Ray."

The girl's head was bandaged, but otherwise she looked none the worse for the incident, Regina noted. It was the first time she had seen Liz without makeup and in a hospital gown, and damn if the girl still didn't look like a runway model.

"Liz?" Renee tried to look at her friend out the corner of her good eye. "Liz? Are you hurt?"

"Oh my God, Ray, look at you," Liz said as she rushed to Renee's bedside.

"I'm okay." Renee managed a smile. "I was just worried about you."

"And I was worried about you," Liz said, stroking Renee's swollen cheek. "They wouldn't tell me where you were, but I tracked you down."

Regina leaned over and whispered in Liz's ear, "We're trying to calm her down. Don't say anything that will get her excited." Liz nodded her assent.

"Liz, I love you so much," Renee said as more tears swelled from her good eye.

"And I love you, too, Ray."

"And, Ray-Ray," Brenda interjected, "your mother loves you, too."

"Isn't that good? We all love each other," the Jamaican nurse said as she approached Renee, hypodermic needle in hand. "Now, how about we give something to Miss Harris to make her feel good?" The nurse stuck the needle into Renee's IV line.

"I just wanted to tell—" Renee started.

"You can tell anything you want when you feel a little better," the nurse cut her off.

"But I just wanted . . ." Renee tried again, but just that fast the morphine kicked in and her eye seemed to roll back in her head. "Oh, that feels good," she murmured.

"That's my job, mon," the nurse said with a smile. "To make you feel good."

Dr. Rosenthal cleared his throat. "And it's my job to ask everyone to clear the room, if you would."

Liz looked up at Dr. Rosenthal with pleading eyes. "Couldn't I just stay with her for a few more minutes?"

"No. You heard the doctor," the nurse said brusquely. "You can stay with her a few minutes another time after she gets some rest."

"And who are you?" Puddin' asked with a smirk. "The enforcer?"

The nurse turned and gave Puddin' a slow up and down look before answering. "As the recovery room nurse, I suppose you could say I am. Now, will you please all leave for the patient's sake?"

"What Nurse Maughn means," Dr. Rosenthal said, "is that—"

"I think they know what I mean," Nurse Maughn said, giving the doctor a meaningful stare.

"I notice you ain't give that nurse that 'I'm Congressman Whitfield' shit, huh?" Puddin' told Charles as they all trekked back to the waiting area.

"No, I know when to keep my mouth shut," Charles said with a grin.

"Yeah, you might be large and in charge," Puddin' said, "but even Jesus Christ don't be fucking with God."

"Puddin'," Brenda said in a shocked voice. "That's blasphemy."

"Brenda, you know what? I'm just so happy that Renee's okay I don't even give a shit about your holier-than-thou bullshit," Puddin' said with a wave of her hand. "Just say a couple of Hail Marys for me when you get a chance, and we'll call it a day."

"Puddin'," Tamika said reprovingly, "Brenda only made a statement. And you don't have to be holier than thou, or even a Christian, to think what you just said was blasphemy."

"It's okay, Tamika." Brenda shrugged. "I'm not studying Puddin'." She turned to Regina. "Why don't you all go home? I'm going to go ahead and sleep in the waiting room until I can see Renee again."

"Well," Regina said, "I was planning to—"

Charles cut Regina off. "Good idea, Brenda. But you don't have a cell phone, do you?"

Brenda shook her head.

"Okay. Then just call on a pay phone or ask if you can use the phone at the nurses' station to let us know when Renee wakes up, okay?" Charles gave her a hug, and David and Tamika followed suit, while Puddin' and Regina looked on.

"Brenda, if you want, I can stay here with you," Regina said finally. "I really don't mind. I'd like to be here when Renee wakes up again, too."

"So would I," Puddin' said. "We are the ones who saved her, you know."

"And Brenda's her mother," Charles said, giving Regina's arm a little squeeze. "So why don't we just let her do her motherly thing, okay? We can all stop by in the morning."

Regina glanced over at Brenda—who was giving Charles an appreciative smile—then gave Charles's arm a return squeeze and nodded. "Just make sure you call and let us know if there's any problem, okay?" she said, giving Brenda a hug. "And you know what? I love you."

"And I love you, too, little sister." Brenda kissed her on the cheek. "And so does my daughter." She gave Regina another quick hug. "Or should I say *our* daughter?"

"Your daughter," Regina said with a smile. "And my niece."

# chapter seventeen

"Good morning, sunshine!"

Regina yawned and stretched before throwing off the blanket and sitting on the side of the bed. She had a slight headache, the kind you get from not getting enough sleep or sleeping too long. She couldn't figure out which it was. She did know that she felt as if she were in a fog. "Mmm . . . what time is it?"

Charles sat down next to her and handed her a cup of coffee. "A little after twelve, so it's actually 'good afternoon,' not 'good morning.' And you got a good seven hours' sleep. Or at least six hours, since you ravished me for an hour."

"What?" Regina's head jerked back. She looked down and found she was wearing a red cotton pajama top. And yes, she was still wearing the panties she had on the day before. But . . . had she . . . ? Had they . . . ?

"Calm down. You're going to spill your coffee." Charles chuckled. "I was only kidding."

"Oh. Well, yeah, I knew you were kidding," Regina said sheepishly, not sure if she was relieved or disappointed.

"No, you didn't," Charles said with a laugh. "I should have kept the joke up a little longer. You should have seen the panic on your face. The thought of making love to me couldn't be that disturbing, could it?"

"I can't believe I slept this late, though," Regina said, ignoring his last question. "What time did you get up?" She took a sip of her coffee, then placed it on the nightstand as the fog lifted and the previous night's events rushed back to her. "Oh God, any word from the hospital? How's Ray-Ray? Did Brenda call?"

"Cool out," Charles said soothingly as he rubbed her back. "Renee's fine. They moved her to ICU right after we left, and they plan to move her into a regular room later today."

"How do you know all that?"

"Well, Brenda's called twice . . ."

"Why didn't you wake me up?"

"Because you needed your rest," Charles explained. "If it were bad news, I would have wakened you, but since everything was all right, I figured I'd just wait until you woke up on your own. I came in a couple of times to check on you. I'd forgotten how beautiful you are when you sleep."

"So Ray-Ray's fine? You're sure?" Regina asked skeptically.

"Fine as can be expected under the circumstances. She's pretty much conscious, but still in a lot of pain, of course. And she's sleeping a lot because of the pain medication, but that's a good thing. She needs as much rest as possible. Brenda's still with her, and I'll take you up to see her later this afternoon, okay?"

"No, I'll just drive up there now," Regina said, looking around for her robe. She put it on and headed to the bathroom, then stopped in her tracks and turned back toward Charles. "You know what?" she said slowly as she moved back to the bed and sat down. "On second thought I'll wait until later. Brenda probably wants, probably needs, to spend time alone with Ray-Ray right now. After all, *she's* Ray-Ray's mother, not me."

"That sounds about right," Charles said with a nod.

Regina stared at Charles, noting for the first time that he appeared to be the one who needed to rest. He looked as if he hadn't slept at all, though when they'd gotten in and he helped her to her room, he had said he would sleep on the living room couch. There were bags under his eyes, and his face had a haggard look. He was also badly in need of a shave.

"Did you get any sleep?" she asked, picking up her coffee.

"No, not really." Charles yawned. "I put the living room back together as best as I could . . ."

Regina sighed. "God bless you. You didn't have to, though. I would have gotten around to it."

Charles shook his head. "When we walked in and saw the mess, you sat down on the couch, and I thought you were going to cry. You didn't, though. You closed your eyes and started snoring. That's when I carried your butt upstairs," he said, chucking her under the chin. "Anyway, I couldn't sleep, so I figured I'd straighten up so you wouldn't have to face it again this morning."

"You're really sweet, Charles," Regina said, then grabbed his hand and gave it a squeeze. "You're really a pretty decent man."

"I've been telling you that for years now, you know, Gina," Charles said softly. He leaned forward and kissed her on the forehead, then on the tip of her nose, and finally on the mouth. She gave a sharp intake of breath when he used his tongue to part her lips and kiss her more deeply, causing her heart to flutter and her body to flush with warmth. He pulled her closer to him, and his lips moved from her face down her neck and to the top button of her pajamas.

She hadn't been with Charles in an intimate way since their divorce, and the memory of their passionate lovemaking mingled with the sensation of his tongue moving down her chest. Why, she wondered as her head fell back and moans that she knew were her own filled the room, had she waited so long? None of the men she'd been with in her life—and she'd been with so many in her youth—had ever made her feel as loved and desirable as Charles did. Not even Little Joe.

Little Joe! His name put a sudden damper on Regina's lust. How could she be ready to fall into bed with her ex-husband when her present lover would be back in the city in just a couple of hours? She needed to get her shit together.

She kissed Charles on the cheek and gently pushed him away and redid her top buttons.

"So," Regina asked in as normal a tone as she could muster, "any updates from the police on catching that asshole?"

She noticed the expression on Charles's face go from surprise to disappointment at her sudden loss of ardor. His brow furrowed and he looked at her quizzically, and it seemed as if he were about to question her about it, but then he simply shrugged his shoulders.

"Yeah, there's been an update," Charles said grimly as he turned away from her. "Get ready for this. They found Robert asleep in his office this morning. You and Puddin' must have really worked him over good because the police took him to the hospital to get him patched up before they could take him to central booking. David and I are on our way to see if we can get in to see him. I actually came upstairs to wake you to let you know I was going when I saw you were already getting up."

Regina jumped up from the bed. "What? Why the hell are you going to see that bastard?"

"Don't worry, we're not going on a buddy tip." Charles gave a harsh laugh. "First off, we might not be able to see him, because they don't allow visitors at booking, but we're going to try to pull some strings. If we do get to see him, I'm going to let him know that if for some reason he gets out of jail, if he ever gets out, I'm going to be waiting for him. I don't care if he does thirty days or thirty years, that bastard's going to know that when he comes out, he's going to have to deal with me.

No one's going to attack my family and think they can get away with it. Not even my ex–best friend."

Regina didn't know how to react at first. The words shocked her, but filled her with a sense of satisfaction and security. It was nice to know that after all their years apart Charles would still feel this strongly about her and Renee.

She slowly sank back down on the bed next to him. "I'm sure that will go over well with the newspapers. I can see the headline now: U.S. congressman, or U.S. senator maybe by then, sent to prison for killing ex-con," she said lightly as she nudged him on the shoulder.

"It will be worth it," Charles said with a sigh. He lay down on the bed, crossed his hands behind his head, and stared up at the ceiling. "Isn't it funny? Robert was my campaign manager when I first ran for Congress. Did a damn good job, too. The man was a born organizer. Now I'm getting ready to put together an exploratory committee for the Senate, and things are 180 degrees different. My once campaign manager is my sworn enemy.

"Who the hell would have thought that it would come to this, huh? I mean, I've known Robert practically all my life. I was the best man at his wedding. He was the best man at our wedding. And now, just six years later, he's in jail for assaulting and trying to rape our niece. Everything seems just so weird and fucked-up."

Charles continued to stare up at the ceiling. "You know, Gina, if only I listened to you when you wanted to cut Robert out of our lives back when he lied to Yvonne about being married, this wouldn't have happened. I mean, I was the one who still insisted that he be our best man, and even be our child's godfather."

"Don't start feeling guilty or blaming yourself. Yvonne's already racked with guilt, and I'm feeling a little guilty myself," Regina said grimly. "If I had just let Ray-Ray know what was going on with Robert instead of trying to shield her, she never would have opened the door for him last night."

Charles shook his head and sighed. "You know, you try hard to protect the people you love, but it just seems you can never do enough. There's so much fucked-up stuff going on in the world."

Regina nodded.

Charles propped himself on his elbow and looked at her. "I know you're going to be mad at me for saying this, but that's why I don't want you to bring lowlifes like that Joe Blayton guy around Camille. I'm not trying to be funny, but I don't even want him around you."

Regina stiffened. "What does Little Joe have to do with this?"

"People like that are unstable, and you never know what kind of crap they're going to do."

"People like what?" Regina asked as she moved away from Charles.

"See, you're getting mad, but I don't even care," Charles said wearily. "People like your Little Joe. Gangsters. Dope dealers. Ex-convicts."

"First off, Little Joe did his time—"

"From what I understand he didn't do all of his time, now, did he?" Charles snapped. "It's my understanding that he was supposed to be doing life without parole but his lawyer got his conviction overturned."

"Well, he did enough time," Regina retorted. "And I'm not saying he's always been a perfect angel, but he's not in the life anymore. So—"

"Well, that car I saw you guys climb into in front of Amy Ruth's looked pretty damn expensive."

"Not that it's any of your goddamned business, but Little Joe made some smart investments before he went in. He owns a piece of two supermarkets and a housing development in New Jersey, to name a few. And—"

"That's bullshit. The government would have confiscated any property or investments he had when they sent him up on that drug racketeering charge because they would have been considered ill-gotten goods."

"Yeah, well, he didn't have them in his name."

"The government has lawyers and accountants that know how to sniff out hidden investments."

"Yeah, well, they obviously weren't as good as Little Joe's lawyers and accountants, okay?"

"You have the nerve to say that with pride in your voice? What the hell is wrong with you? And of course, you know how helpful it was to my possible Senate run to have the people I was schmoozing see my ex-wife with a thug ex-con."

Regina sucked her teeth. "Look, I didn't know you were in New York. Maybe if you'd let me know ahead of time, Little Joe and I would have been more discreet as to where we decided to go eat."

"Damn it, Regina, what the hell is wrong with you?" Charles stormed. "It's not just about your being seen together. I could explain that away if I had to, but it's about your being with someone like him in the first place."

Regina jumped up from the bed. "There's nothing wrong with me except that I forgot what an asshole you can be sometimes."

Charles stood up and faced her. "Oh, so now I'm an asshole, huh?"

"Yeah." Regina folded her arms over her chest. "You are."

"And why is that?"

"Because you don't even know Little Joe and you're tearing him down. You're judging him on what people have told you about his past. I got news for you, Charles. Little Joe isn't the only one with a past, or have you forgotten? I mean, after all, you married me knowing that I hadn't always been a saint."

"Yeah, but you weren't a dope dealer. Look at all the shit David and Tamika are going through right now because of dope dealers. And you want people like *that* around Camille? And even if he's not actually dealing drugs anymore, you can't tell me you know for sure he's all on the up-and-up. You don't know what that man is doing or what kind of violence he's capable of. God damn it, Regina. Hasn't what just happened to Renee knocked any kind of sense into you? To hell, do what you want. I'm out of here," Charles yelled, walking out of the bedroom.

"You know what? Fuck you, Charles," Regina shouted, storming out after him. "What happened to Renee doesn't have anything to do with Little Joe or 'people like that.' Get this straight, you bastard. It was Robert—in other words, someone like *you,* with a privileged background and an Ivy League education—that attacked Ray-Ray."

"Go to hell, Regina," Charles said as he walked down the steps with Regina on his heels.

"No, you go to hell, you fucking stuck-up motherfucker. Who the fuck do you think you are, coming into my house and telling me who I should or should not have around Camille?"

"I happen to be her father, and I care what goes on in her life," Charles said, and snatched his coat from the hallway closet.

"And I happen to be her mother. Are you suggesting that I don't care about what goes on in her life?" Regina said defiantly, blocking the front door so he couldn't leave.

"You sound as trashy as Puddin'," Charles said in a disgusted voice.

"Fuck you, Charles. You don't like me talking like this, don't piss me the fuck off," Regina spat out. "You think I don't have good enough fucking judgment to know who I should bring around Camille? You think I'm some kinda fucking chickenhead? You didn't even ask me if Little Joe had been around Camille or had ever met her. For that matter, you never bothered to ask what my relationship is to Little Joe. You saw us together that one time, and you just go jumping to all kind of fucking conclusions."

"So then you admit you have a relationship with him, huh?"

"Yeah, that's what this is really about, isn't it? You wanna know if I'm screwing Little Joe," Regina said with flared nostrils and narrowed eyes. "I don't know how many times I've already told you 'fuck you,' Charles, but I'm going to say it again. Fuck you, Charles, and fuck the horse you rode in on."

"Why don't you just move so I can get the hell out of here?"

"Best idea I've heard all day." Regina turned, unlocked the door, and flung it open. She slammed it shut after Charles walked out, almost hitting him in the back of the head.

She was halfway back up the stairs when the doorbell rang.

"What do you want?" she demanded through the closed door.

"Let me in, I want to talk to you."

"Charles, believe me, if I open this door, you're gonna wind up a battered ex-husband," Regina said with a sarcastic laugh. "You'd better split while the splitting is good."

☙

The phone was ringing when Regina stepped out of the shower, and she momentarily considered not answering it in case it was Charles, but changed her mind since it might be the hospital calling.

"Hello," she said cautiously.

"Hey you."

"Oh hey, Little Joe." Regina glanced at the clock. It was almost 2:30 p.m. Little Joe's plane must have just touched down.

"So what's going on? Is your niece okay?"

"She's going to be in the hospital for a while, but she's going to be fine," Regina said. "I'm on my way to see her now."

"Well, I'm not even gonna ask you if you want me to meet you up there, since it's obvious you wanna keep me as your down-low lover, but just call me on my cell if you need anything, okay?"

"Okay."

"And what about the muthafucka that put her in the hospital? Police catch him yet?"

"Yeah, they caught Robert this morning. It would have been nice if they had shot him on the spot, but they took him to the hospital to patch him up, then hauled him off to Rikers Island."

"Why did they have to patch him up?"

"Shoot, me and Puddin' put a beating down on him when we caught him up in here. That bastard was punched, kicked, smashed with a baseball bat, and stabbed."

"Damn! My girls!" Little Joe laughed. "So is Camille still with your ex?"

"Actually, Charles is here in the city, but he left Camille in Philadelphia with his mother. Why?"

"Yeah, I shoulda figured he'd be there."

"Is that a problem?" Regina asked.

"Naw, ain't no problem, and keep that attitude out your fucking voice." Little Joe chuckled. "Look at you trying to pick a fight with your pint-size self. But listen, call me when you finish up at the hospital so we can maybe get together for dinner."

"Okay."

"Okay." And with that, the line went dead, but two seconds after Regina put the receiver down, the phone rang again.

"Hello."

"Hey you. I meant to ask yesterday, but then all this shit came up, but how's things going with Tamika? Anything new?"

"You mean with those drug dealers? She didn't mention anything, so I assume not."

"No, huh? Yeah, well, make sure you remember to call me when you finish up this evening. Talk to you later." And once again the phone went dead.

Regina quickly dressed and headed out to pick up Tamika

so they could go to the hospital together. Since Charles had flown into New York in a helicopter, he didn't have a car at his disposal, so David had driven him to central booking, leaving Tamika in need of a ride to the hospital.

"Girl, you need to listen to this," Tamika said a few minutes later as she climbed in the passenger seat of Regina's car. She held up a microcassette tape recorder.

"What is it?" Regina asked.

"The tape from my answering machine. I didn't check the machine until about an hour ago, but this message was on it." Tamika hit the play button on the recorder.

*"Mr. and Mrs. Corbett, I hope you recognize my voice and know who this is . . ."*

Tamika hit the pause button. "It's one of those drug dealers. The one named Jerry who first came to my door." She hit the play button again.

*". . . but I'm calling to apologize for any problems you had recently, and let you know I don't think you're gonna have more problems. So please don't worry anymore, and please tell your friends that they ain't gotta worry because everything's cool."*

"Get the hell outta here," Regina exclaimed as she turned the car onto Lenox Avenue.

"Ain't that something!"

"Yeah, it is. Do you think it's for real? Do you think he's serious?"

"You know," Tamika said as she slipped the recorder back into her pocketbook, "for some reason I think he is. I don't know why, but I really do."

"Well, I wonder what happened to cause this sudden change of heart. I mean . . . wait a minute. Do you know when that call came in?"

"The time and date stamp indicated it was recorded about nine last night. I guess we were over at Yvonne's. Why?"

Regina paused. "Well, I spoke to Little Joe about an hour

ago, and he made it a point to ask if there was anything new with you."

"Really?"

"Yeah." Regina shrugged. "But it could just be that he was worried since he knew about your problem."

"Yeah, it could be," Tamika agreed.

"But the deal is that we had already hung up and he had to call back just to ask that one question . . ." Regina's voice trailed off. "And then he seemed surprised when I said there was nothing new."

"You don't think that—"

Regina cut her off. "I don't know what to think. How about we just leave it like that?"

"Yeah, I mean, but even if someone did reach out to this Jerry guy, it's not like I would be mad," Tamika said slowly. "In fact, I'd be grateful."

"I'm sure you would," Regina said, looking straight ahead. "But of course, there's really no real reason to believe that someone did. It could be that Jerry and his crew decided they've done enough already and there's no reason to bother you anymore."

"That could be."

"Yeah."

"Or it could be that someone did reach out," Tamika said with a shrug. "And that would be a good thing, not bad."

"Right. But we don't know that's what happened."

"We could ask. Or you could ask."

"I could, but I won't."

"Why not?"

"Because . . ." Regina hesitated as she tried to figure out exactly what to say. If Little Joe had indeed found the guys and convinced them to leave Tamika and David alone, that was something she should be happy about. But it would depend on how he convinced them. If he had just simply talked them into it, that was one thing. If he had threatened them, or actually had one of them hurt to show he was serious, that would be a whole other thing. And Regina knew Little Joe was more than capable of going that second route. And she just really didn't want to know. Especially since she'd just had the argument with Charles about whether or not Little Joe had changed his ways.

She took a deep breath. "Just because," she finally answered Tamika as they pulled up in front of the hospital.

"Mrs. Corbett," someone called as they got out of the car.

The women turned around and saw a tall, thin, copper-skinned man wearing a New York Giants athletic shirt, baggy blue jeans, and untied Michael Jordan sneakers waving in their direction.

Regina grabbed Tamika's arm. "Is that one of them?"

"One of who?"

"One of the guys who's been bothering you!"

"No," Tamika said as she waved back. "That's one of David's clients. Would you believe he's almost forty years old? He dresses like he's a teenager, doesn't he?"

"Whew!" Regina said as they walked to the hospital entrance. "That's a relief. I thought we mighta had to give someone a beat-down out here on 135th and Lenox."

"Mrs. Corbett," the man said, approaching them. "Howya doing? Got a couple of minutes?"

"Um, sure, Mr. Riggs," Tamika said a little nervously.

"Call me Spider."

"Thanks. And this is my friend Regina Harris."

"How do you do?" Regina said, extending her hand.

"Fine. Fine." The man grabbed her hand and gave it an absentminded shake, then addressed Tamika again. "Mind if we talk privately for a minute?"

"Sure," Tamika answered again. "Regina, why don't you go on upstairs? I'll catch up with you in a minute."

Regina gave Tamika an "are you sure" look and received an assuring "I'll be okay" nod in return.

"Okay, girl," Regina said. "I'll see you in a few, I guess."

# chapter eighteen

Aunt Gina, you missed it!" Renee's voice rang out as Regina entered the room.

"How are you feeling, sweetie?" Regina bent down and gently kissed her niece on the cheek. "Hey, Liz," she said to the girl who was sitting in a chair next to Renee's bed. The bandage on Liz's head was smaller than it was the night before, and she was dressed in her usual uniform of tight jeans and slinky blouse.

"I'm feeling okay, but you missed it!" Renee said excitedly.

"Hi, Miss Regina," Liz said with a huge smile.

"Okay, what did I miss?" Regina placed the flowers she had purchased at the hospital gift shop on the nightstand next to Renee's bed.

"Mommy just threw her preacher man out on his butt!" Renee started laughing, then winced and pressed her left hand against her ribs. "Dang, it hurts when I laugh."

"Preacher man? What preacher man?" Regina asked.

"Father Destiny. The guy who heads the Church of Unified Reformers that Mommy goes to," Renee answered with a little chuckle. "He came up here so he and Mommy could pray for me, which you know I wasn't all that hot about, anyway. But then when they got up off their knees, he told Mommy that he was sure she knew that God had punished me because I was a miscreant and sexual deviant who strayed from the path of righteousness.

"You shoulda seen Mommy's face. I thought she was going to hit him!" Renee was struggling not to laugh again. "She went off on him, telling him that she called him in here for prayers and support and that if he thought he was gonna come up in here and call her daughter names, he had another thought coming. She even said that if God wanted to punish anyone, it would be someone like him lining his pockets with poor people's money and buying a new car every year when some of his followers couldn't even pay their rent."

"Yeah, she read him up, down, and sideways," Liz said. "He ran out of here so fast he left his Bible."

"And then he was scared to come back in the room with Mommy in here, so he sent a nurse in after it," Renee added.

"Get outta here," Regina said in amazement. "Where's your mom now?"

"Right here," Brenda announced as she walked through the open door. "I was down at the lobby reception desk letting them know that if that fake man of God tries to get in here again, they should throw him out on his ass."

"Whoa," Regina said, giving Brenda a hug, "I'm scared of you."

"Here, Miss Brenda," Liz said, getting up and offering Brenda her chair. "You look like you need to catch your breath."

"That's okay," Brenda said in a sharp voice. She walked over and sat on the windowsill. "You go ahead and keep the chair. I'm okay over here."

Regina noticed Renee and Liz share a worried look, and she started to say something, but Brenda spoke first.

"I didn't mean to snap at you, sweetheart," Brenda said, addressing Liz. "I'm still worked up over that short, fat bastard."

"That's okay, Miss Brenda," Liz said demurely.

Brenda fell silent for a moment, then finally said, "Look, I apologized to Renee earlier, but I want to apologize to you, Liz. And to you, too, Gina."

"For what?" Regina said as she sat down next to Brenda.

"For being such an idiot, I guess." Brenda lowered her eyes. "I don't know what was wrong with me. I didn't have any business listening in on Renee's telephone call when she was talking to Liz, and I must have been out of my mind to throw my only daughter out because of whom she chooses to love."

Brenda looked up at Liz. "I've already told Renee that I want her to come back home to me when they let her out the hospital, and I want you to know that you're always welcome in my house. Anyone who loves Renee is welcome in my house."

"Thank you, Miss Brenda," Liz said with a smile. "I really appreciate that."

Regina put her arm around Brenda's shoulders. "You know I really love you," she whispered in her sister's ear.

Brenda shrugged. "And I want to apologize to you, too. I said some really foul things to you."

"That's okay." Regina gave Brenda a little squeeze.

"No, it's not okay," Brenda said, shaking her head. "I gotta tell you something, sis." Brenda took a deep breath and looked away from Regina. "I think—no, I *know*—that I've been jealous of you for years now. And not because you're successful or anything, but because of your relationship with Renee. I've always felt like she considered you her mother, and I was just someone she had to live with."

"Oh, Brenda . . . ," Regina started.

"I told her she shouldn'ta felt like that," Renee interjected.

"Maybe I shouldn't have, but I did," Brenda said miserably. "I mean, you were really the one who raised Renee. She barely even knew I was her mother until you were shot and she came

to live with me when she was six. And I've tried to make it up
to her . . ."

"You have, Mom!"

". . . but she and I never formed the bond that you two have.
I thought that maybe after Camille was born, you and Renee
would become more distant, but you didn't." Brenda let out a
deep sigh. "But that's understandable. You were her mother for
the first six years of her life while I was out running the streets.
I can't erase that. I shouldn't have wanted to. And I sure
shouldn't have been jealous."

Regina sighed. "Shoot, now I guess I have to apologize,
too."

"For what?" Brenda looked at her quizzically.

"Well, I said some pretty wicked stuff that night to you,
too, remember? And also . . ." Regina hesitated. "And also, I
know sometimes I overstep my bounds when it comes to
Renee. But, you know, it's hard sometimes to figure out how
much I'm allowed to do as an aunt and at what point it be-
comes me acting like I'm her mother."

"Aww," Renee said with a grin. "You two just love me so
much."

"Oh, shut up, Renee," Brenda said with a laugh.

Regina gave Brenda a nudge. "You took the words right out
of my mouth."

"Anyway," Regina said, turning to Renee, "what's your
prognosis? Are you going to live?"

"I still got a lotta pain, but the nurse comes in with medication every couple of hours, so it's bearable. And my arm and
leg itch under the casts, so that's uncomfortable. But the doctor said I might be able to get outta here in about two weeks."
Renee sighed. "I can't wait. The food here sucks."

"What about your eye?"

"A doctor came and looked at it this morning. He said it
was a scratched retina and it'll probably heal itself with no
damage."

Regina shifted uncomfortably in her seat. "Listen, I guess you and Liz need an explanation about why Robert did what he did—"

Renee cut her off. "Oh yeah! I forgot to tell you. Aunt Yvonne was by here about an hour ago. She told me about Uncle Robert." Renee wrinkled her nose. "I don't think I'm gonna call him uncle anymore."

"I don't blame you," Regina agreed.

"Anyway, she was real beat up, too. And she told me they locked him up. The police were here, too, and they took me and Liz's statements. I hope you know I'm pressing charges. How do I do that, anyway?"

"You can talk to Uncle David and Uncle Charles when they get here. I'm sure they can tell you." Regina shook her head. "You know, I came over here thinking you'd be moaning and groaning in pain, and here you are all cheery and talking up a storm. It must be nice to be eighteen." Regina turned to Liz. "You know what? I'm sorry. I didn't even ask how you were feeling."

"I'm doing fine." Liz touched her bandaged head. "A little bit of a headache, but nothing two Tylenol don't take care of."

"Fuck some Tylenol," Puddin' announced as she strode through the door, followed closely by Tamika. "Let me know if you ever need any real drugs, girl. I'll hook you up."

"Hey, Aunt Puddin'!" Renee exclaimed. "I bet my drugs are better than yours. They're giving me morphine."

"Aw, isn't that cute?" Puddin' chuckled as she bent down and kissed her on the cheek. "A fledgling junkie."

"How you feeling?" Tamika said when it was her turn to kiss Renee.

"I'm okay. Well, you know, not exactly okay, but I'm okay," Renee answered. "The doctors said I might be able to go home in about two weeks."

"Hi, Miss Tamika. Hi, Miss Puddin'," Liz said meekly.

Puddin' gave her a nonchalant nod, but Tamika walked over and hugged the girl.

"How are you feeling, Liz?" Tamika asked as she caressed the girl's face.

"I'm doing really well, thanks." Liz looked up at her with a bright smile.

"You sure?"

"Yes."

"Listen," Tamika said slowly, "you live in the Bronx, don't you?"

Liz nodded.

"Well, I was thinking. I know you're going to want to spend every waking minute in this hospital with Ray-Ray, so since I only live a few blocks away, why don't you stay with me for a while? David and I have plenty of room, and that way you don't have to be traveling the subway late at night to get home, or wasting money on cabs."

Regina couldn't believe her ears. Why would Tamika . . . and then it hit her. Tamika had remembered what she herself had forgotten—Liz's father. Tamika obviously thought him an unfit, or at least an unstable, father.

"Oh, I wouldn't want to impose, Miss Tamika," Liz was saying.

"It wouldn't be an imposition at all. David and I have plenty of space. You can even have your own room."

"Ooh, Aunt Mika, that would be so cool," Renee said excitedly. "Liz, you gotta do it. That would be so cool!"

"Yeah, that does sound kinda cool." A grin slowly appeared on Liz's face. "I'll just go home after visiting hours tonight and let my father know and pack up a few clothes."

"Tell you what," Tamika said, giving the girl another hug. "David will be here any minute now, and I'm sure he won't mind driving you home and bringing you back."

"Tamika, that's nice of you to offer and everything, but you don't think her father would mind?" Brenda asked.

"Give him a couple of drinks," Puddin' exclaimed, "and he probably wouldn't even notice she's gone."

"Puddin'!" Regina said as a warning, but it was too late. Liz's face reddened, and she shifted uncomfortably in her chair, her eyes downcast as she fidgeted with her pocketbook.

Brenda leaned in close to Regina's ear. "Oh dang, something's going on here, huh?" she whispered. "I didn't know, or I wouldn't have said anything."

"You couldn't have known," Regina whispered back. "I'll fill you in later."

"I guess you met Frank last night?" Liz said in a small voice. "He's not really as bad as all that. He just like to get his drink on every now and then. He's usually pretty harmless."

"Liz," Renee said softly, "I can't get up and hug you right now, so why don't you come here and hug me?"

"I'm okay, Ray," Liz said, still looking down.

"Stop lying and come here."

Liz shook her head.

"Okay, then," Renee said, and struggled to sit up. "I guess I will have to go over to you."

"Renee!" Regina and Brenda said simultaneously as they jumped from the windowsill and rushed over to her.

"I'm fine," Renee said, but she grimaced in pain and fell back onto the bed. "I'm fine. Just let me catch my breath."

"Just lie down, Ray." Liz walked over and took Renee's hand. "I'm right here."

"Listen, you can't pay Aunt Puddin' any mind. She's just insensitive and mean sometimes," Renee said, squeezing Liz's hand. "Isn't that right, Aunt Puddin'?"

"Well . . . ," Puddin' started.

"She's just insensitive sometimes," Renee continued. "But you've got to learn to ignore her like everybody else does."

"Girl, you'd better watch what the fuck you say—"

"Why, Aunt Puddin'? You don't watch what the fuck *you* say," Renee said without looking at her. "You say whatever comes into your head without stopping to think how other people are gonna feel about it. Why should you be the only one?" She squeezed Liz's hand again. "Like I was saying, Aunt Puddin' is insensitive, but she isn't really mean. Or she wasn't trying to be right then."

"It's okay, Ray," Liz said grimly. "She was right in what she—"

"No, she wasn't," Renee interrupted. "She had no place saying that."

"But just so you know," Liz said with tears in her eyes, "like I said before, Frank like his drink, but he's never been abusive. So please don't feel sorry for me or that you have to protect me. Not from him. He really does love me." She turned to Tamika. "I would like to take you up on your offer, but not to get away from Frank. Just so I can be nearer to Ray."

"Sure, honey," Tamika said. "And you don't have to go back to your father's tonight to get your clothes. I'm sure I have some clothes you can wear for a while."

"Liz is too tall and skinny to wear your clothes, Aunt Mika," Renee said cautiously. "Maybe Aunt Puddin' can loan her some of her clothes."

Puddin' snorted. "Yeah, I got some shit you can wear. But, Ray-Ray, if you ever try to play me again, I swear I'll forget about the beat-down you already got and I will jump in your shit, hear me? And Gina's, too, if she gets in the way."

"Yeah, not fucking likely," Regina said with a harsh laugh.

"And you'd have to come through me, too," Brenda added dryly.

"Yeah? Well, ain't neither of you ain't saying shit I can't handle," Puddin' growled. "I'll—"

"Y'all don't need to fight. I 'pologize," Renee said quickly.

"You just oughta," Puddin' snapped. "I love you like you was my own blood, and I think I proved that a bunch over. If I said something outta line, then I apologize, but—"

"You just oughta," Renee said lightly, causing everyone—including Puddin'—to laugh.

"Well," Puddin' said, "I ain't mean to hurt your feelings, Liz, okay? I was only trying to make a joke. We cool?"

Liz smiled and nodded just as the nurse walked in.

"Good evening, Miss Harris. Evening, Harris family. Everybody doing well?" She didn't wait for an answer as she began to check Renee's vital signs. "Are you experiencing any pain, dearie?"

"No, but I am a little sleepy," Renee said with a yawn.

"Why didn't you say something, baby?" Brenda kissed Renee on the cheek. "I'll put everyone out so you can get some rest."

"Mom, you should go home and get some rest, too. I don't need a babysitter."

"No, I don't mind staying," Brenda protested.

"Mom, I'll be all right! Go home." Renee yawned again. "I'll see you in the morning, okay?"

"Well . . ." Brenda hesitated. "Well, okay. But I'm going to stay over at your Aunt Regina's house tonight instead of going all the way to Queens. So if you need me, just call and I'll be here in a few minutes." She looked at Regina. "You don't mind me staying over, do you?"

Regina waved her hand at her sister. "Girl, please. You know you don't even have to ask."

⤳

"Hey, Mika," Regina said as they walked out of the elevator and into the lobby. "What was it that guy wanted to talk to you about? What's his name, Spider?"

"Yeah, I was going to tell you about that," Tamika said in a low voice so that the others, who were walking ahead of them, wouldn't hear. "He said that he heard we was having a little trouble and that he was glad my people straightened it out, but next time we run into a problem we should let him know 'cause he's got some juice, too."

"Oh really?" Regina's eyebrow shot up. "So did you ask how he heard about it?"

"Yeah, but he got vague on me—you know how they get—and just said he heard something about it on the street."

"And he said it was *your* people that straightened it out, huh?"

"Yeah, but then when I was leaving, he told me to tell my uncle that Spider said hello."

Regina's stomach sank. Little Joe had introduced Puddin' as his niece when he was defending her at the Rob-Cee listening party; it was a safe bet he was calling himself Tamika's uncle now. There was no use in trying to make believe he hadn't gotten himself involved. The only question now was just how involved. Before she could ask Tamika anything else, she saw David coming through the hospital doors.

"Hey," he said after he gave Brenda and Liz a hug and kissed Puddin', Regina, and Tamika on the cheek. "Visiting hours are over already?"

"No, but Ray-Ray was tired, so we decided to give her a break. How'd it go at central booking?" Tamika asked, linking her arm through his.

"Isn't Charles with you?" Regina asked before he could answer Tamika.

"He had me drop him at the airport so he could rent a car. He should be here soon," David answered. "I'd better call him and tell him to meet us at the house."

"How'd it go at central booking?" Tamika asked again.

David shook his head. "It was a mess. Robert was slobbering and clawing at us, telling us how sorry he was and how he couldn't even remember what had happened."

"Yeah, right." Puddin' sucked her teeth. "I bet that muthafucka remembered that knife I stuck between his shoulder blades."

"Then he started talking about how his life was so messed up, and that he knew he's going to straighten up and kick his drug habit," David continued. "And the crazy bastard asked if I would represent him at his arraignment hearing and get him released on his own recognizance so he could try and square everything with the Bronx D.A. so he won't lose his job."

"Get the hell outta here!" Regina said in amazement. "What did you say?"

"Hell. I was going to punch the shit out of him, but I couldn't because I was too busy holding Charles back," David said with a snort.

"Do you think he's going to get out?" Brenda asked nervously.

"You've got nothing to worry about." David put his arm around her and drew her close to him. "We've already called the Manhattan D.A.'s Office and talked to the ADA who's caught his case. Believe me, he's not going to get out on bail; they're charging him with three counts of assault, three counts of attempted murder, two counts of attempted rape, and one count of breaking and entering. And they're not going to offer him a plea, either. That boy's going to do some real time behind all this shit."

# *ℐ*chapter nineteen

*Police report that the body of a nineteen-year-old man was found early this morning in Harlem. The man, who has not yet been identified, was shot once in the back of his head, according to police officials. His body was found on 123rd Street on a known drug corner, around 4:30 a.m. Police say they have no suspects at this time, and they don't know if the shooting was drug-related. In other news . . ."*

Regina clicked off the radio and pulled her car over to the curb. One Hundred and Twenty-third Street. Wasn't that the street Tamika said the thugs who had been harassing her family hung out on?

Regina bit her lip and tapped her fingernails against the steering wheel as she stared out the window at nothing. Little Joe couldn't have done it because he wasn't in New York until 2:30 this afternoon, she tried to reason to herself. But she knew that didn't mean he didn't have it done; he had enough practice doing that when he was on the council. There was only one way to find out for sure, she decided as she put the car back into gear, and that was to ask him. She'd have the opportunity to do just that in a few minutes, since she was only a few blocks away from the Flash Inn, where she had agreed to meet Little Joe for dinner.

Little Joe was already seated at his usual table when she walked in. He smiled when he saw her, but try as she might, she couldn't bring herself to return the smile.

"You're looking good. California must agree with you. You look all relaxed and everything. And I can't believe you actually managed to get a tan," she said after she gave him a quick peck on the lips and sat down. "You were only there two days."

"Well, like they say, when in movieland, do as the movie stars do, so I spent a little time at the beach frying myself up." Little Joe looked at her quizzically. "What's wrong with you?"

"Hmm? Oh, nothing," Regina said as she placed her napkin in her lap. "Just had a hard day is all."

"Yeah, yeah, that's right." Little Joe nodded. "How's your niece?"

"She's going to be fine." Regina opened the menu the waiter handed her. "Do you know what you're going to get yet?"

"Gina, what the fuck is wrong with you? Why you rushing and shit?" Little Joe's lips curled as he talked. "You act like you don't wanna be here."

"No, I'm sorry." Regina put the menu down and smiled at Little Joe. "I am being rude, but I don't mean to. Like I said, I'm just out of it. I probably shoulda canceled. I'm really sorry."

"Yeah, well, I woulda understood, but I still woulda been pissed off," Little Joe said coldly. "Your man just got back in town, you're supposed to want to spend a little time with him, ya know. Or don't you know?"

"I do know, and like I said, I'm sorry." Regina reached over the table and took Little Joe's hand. "How about we order a drink and maybe an appetizer and you tell me how it went in L.A.?"

"It went good. It went real good," Little Joe said after he ordered Regina an apple martini and a shrimp cocktail and a whiskey sour and an order of fried calamari for himself. "They had a limo waiting for me and my boy at the airport, and they put us up in a suite at the Ritz Carlton."

"Ooh, must be nice," Regina gushed.

"And I thought I was supposed to be just meeting with Tecumseh Joseph, but when I got to his office, he was there with a producer and a screenwriter. He said he wanted them to meet me because they would be the ones helping to develop the screenplay if we decided to go ahead and do a movie based on my life."

"Wow. So what did you guys talk about?"

"They musta done their homework, because they knew a lot about me. Or at least about my street life. They did ask me a few questions about my life growing up, though. And they asked me how much I would be comfortable having put into a movie. Like would I be willing to name names and shit."

"What did you tell them?" Regina asked excitedly.

Little Joe took a swig of the whiskey sour the waiter had put in front of him. "I told them that I might be willing to name a few names—"

"You're kidding!" Regina's eyes widened.

"Calm down." Little Joe chuckled. "You know I wouldn't give 'em any names that ain't already been made public, and I wouldn't connect them names with any crimes that they ain't already been convicted of."

"Okay."

"And I told them I ain't fessing up to no shit that's gonna put my ass back in jail."

"I hear that," Regina said as she sipped her martini. "But then again, you ain't never been stupid."

"And I told them that I wouldn't tell them shit about shit unless the price was right." Little Joe grinned. "But you know that."

"So how much are they talking?"

"First they said a flat ten grand, but when I started to get up and walk the fuck out, they started talking a little bit a sense. They said they'd pay me fifteen thousand to sit down with them and give enough to do—what's that called?—a treatment, and then fifty thousand if they show the treatment around and get some bites and then write a script. That only comes up to sixty-five grand, and I wasn't really feeling that, but then they said they could hire me as a consultant for the movie, so I could make another eighty or ninety for that."

"Oh my God." Regina leaned back in her chair. "You'd be making some dough. So are you going to do it?"

Little Joe shrugged. "I told them I'd think about it and get back to them in like a week."

"Yeah?" Regina said as she bit into a shrimp.

"Yeah, and I also told them two more things." Little Joe grinned.

"What?"

"I told them that if I let them make the movie, they had to have Jamie Foxx play me, and that if I decided not to do the movie and they went ahead with it anyway, I was gonna come back to L.A. on my own dime and personally fuck all of them up." Little Joe's grin widened. "We all laughed, and then I said I was only kidding about the Jamie Foxx thing, but I was dead serious about the fucking people up." Little Joe laughed.

Regina felt a knot in her stomach at his words, because they served to remind her about the question she promised herself she was going to ask. Now, she decided, was as good a time as any. She took a large sip of her martini for courage.

"Listen," she said as lightly as she could. "Remember you asked me if there was anything new with the Tamika thing?"

"Uh-huh," Little Joe said in a nonchalant tone.

"Well, would you believe that one of them left a message for Tamika and apologized for bothering her family and promised there wouldn't be any more trouble?"

"Good," Little Joe said as he picked up his menu. "You decided what you want for an entrée yet?"

Regina stared at Little Joe's expressionless face. If he had something to do with the turnaround, he wasn't giving up the info.

"And I heard on the news that the police found a body up on 123rd. It was one of the boys that was messing with Tamika," Regina lied in an attempt to get a reaction. "Ain't that some shit?"

"Ain't it, though?" Little Joe put down the menu and looked at Regina. "I'm getting the Creole chicken. What you want?"

Regina looked Little Joe straight in the eye. "So did you have anything to do with it?"

"With what?"

"With those boys changing their minds?" She caught herself before she could add, "and getting the boy killed."

Little Joe leaned back in his chair, but his eyes never wavered from her. "Why you gonna ask me some shit like that?" he said softly.

" 'Cause I wanna know."

"You know I was in California. So how could I have something to do with it?"

"I didn't say you did, I'm just asking."

"Why are you asking?"

"Because I want to know." Regina bit her lip. "Because I'm hoping you didn't, but I need to be sure. We both have a past, but I'm hoping that it *is* our past. I'd hate to find out that you'd be involved in someone getting hurt or getting killed." Regina paused. "I don't think you'd be involved or that you are involved," she lied, "but I just want to ask to be sure."

"Is that a fact?" Little Joe's lips curled into a sneer. "You wouldn't want me involved in someone getting hurt, huh? Was you fucking thinking like that when you dragged my ass out to Brooklyn to clean up that shit for your girl Puddin'?"

"That was different," Regina said quickly. "I knew that your just being there was going to cool that out, and that you wouldn't have had to actually do anything."

Little Joe suddenly leaned over the table and grabbed Regina's chin in his hand. "Don't play me, Regina. We both know if some shit had went down, I woulda stepped up to the plate. And we both know that you was counting on that shit. Don't fucking play me, now."

Regina tried to wrest her face from Little Joe's grasp, but he squeezed harder.

"Don't think you can have me step into a role and then step out at your fucking whim, hear? I'm not your fucking puppet. And I'm not some little punk you can try and make feel bad just 'cause *you* do. You got that?" He let go of her and leaned back in his chair. "You should be glad someone took care of that shit for Tamika."

Regina jumped up from her seat, grabbed her purse from the table, and all but ran out the restaurant.

She fumbled with her keys before unlocking the car door and jumping in. She was getting ready to pull off when her cell phone rang.

"Hello," she said as she wiped away tears she hadn't realized were streaming down her cheeks.

"Gina? Where are you?" Charles asked urgently.

"Why? What's wrong?" *Oh shit,* she thought, *please don't tell me the hospital called to say something's wrong with Ray-Ray.*

"Look, I'm here at my hotel, and I just got off the phone with the Manhattan D.A.'s Office. Robert's dead." Charles's voice cracked as he talked. "They got a call from Rikers."

Regina almost dropped the cell phone. "Oh my God," she said softly. "He committed suicide?"

"No," Charles said, tears evident in his voice. "They don't know for sure if it was a guard or another inmate, but someone attacked him."

"Attacked him?"

"They castrated him, Gina," Charles said through soft sobs. "They castrated him and stuck his genitalia in his mouth."

Regina's head started whirling, and her stomach lurched violently. She dropped the telephone on the seat and barely got the driver's door open before she vomited.

# chapter twenty

Regina paused in front of Charles's hotel room at the Plaza and took a deep breath. She had called him back after she had pulled herself together in her car, and the pain in his voice was so acute she knew she had to be there for him, just as he'd always been there for her. But the closer she got to the Plaza, the worse she felt for herself; she was racked with guilt. The words she had told Little Joe kept playing over and over again as she drove.

*Little Joe, Robert simply can't get away with this shit—beating up a kid and then trying to rape her. He just can't. Someone needs to catch him, cut off his dick, and shove it up his fucking mouth.*

If there was the least bit of doubt about Little Joe's involvement in Tamika's situation, there wasn't the slightest when it came to Robert's death. Little Joe must have called in some favors or paid someone to do the dirty deed. The bottom line was he was directly responsible, although no more responsible than she. She should have known better than to say some shit like that to Little Joe.

She called Tamika while driving to the hotel and found out

that David had already informed her of Robert's grisly death. They were both on the way to Mama Tee's to break the news in person to Yvonne. Regina contemplated telling Tamika she'd meet her there so she could also show her support, but she decided against it. She also contemplated telling Tamika of her suspicions about Little Joe's involvement in Robert's murder but decided against that, too. She might share it with her later on, but for now it was best to keep her mouth shut.

She took another deep breath, then finally knocked on the hotel room door.

"Regina. Thanks for coming," Charles said when he opened the door. "But you know what? Why don't we go downstairs to the bar? I really need a stiff drink. Maybe two or three."

Regina shook her head as she walked into the room. "Charles? Would you mind much if we had room service bring us up some drinks? I'm not really up to being in public right now." She looked at his red eyes and worn face. "You don't look like you need to be in the public eye, either, Congressman."

Charles nodded, then bent down to give her a peck on the lips, but she averted her face. "Sorry," he muttered, and backed away.

Regina caressed his shoulder. "It's not what you think. I was sick to the stomach after you told me what happened to Robert, and I didn't want to make you nauseous."

"Damn, Regina, I'm sorry." He grabbed her in a bear hug, pressing her face hard against his chest. "I shouldn't have told you on the telephone. And I sure as hell didn't have to go into graphic detail like that. That was just inconsiderate of me. Are you okay?"

Tears sprang to Regina's eyes as she inhaled Charles's musky cologne. Here he was in pain because of the death of his childhood friend, and he was worried about her. *Oh God,* she thought, *I can't ever let him know what I did. He'd never forgive me. And I don't know if I can live without Charles in my life.*

She pulled away from him and flashed a weak smile. "Please! I should be asking if you're okay, Charles."

Charles turned and walked over to the bed and sat down, hunched over. "You know, I hated him because of what he did to Renee. I really wanted to hurt him. Hurt him bad. But at the same time, he was my oldest friend. He was like a brother." He covered his face with his hands, and Regina could see him using his index fingers to wipe the tears that formed in the corners of his eyes. "I guess I'm conflicted. He was really messed up, but it's like we were saying just this morning . . . he was a big part of my life. He was there the first day we met. He was my best man and our daughter's godfather. And I loved him."

Regina sat next to him and started rubbing his back.

"I would never have let him near me or my family again," Charles continued, "but God, I didn't want him to die. And especially like that."

"I know, Charles," Regina said soothingly. "I know."

"I'll be okay." Charles lifted his head and openly wiped his tears away. "This has just been a hard couple of days for all of us, hasn't it, baby?" He grinned. "Oops, that's right. I'm not supposed to call you baby, right?"

Regina smiled and put her head on his shoulder. "Well, I guess I don't mind right now, sweetheart."

Charles put his arm around her shoulder and kissed her on the forehead. "Have I thanked you for coming over here tonight?"

"Yep."

"Have I told you I still love you? That I've always loved you and that I always will love you?" Charles asked gently.

Regina looked up at him. "Not in so many words, but I know."

"Did you know that I've always thought, always hoped, that you and I would get back together?"

Regina looked down and said nothing, not knowing what to say.

"When I left your house this morning, and then I knocked on the door and you wouldn't let me in . . ." Charles took a deep breath. "Well, I was coming back to apologize, because you were right. Or partially right, anyway. I do think I have a right to not want that Blayton character around Camille, but I think I really just as much don't want him around you. And not just because he might hurt you—although I'm not as clear-cut that he's not capable of doing so—but because I don't want any man around you like that.

"I know we're divorced and that you can see who you want, and I've always assumed you have gone out. But it's one thing to assume it. It's another to see it," Charles continued. "And as for his past, can I tell you the truth about something? To be honest, I don't think it bothers me as much that he has a criminal past as the fact that he has a past with you. I know I can stand my own against any Johnny-come-lately that tries to step into the picture, but I mean . . . I don't know . . . you might have loved him as much as you loved me. I don't know if I can handle that."

Charles looked at her as if he was waiting for her to say something, but when she didn't, he averted his eyes. "Look, I'm sorry to babble on like that. I'm just unhinged, I guess." He leaned over and picked up the telephone from the nightstand. "Guess I'll order that room service."

Regina stood up. "Listen, do you mind if I use your toothbrush? In fact, would you mind if I took a quick shower?"

"I wouldn't mind at all."

❧

*He loves me, always has, and always will,* Regina mused as she stood in the bathtub and let the water beat down on her chest while she lathered her stomach. Yes, she had always known it, but it felt so good to hear it. Especially from a man she loved, always had, and probably always would. But then, hadn't she felt the same way about Little Joe? And no matter what he had done, she had no doubt that he loved her. In fact, she was sure that he'd done what he'd done because he did love her. *How touching and sickening at the same time.* It was a true love, but a dangerous one. Not like what she and Charles shared. *I wonder if I should get back with Charles,* she thought. *I wonder if I could.*

Her thoughts were interrupted by a knock on the door. "Yes?" she yelled over the shower.

Charles opened the door a crack. "I just wanted to know if you wanted me to send your clothes down to the laundry service. They have that one-hour expedited service. And you can wear one of the hotel robes until they get back."

"That sounds good," Regina said, sticking her head out from behind the shower curtain. "But listen, how about since you're in here, anyway, why don't you get in the shower with me so you can wash my back?"

Charles paused and looked at her long and hard before answering. "No," he said slowly. "No, I think I should probably pass right now."

Regina blinked a couple of times, then jumped out of the tub and grabbed a towel, which she quickly wrapped around herself. "I'm sorry, I wasn't suggesting it for the reason you might have assumed," she said, avoiding his eyes. "I just—"

"Hey, shush now, I wasn't assuming anything," Charles said gently. "Now, hurry and get dried off. Our food and drinks should be here any minute."

"That's okay. I'm just going to get dressed and leave." She tried to nudge him out of the bathroom so she could close the door. Charles, however, refused to budge.

"Why do you have to leave all of a sudden?" he demanded as he crossed his arms over his chest.

"I just do."

"No, you don't." Charles walked past her and picked up her dress and threw it over his arm. "If you do, you're leaving in your underwear or in a robe," he said as he walked out of the bathroom.

"Oh, try me," Regina spat out. She tried to slam the door after him, but he whirled around in time to block it with his elbow.

"Regina, listen to me," he said urgently. "This isn't making any sense. You know what? You want to leave, go ahead. I won't try and stop you. Here," he said, pushing the dress into her hands. "I shouldn't have tried in the first place. But I think we should try and figure out why it is that we start out so well and end up yelling and pissed off. I'm getting tired of it, and I sure as hell am not up to it right now."

He walked out of the bathroom, gently closing the door behind him.

*Damn,* Regina thought. *What the hell is wrong with me? Here's this man who's always been there for me, and I get pissed and I'm ready to walk out on him when he needs me. And why am I pissed? Because I feel like he rejected me? Hell, I must have rejected him at least three times in the last couple of weeks, and he's never caught an attitude.*

She started drying herself so furiously her skin was turning red. *And what made me all of a sudden put the moves on him, anyway? Because I feel sorry for him and what he's going through right now? Because I feel guilty about what happened to Robert? Because I'm mad at Little Joe?*

She peered at herself in the steamed-up bathroom mirror. *Because I've made a choice?*

She threw on the white plush terry-cloth robe provided by the hotel and meekly walked back into the suite.

Charles was lying on the bed, fully clothed, his arms crossed under his head while he stared up at the ceiling. The room service cart was next to the bed, untouched. She sat down beside him. "I'm sorry," she said simply. When he didn't say anything, she added, "Very sorry. And I would like to stay if you don't mind."

Charles reached up and stroked her neck for a few seconds, then gently pulled her down on the bed next to him. He kissed her softly on the lips, on her eyelids, and around her face as he undid her robe.

"Charles?" she said tentatively as his kisses moved lower down her neck, her breasts and stomach, and beyond.

"Charles?" she said again as he used his tongue to part the lips of her vagina, then flitted it around her clitoris. "Oh God, Charles," she moaned. Her breath was coming in gasps, and she couldn't keep her eyes open as a warm sensation surged through her body. It had been too long since she'd had someone make her feel like this, like she was simply floating on air. Little Joe loved getting oral sex, but he would never even consider giving it in return. Charles, on the other hand, was an expert in that area—as he was in the process of proving.

She could feel herself on the brink of climax, and she tried to pull Charles up, but he ignored her and kept on licking, sucking, and nibbling and driving her crazy. Her body tensed, and she clenched and unclenched her fists and rolled her head from side to side, trying—why, she did not know—to stop herself from exploding. But it was no use.

"Oh God. Oh God. Oh, Charles. Oh, Charles," she said in gasps. "Oh no, baby. Oh, please stop. Oh, don't stop. *Oh God!*" she screamed, finally letting go. "Oh, baby, I'm coming. I love you!"

Her body went limp on the bed, and her eyes closed as she tried to catch her breath. She reopened them when she felt Charles lowering his now naked body over hers. She reached up and pulled him into a deep kiss as she rubbed his smooth chest and he rubbed her still-erect nipple. She reached down and grabbed his thick eight-inch penis and started stroking it up and down as she nibbled his ear.

"Oh God, you feel so damn good, Gina," Charles moaned. "God, I'd almost forgotten how good you feel. How good you taste."

"And I'd forgotten how good you make me feel, Charles," Regina whispered in his ear. "Nobody can make me feel as good as you."

"Oh, baby, I hope you mean that."

"Oh God, I do." She guided the head of his penis to the portal of her vagina. "And I want you. I want you right now."

"Are you sure?" Charles said as he looked directly into her eyes.

"Yes. Oh yes," Regina said, lifting her hips, trying to force him in. But Charles raised himself ever so slightly out of her reach.

"Are you ready for me right now?" he asked as he lowered himself again so that he was once more at the tip of her entrance.

"Oh God, Charles," Regina moaned. "I've never been more sure of anything in my life."

"Neither have I," Charles said as he kissed her on the lips, then slowly—so very slowly—pushed inside her.

"Oh damn!" Regina felt herself on the edge of climax almost the moment his head penetrated her. "Oh my God." Charles was deliberate, and so attentive—touching and rubbing all over her body as he stroked in and out of her—that she found herself sobbing with enjoyment. She suddenly wrapped her legs around him as she felt herself ready to climax, and she thrust up as hard as she could.

"Oh fuck, Gina, stop. You're going to make me cum," Charles moaned. "I don't wanna cum yet, baby."

"Why not? You're making *me* cum," Regina said through her gasps. "You're making me cum right now. Oh God. Right *now*!"

"Oh *damn*!" Charles's eyes seemed to roll into the back of his head as he collapsed on top of her.

"Oh God, Gina, I love you so much," he said when he finally recovered a few minutes later.

"Same here, Charles," Regina said, and cuddled closer to him.

He propped himself up on one elbow and stroked her hair, which was still damp from the shower. "So no regrets, then?"

Regina looked at him quizzically. "No. Why?"

"Honestly?" Charles traced his finger along her face. "As much as I wanted you, I was afraid that I might have been taking advantage of you. You're probably in a pretty vulnerable state right now with everything that's been going on . . . especially with what just happened to Renee."

"You don't have to worry about that," Regina said lightly, then began to nibble at his throat. "I'm a big girl, and I know what I'm doing."

"Yeah, you certainly seem to." Charles grinned. "And I sure love the way you do the things you do." He groaned as she started massaging his limp penis back into action. "I really do."

# chapter twenty-one

Uncle Charles, I don't want you to see me like this!" Renee used her one good arm to pull the hospital bedsheet over her head to hide her still bruised and swollen face. "Why didn't you tell me he was with you, Aunt Gina? You didn't even tell me he was back in town."

"He drove in this morning to bring Camille home, Ray-Ray. And please, believe me, he's seen you looking a lot worse," Regina said as she yanked the sheet off her niece's head and bent down to give her a kiss. "How are you feeling, sweetie?"

"I'm feeling fine," Renee answered glumly, turning her head away from Charles.

"Stop acting silly, silly," Charles said with a grin. "You're still the most beautiful girl I know besides your aunt."

"Ain't this some shit? Here you are a lesbian and you still got a crush on Charles." Puddin' snorted. "Girl, you'd better bone up on your butching skills."

"Huh?" Charles looked at Puddin', then Regina. "What's she talking about?"

"Oh shit, you didn't know?" Puddin' asked him. She started

laughing when she saw the angry look on Renee's face. "Aw naw, naw, naw. Hell, don't be getting mad at me. You came out the closet to everyone else, I thought you told him."

"My daughter's a lesbian is what she's talking about," Brenda said from where she sat in the corner of the room. "And we're all very proud of her."

"Really?" Charles fixed his stare on Regina. "An actual lesbian and not just a tomboy?"

"An actual lesbian," Regina said, trying to hide her smile as she walked over and gave her sister a big hug.

"I see," Charles said, rubbing his chin. "I mean, I guess I see."

"It's not a big deal, Uncle Charles," Renee said in a defensive voice. "It's not like I'm any different, you know. I'm still Renee."

"Come on, you know I know that," Charles said, and grabbed her good hand and gave a squeeze. "Just like you know you'll always be my girl. You just caught me by surprise is all."

"I was going to tell you the night we had the pizza party at my house last week, but I didn't get a chance," Regina said, busying herself with rearranging flowers in the vase on the nightstand.

"Uh-huh, I see." Charles turned his attention back to Renee. "So do you, like, have a girlfriend or anything?"

"Yeah. You remember Liz, right? I introduced the two of you, as a matter of fact," Renee answered. "She was at the pizza party."

Charles looked around the room. "And everyone knew but me?"

Brenda grinned. "Even your daughter, Camille, knows."

Regina looked at Brenda and mentally shook her head. Her sister had done a total 180-degree turn. She'd been not only courteous but almost downright maternal to Liz since Renee's hospitalization; and now she was actually joking about Renee's homosexuality. It seemed it took almost losing her daughter to make her fully accept her.

"Aunt Gina? How come you guys didn't bring Camille?" Renee asked, interrupting her thoughts. "I miss her."

"She misses you, too, sweetie, but hospital rules won't let young children make hospital visits. I'll have her give you a call, okay?" Regina smiled. "By the way, anyone seen Tamika? We stopped over her house to see if she wanted to come to the hospital with us, but she wasn't home."

"She called me a little while ago," Puddin' said. "She's been spending a lot of time with Yvonne, trying to make sure she's okay. Miss Thang keeps saying she's fine, but I think she's on the verge of a nervous breakdown. Mika thinks so, too. I'm going over there when I leave here."

"Maybe I should go, too." Regina took a deep breath. In the week since Robert's death Yvonne tried to act as if his passing didn't bother her, as if admitting that it did would be an act of betrayal against her friends. Both Tamika and Regina had tried to assure her that it was understandable that she would feel some grief, since she had once loved the man, but Yvonne kept brushing them off, saying that was nonsense. Regina winced when she thought what Yvonne would do if she found out that Little Joe was responsible for Robert's murder, or that it was Regina's words that instigated it.

For that matter, she wondered what Charles would do if he found out. She still hadn't told anyone, and she wrestled about whether or not she should confront Little Joe on it. They hadn't talked since that night in the restaurant, but he'd been leaving messages on her home and cell phones. She knew she'd have to get back to him sooner or later, or he would likely pop up at the most inopportune time.

"Well, you can't leave right now, Aunt Gina," Renee protested. "You and Uncle Charles just got here!"

"Actually, I was really just dropping your Aunt Gina off because her car's in the shop, but I wanted to at least stop by and give you a quick hello." Charles stood up and kissed Renee on the cheek. "I've got a meeting in Brooklyn in about an hour, and I want to beat the traffic." He turned around and almost bumped into a nurse who had suddenly appeared at Renee's bedside.

"And you, my dear, have a meeting yourself," the nurse told Renee. "We've got to get you downstairs for an MRI."

Brenda stood up. "Why does she need an MRI? No one told me about an MRI."

"It's just routine, ma'am," the nurse said as she prepared to wheel Renee's bed out of the room. "She's going to be leaving us in a couple of days, and we just want to make sure everything that's supposed to be healing is healing. But not to worry, I'll have her back up here in about a half hour."

Charles walked over to Regina and put his arm around her waist. "Well, then, I'm out of here, okay? You want me to call you later? Maybe have dinner?"

Regina hesitated. Camille had already begged to stay over at Tamika's house to play with Darren and Sissy, and it was the perfect opportunity to go ahead and meet up with Little Joe and get the confrontation over and done with. "How about we take a rain check? I'm going with Puddin' to meet up with Tamika and Yvonne, you know?"

"Yeah, yeah, I know how you guys are." Charles kissed her on the cheek. "I've been in love with you long enough to know how the Four Musketeers hang."

Regina turned to Brenda after Charles left. "You want to hang out with us, sis?"

Brenda shook her head and put two chairs together to make a bed. "I'm going to catch a quick nap. I want to be here when Renee gets back to make sure the tests all come out okay."

"They probably won't have the results right away," Regina said. "You sure you don't want to come?"

"No, you go ahead," Brenda said with a wave of her hand. "I'll see you at the house tonight, okay?"

"Okay, then." Regina gave her sister a kiss on the cheek. "Love ya."

"Love ya back."

❧

"So are you and Mr. Congressman getting back together?" Puddin' asked as she and Regina walked the ten blocks from Harlem Hospital to Mama Tee's house, where Yvonne was still staying. "You've been looking mighty lovey-dovey lately."

Regina shrugged, then shook her head. "No, I don't think so. I'm not moving back to Philadelphia, and he can't move back to New York, so it wouldn't work."

"What if he wasn't in politics and didn't have to live in Philly? What about then?"

"They'd be together in a New York minute," Tamika said as she came up behind them.

"Hey, where'd you come from?" Regina said after the three women hugged. "Puddin' said you were at Mama Tee's with Yvonne."

"I was, but I couldn't do anything with her, so I gave up and was waiting for the bus when I saw you from across the street. You guys just leaving the hospital?"

Regina nodded. "I might go back later before visiting hours are over tonight. I'm not sure. So where are you heading, then?" Tamika shrugged.

"Well, then, let's go back to your house," Puddin' decided for them. "And let's jump on the subway. I musta been fucking crazy to let Regina talk me into walking as far as I have already. My feet are fucking killing me."

Once they reached the 145th Street subway station and stepped onto the platform, Tamika turned to Regina and Puddin'. "Ya'll were talking about you and Charles getting back together?"

"Yeah, Regina said she can't because she doesn't want to

move back to Philly," Puddin' said as she walked over and took a seat on the wooden bench.

"That's not what I said," Regina said after she and Tamika sat down next to her.

"Pretty much what you said." Puddin' slipped her shoes off and used one foot to massage the other.

"I already told her I'd like to see them get back together." Tamika nudged Puddin' with her elbow. "I wouldn't want to see Regina move back to Philly, though." She turned to Regina. "But what's up with you and Little Joe? You still not talking to him?"

"Yeah, why are you spazzing on Uncle Joe?" Puddin' asked. "You've been tight-lipped about him ever since he got back from L.A. What happened down there?"

"Well, he's considering doing the movie," she said.

"And you're pissed with him about that?" Tamika asked. "Why?"

Regina shook her head. "No, no. I don't care one way or the other."

"Mika told me about him getting those dealers off her back. I know you ain't mad at him about that shit," Puddin' snorted. "Shit. We should be giving him a medal. And who the fuck cares if he had to knock off one of those thugs to make a point? One less piece of scum in the world, I say."

Regina looked at Puddin' and then Tamika. "I want to tell you guys something, but you have to promise not to tell anyone." She glanced around to make sure no one was within earshot. "Not even Yvonne or David. And especially not Charles. You've got to promise."

"Okay," Puddin' said slowly. "Seems like this is gonna be some deep shit."

"Very deep." Regina sighed. "I got your words on this?" She waited until both women nodded, then took a deep breath. "Little Joe called me that night Robert attacked Ray-Ray, and of course, I was so upset I was damn near hysterical, ya know?

Anyway, I told him what happened, and that I hoped Robert got caught and someone cut off his dick and shoved it in his mouth for what he'd done."

"Oh shit," Puddin' said in almost a whisper.

Tamika gasped.

Regina could hear the rumble of the train pulling into the station, but neither she nor her friends made a move to get up. They sat there as the train stopped, then pulled away, still not saying anything.

"That is some very deep fucking shit," Puddin' finally said. "I don't even know what to say. Damn."

"Oh damn, Regina." Tamika shook her head, then reached over and rubbed Regina's back. "You must be going through pure hell. What did Little Joe say when you talked to him about it?"

"I haven't said anything to him about it. The ironic thing is we went out to eat and had a big fight when I suggested that he had been involved in your thing, Mika, and that I didn't approve." Regina threw her hands up in the air and let them fall back into her lap. "I mean, he *really* blew up. He didn't say it was true, and he didn't say it wasn't true, but he said I was being hypocritical because I set him up to play savior with that Rob-Cee thing."

"Didn't I—"

"Save the 'I told you so's,' Mika," Regina snapped. "You were the one who told him about those guys' names, you know."

"But I didn't think—"

"Yeah, well, neither did I when I said what I said about Robert." Regina shook her head and sucked her teeth. "How the fuck was I supposed to know what he was going to do?"

The women fell silent as yet another train entered and left the station.

"You ever hear the parable about the swan and the scorpion?" Tamika said after a while. "There was this scorpion who wanted to cross this wide lake, but scorpions can't swim. So he went to the swan and asked if the swan would take him across. The swan turned him down, saying he didn't trust the scorpion not to sting him. The scorpion pleaded and pleaded, and finally, the swan told the scorpion to climb on his back and he'd take him across. So the scorpion climbs on the swan's back, and they're about in the middle of the lake when suddenly the scorpion lashes out and stings the swan on the neck.

"Of course, the scorpion sting is fatal, so the swan begins to sink into the water, taking the scorpion down with him. Just before they drown, the swan asks the scorpion why did he sting him when he knew that by doing so he had killed both of them. The scorpion looked at him and said, 'Because I'm a scorpion, and that's what I do.'"

"Hmm, yeah." Puddin' nodded. "I can see how it kinda fits here. Kinda, anyway."

"You tell him about Rob-Cee, and he takes care of that for Puddin'," Tamika said. "I tell him about my problem, and he takes care of that for me. You tell him about Robert, and he takes care of that for you."

"And for Yvonne, too, I guess," Puddin' added. "Rob-Cee doesn't know how lucky he is. He coulda wound up like that drug dealer or Robert. I gotta figure out how I could use that to my advantage."

Both Tamika and Regina looked at Puddin' and shook their heads.

"You know what, Gina?" Puddin' continued. "Remember that shit we were talking about at the restaurant that day? About you trying to stop yourself from getting payback on people? Looks like maybe you just found someone to do it for you. Whaddya think?"

Regina's head jerked back, then she swung around to face Puddin'. "Oh no, uh-uh. That's not the deal at all. How can you say some shit like that? You think I planned all this?"

Puddin' shrugged. "Don't get all excited. It was just a question."

Regina glared at her for a moment, then sat back and stared straight ahead.

"So what are you going to do now?" Tamika asked.

Regina shrugged. "Hell if I know."

"Well, one thing for sure, you really do need to make sure that you don't tell Yvonne or Charles, because even though it's not your fault, they would still never forgive you," Tamika said after some thought. "And I think you're right to avoid Little Joe. At this point we don't know what else he's capable of."

Regina shook her head. "No, I think you're wrong there. He's been blowing up my phone for the past two days. I think it's best I meet with him and get this straightened out."

"Yeah, we don't want him to come looking for her," Puddin' agreed. "But I say we go with her."

"Oh God!" Tamika said with a sigh. "But yeah, maybe you're right."

"Nope. I gotta do this on my own," Regina said, folding her arms across her chest. "I don't even know if I'm going to bring up the Robert thing. I'll just tell him that I don't think we should see each other anymore and just leave it at that."

"You think he'll just leave it like that?" Tamika asked.

"Yeah, yeah, I think so," Regina said hopefully.

Puddin' shrugged. "Look at it like this. We all heard the stories from back in the day about Little Joe having people rubbed out, but we never heard any stories about Little Joe having bad breakups with women. His philosophy was always like easy come, easy go."

"Yeah, but he might not have been in love with all those women he was running back in the day. He's in love with Regina, so it might be different."

"He told you he's in love with you, Gina?"

Regina nodded.

"Yeah," Puddin' said. "Well, then, you just might be fucked."

# chapter twenty-two

thought you was going to stand me up."

Regina smiled nervously as she sat down at the table across from Little Joe. "Camille's staying over at Tamika's tonight, and I wanted to make sure she was settled in before I left her. Then I had to wait for a cab because my car is in the shop to get new brakes put on. I tried to call you on your cell, but it kept going straight to voice mail."

Little Joe snapped open his cell phone, then snapped it closed. "I didn't realize my battery is low. I'll recharge it when I get back in the car." He slipped the phone in his pocket. "So? You were calling me to cancel on me or something?"

"No. No. I just wanted to let you know I was running late." Regina sighed inwardly. Little Joe was obviously in a mood. The night wasn't going to be easy.

"You want to order something to eat, or should we just get

drinks?" Little Joe leaned back in his chair and studied Regina. "I don't want to keep you out too late."

"Well, uh, I guess it's up to you," Regina said in a state of confusion. She had expected him to be mad or emotional, but why would he insist on her coming out to meet him just so he could treat her so coldly? she wondered. She'd never seen him like this before. Nor did she like it.

"Just drinks, then." Little Joe waved to the waiter, who hurried over and took their drink orders.

"So how's your niece doing?" Little Joe said after the waiter left. "Still in the hospital?"

Regina nodded. "She's doing a quick mend, though. The doctors say they'll probably release her tomorrow or the next day."

"And Yvonne?"

"She's doing okay," Regina said cautiously. "Physically, anyway. She's upset about Robert's death. I guess you heard about that. It was in all the newspapers."

"I read a couple of stories about it," Little Joe said in a nonchalant voice, though he looked at her as if he dared her to go further.

*Okay, if that's how he's going to play it, then that's that,* Regina decided. She picked up the menu and flipped through it, pretending to look over the entrées when she was really wondering when Little Joe was going to finally tell her why he wanted to see her.

"So you wanna tell me, or you want me to tell you?" Little Joe said when the drinks arrived.

"Tell me what? Tell you what?" Regina said as she stared into her martini.

"That it's over." Little Joe took a deep swig of his whiskey sour. "I thought we'd get some closure on this shit rather than just slink out of each other's lives, ya know?"

"You want me to come meet you so we could break up properly?" Regina said slowly. "That's very, uh, nice of you."

"Yeah, that's me. Nice." Little Joe gave a mean little laugh. "But let me ask you something on the up-and-up. Do you think you really know what the fuck you want? Do you? 'Cause you sure confuse the shit outta me."

Regina looked down at the table. "I'm sorry if I sent you mixed signals . . ."

"Aw naw, naw, naw." Little Joe shook his head. "Mixed signals, my ass. Own up to your shit, Regina."

"What do you mean?"

"Mixed signals is when someone sends out a signal saying one thing, then turns around and sends a signal that says something else. What you do is send out a signal, wait until someone takes action based on that signal, and then say the signal never existed. That's really fucked-up."

"Look, I'm—"

"And it's a fucked person that would do it," Little Joe continued, then took another gulp of his drink. "I expected better of you."

"Little Joe, I'm—"

"I don't know why I expected better, though. You're pretty good at treating people like shit, aren't you?" Little Joe leaned over the table. "I may not have been the best man in the world, but I honest to fucking God did the best I could by you. I treated you like a queen, Regina. How did you treat me? I wasn't even good enough to be introduced to people. You fucking ashamed of me? Don't even answer. It'll just piss me the fuck off."

"Okay, so you just want me to apologize?" Regina chewed her lip as she felt her face heat up. "I apologize, okay?"

"You ain't learn to check your attitude at the door yet, huh?" Little Joe said with a sneer. "Yeah, go ahead and get your shit off, Gina."

"I don't have any shit to get off. In fact, I just apologized, didn't I?" Regina crossed her legs under the table in an effort to keep herself under control. This wasn't the way the evening was supposed to go. She was supposed to be confronting him; instead, she was being chewed up and spit out. And it didn't help that she knew every word he said was true.

"That's a real fucked-up apology," Little Joe snickered. "But I guess it's the best you're capable of, huh?"

"Yeah, well, maybe it is," Regina said defiantly. "But—"

"Yeah, well, then, in the words of Donald Trump, you're fired. Now get the fuck out my face," Little Joe said, and leaned back in his seat.

Regina's mouth dropped open. "What?"

"You fucking deaf? Get the fuck to stepping."

Regina gasped. She couldn't believe it. She wanted to lash back at him, but the lump that suddenly lodged in her throat prevented her from speaking. And besides, what really could she say? She, who never let anyone get the best of her in an argument, suddenly had no comeback. She knew she deserved every word he said, but did he have to be so damn hurtful? She fought back her tears as she slowly got up from the table, picked up her purse, and walked out the door, head held high.

She walked down the block in search of a taxi, still trying to hold back her tears. She waited until the light was green before stepping into the street, never noticing the gray Ford Taurus speeding around the corner. She gasped as someone pulled her back in the nick of time.

"Regina, you're trying to get killed?" Little Joe pulled her into his arms.

She struggled to break free as her tears started flowing. "Let go of me, okay? I'm fine."

"The hell you're fine. Didn't anyone tell you to look both ways before crossing the damn street?"

Regina managed to pull away, but then leaned against a parked car, buried her face in her hands, and started sobbing.

"Regina, stop crying," Little Joe said as he tried to hug her. "I'm sorry."

"What are you sorry about?" Regina said, trying to turn

away. "I'm the one who did all the dirt, right? I'm the one who's supposed to be apologizing, aren't I? And besides, I'm not crying."

"You ain't crying, huh? Well, baby, you're leaking water from your eyes." Little Joe stroked her hair. "And I am sorry. Really sorry."

He tried to pull her away from the car, but she refused to budge. "Gina," he said, giving up and leaning against the car with her, "I apologize. I was so fucking mean, and I was extra mean on purpose. I wanted you to cry, or at least I thought I did."

"I'm not crying."

"Oh yeah, I forgot." He put his arm around her shoulders and pulled her closer to him. "Gina, I'm sorry. I jumped on you like that because I was mad, but also because I think maybe subconsciously I wanted to make sure I burned whatever bridges we have. I needed to make sure there was nothing for us to be tempted to cross back over."

"What do you mean?" Regina sniffed.

"I truly love you, and I believe you love me, but we just ain't what each other need." Little Joe grimaced as he talked. "I don't fit in your world, and you don't fit in mine anymore. There was a time when you never woulda fucking asked me about what I did to who. You'd just take it for granted I did it and be proud as hell that I did. That's the Regina I knew. That's the Regina I thought I was coming home to.

"And I thought about, well, trying to slow my roll when it comes to you, but I know me. And anytime I feel like you're threatened I'm going to take steps to remove that threat. That's just who I am. And I fucking like who I am."

"I like who you are, too," Regina said softly. "But yeah, I know what you mean."

"And I like who you are, too," Little Joe said as he caressed her face. "But it wouldn't work. And I'm just fucking pissed off about that shit that I just, I guess, unloaded on you. You ain't deserve all that. I'm sorry."

"Why? Just about everything you said was on the mark."

"Yeah, that's true. But I still ain't had to come at you like that. So take the fucking apology, okay?" Little Joe put his hands in his pockets and stared up at the sky. "And take your little ass home before I start blubbering or some shit."

Regina wiped her eyes and looked at Little Joe. "So this is it, huh? We're not going to see each other again?"

"You trying to say that there ain't a little part of you that's glad about that?" Little Joe challenged her. He snorted when she looked away. "That's what I thought."

Regina put her head on his shoulder. "But I do love you, Little Joe."

"Feeling's mutual, Regina. You'll always be my Satin Doll."

∽

Regina could hear the telephone ringing while she unlocked the front door, and she nearly tripped over the umbrella stand, trying to answer it before it stopped.

"Hello."

"Hey, baby," Charles's voice came through. "So good to be able to call you baby again."

Regina smiled. "So good to hear it again. What's up?"

"Nothing much. I just wanted to call and tell you that I love you. And I was wondering if you might be free for a late dinner, since it seems you got home from Yvonne's kind of early. How is she, by the way?"

"Actually, we didn't go over there. We saw Tamika on the way, and we all just hung out for a little while." Regina twirled the telephone cord around her finger as she told her half-truth. "But," she continued, "I'm kind of tired, so can I get a rain check?"

"No problem. Since I don't have to be back in Philly until

Monday, maybe I can take you and Camille to the movies this weekend. And maybe I can get you to marry me again?"

"Charles!" Regina took a sharp breath.

"You don't have to answer now," Charles said hurriedly. "I know you need time to think about it. But, Regina, you and I both know that we're still in love. And we both know that we're good together."

"I know," Regina said in a low voice.

"The only problem that I can see is that I know you won't want to move back to Philly, and I have to live in my voting district. But I know we'll be able to work something out. I wouldn't be the first or only congressman to only spend weekends in the house that he keeps in his home district. Or the first senator."

"Probably not," Regina said with a light laugh.

"So will you think about it?"

"I will."

"I love you, baby."

"I love you, too, baby."

*Funny how things turn out,* Regina thought as she hung up the telephone and sat down on the couch. *Who would have guessed that I'd be dumped and proposed to in the same night?*

She leaned back and closed her eyes. She was going to miss the hell out of Little Joe, but he was right. She loved him, but she probably loved the gangsta in him even more, she admitted to herself. And yet she couldn't stand to be around someone who did the things gangstas do.

As for Charles, well, she didn't know if it would work out, but it felt good having the chance to see if it would. At the same time, it felt strange knowing she was now more comfortable in his world than in Little Joe's—the world she had thought was her own.

# chapter twenty-three

Ray-Ray, I know you didn't cook this," Regina said as she took another forkful of the candied yams.

"How do you know I didn't?" Renee grinned.

"Because the last time you tried to cook candied yams it tasted like burnt orange string," Brenda said, helping herself to more corn bread stuffing. "And my kitchen smelled like burnt molasses and sweet potatoes for two days."

Renee smiled and took Liz's hand. "Which is precisely why Liz won't let me anywhere near the stove. But I did open the can of cranberry sauce."

"I wondered why the cranberry sauce tastes like crap," Puddin' said as she moved back from the table and loosened her belt. "And as for the milky yellow stuff you served before dinner, thank God I brought a little taste of rum with me to turn it into eggnog."

"Aunt Puddin', I love you, but this is the last time I invite you over for Thanksgiving dinner." Renee grinned again.

"Don't listen to Puddin'. Everything's delicious," Tamika interjected. "Too bad David went to his mom's in Philly, be-

cause he would have loved it all, too. Liz, you've outdone yourself. And, Renee, the cranberry sauce is simply delicious."

"And so is the eggnog," Yvonne said, looking pointedly at
Puddin', who ignored her.

Regina smiled as she looked around at the people gathered
at the dining room table in Renee and Liz's apartment. It was
hard to believe that only five months had passed since she had
sat in a hospital room praying for her niece's recovery. Neither
girl bore any signs that they had ever been attacked. And it was
good to see Yvonne finally out and about. It had taken her a
good three months to come out of the blue funk she had de-
scended to after the attack and Robert's subsequent death.
Maybe she was finally able to wrap her mind around the fact
that what happened wasn't her fault.

Puddin' took a large swig of her doctored eggnog. "Yeah,
well, Ray-Ray, since you won't be inviting me to your house
next year for Thanksgiving, I'm not inviting you to my house
for Christmas this year. You can come, though, Liz."

"Your house?" Regina raised her eyebrow.

"Yeah, my mansion, actually," Puddin' said as she gave an
obviously faked yawn.

"You been smoking too much of that shit," Yvonne said
with a laugh.

"So you've got a mansion, huh?" Regina said, pushing her
plate back. "What? You snagged yourself another rich rap
artist?"

"Who needs a rich rap artist when I got this?" Puddin'
pulled a piece of paper from her pocket and put it in the middle of the cluttered dining room table.

"What's that?" Regina reached for the paper, but Yvonne
was quicker.

"A lottery ticket," Yvonne said as she looked at Puddin'
quizzically.

"Not just a lottery ticket," Puddin' said nonchalantly. "A
New York State lottery ticket from last night's drawing."

"Oh my God, you're kidding!" Tamika jumped from her seat and ran over to Yvonne, who was looking at the ticket in disbelief. "That's the winning ticket?"

Puddin' shook her head. "Nope."

Yvonne lightly tapped Puddin' on the head. "See? Why you wanna try and get us all excited again? You ain't shit."

"Hold up. Hold up. It may not be the winning ticket. But it's still a winner. I got five numbers out of six on that puppy, ladies," Puddin' said with a grin.

Renee stared in disbelief. "Aunt Puddin', are you for real?"

"Did you double-check the numbers?" Regina asked breathlessly.

Puddin' grinned and nodded. "And I made sure it was for the right drawing."

Yvonne slowly stood up, now holding the ticket in both hands. "Puddin'," she said in a dazed voice, "how much is this ticket worth?"

"Not quite enough to buy Regina her own magazine; pay for Tamika's second year of med school; buy you a husband, Yvonne; and buy myself a cocaine farm in South America and a private jet with a pilot to bring me fresh stash every week. But"—Puddin' got up from the table and did a little dance—"enough to be living really large for a really long time. Eight hundred and seventy thousand dollars."

All the women in the room started screaming and joined Puddin' in her dance.

"Mom, what's going on?" Darren said as he ran into the dining room, followed by Sissy, Johnny, and Camille. "Why's everyone screaming?"

"Because we're fucking rich!" Puddin' hooted.

"Puddin', watch your . . . oh, the hell with it!" Tamika started laughing. "Kids, your Aunt Puddin' just hit the lottery. She's rich!"

Puddin' grabbed Renee by the shoulders. "Ray-Ray, I'm going to buy you and Liz a brand-new condo."

"Ray just applied for early admission to Temple, so can the condo be in Philadelphia if she gets in?" Liz asked excitedly.

"It can be any-fucking-where your little hearts desire," Puddin' said grandly. She then turned to Brenda. "And I'm going to buy you your own cult so you can make up your own rules instead of following every-fucking-body else's."

Brenda started laughing. "Girl, I would smack you, but I'm not in the habit of hitting people who have enough money to buy the island of Manhattan."

"Puddin'," Yvonne said suddenly, "you need to keep this ticket in a safe place until you cash it in. The lottery office isn't open again until Monday because of the holiday, right?"

Regina snapped her fingers in the air. "I know the perfect place."

"Where?" Puddin' asked.

"I believe the Ritz Carlton in Albany has private vaults in each of their suites," Regina said with a grin. "What say we grab a limo right now, we and the kids all pile in, and take a trip to Albany? We can spend the weekend there in a couple of luxurious suites and go to the lottery office on Monday."

"How the hell are we going to afford a limo to take us all the way to Albany?" Yvonne asked skeptically.

"Puddin's boyfriends aren't the only ones with American Express cards. I'll just charge it now and pay for it later." Regina turned to Puddin'. "Actually, Miss Rich-Ass Thang will be the one paying for it later."

"It'll be my fucking pleasure," Puddin' said grandly. "But how are we going to get a limo on Thanksgiving night?"

Tamika snapped her fingers. "David's client Spider—he owns a limo service. I bet if I call him, he can get us one tonight. We might have to promise him a big tip, though."

"Tell him we'll give him a five-hundred-buck tip," Puddin' said. "Fuck it, make it an even thou."

"Okay, Tamika, you call Spider, and everyone hurry up home

and pack, and we'll meet back here in two hours," Yvonne said excitedly.

Regina closed her eyes and took a deep breath. "This is so much like a dream I'm tempted to ask someone to pinch me. But I won't," she added quickly when Brenda walked over to her. "But I will say this. I love all you guys, and, Puddin', this couldn't have happened to a better person."

"It happened to all of us," Puddin' said as she stuffed the bottle of rum into her bag. "We're still the Four Musketeers, you know."

"All for one and one for all," Regina said as she, Puddin', Yvonne, and Tamika clasped hands.

"Now," Regina said with tears in her eyes, "let's boogie."

# reading group guide

## DISCUSSION QUESTIONS

1. Now that Regina has "made it" and lives a middle-class existence, should she cut off old friends like Puddin', who continue to live and revel in ghetto life?

2. Is Ray-Ray at eighteen too young to declare herself a lesbian?

3. Why do you think Brenda keeps changing religions?

4. Do you believe Little Joe really loved Regina? Do you believe Regina really loved Little Joe?

5. What does Regina mean when she calls Little Joe "thug romantic"?

6. Overall, would you say Little Joe is a "nice guy" or a "bad guy"? Would *you* want him as a friend?

7. Did David do the right thing by throwing out the drugs? Would it have been better for him to simply return them to the

dealer? Should he have turned the drugs over to the police, knowing they might implicate his stepson?

8. Do you think Regina told Little Joe about what Robert did hoping that he would have him killed?

9. How would Yvonne and Charles have reacted if they had found out that Robert was killed in the manner that Regina had suggested to Little Joe? Would their reactions be appropriate?

10. How important are your friends and family to you? How far would you go to help them and protect them?

More sizzling fiction
from KAREN E. QUINONES MILLER!

Please turn the page
for a preview of

# Passin'

Available in paperback
Winter 2008

Didn't I tell you, Mama? Her skin is so thin and light you can see her little blue veins. I'm telling you she's gonna have skin as white as Meryl Streep's. And look at that blonde hair. That ain't no hair's that's going to be napping up!"

"And her eyes," Cecilia said excitedly. "You know, Evelyn, I told Peter when he first started talking about marrying Rina, I said, 'Well, her skin might be a little too dark for my taste but at least she ain't no ink spot. And if even only one your kids get them blue eyes Rina's grandmother had, it'll all be worth it.' Their first child didn't get 'em, but they lucked up with this one."

Rina didn't bother to fake a smile for her mother-in-law and sister-in-law since they didn't bother to acknowledge her but instead focused all of their attention on the two-day-old baby she'd just finished nursing in the hospital room. She wasn't surprised or hurt—her relationship with her in-laws had always been, at best, strained. Truth be told, the relationship was horrible. Mother Jenkins had never forgiven her for marrying precious little Peter, the matriarch's youngest son. The Jenkins were all light-skinned—what was called "light-bright and damn near white"—and made it a point of marrying people with matching complexions. Peter, who was the color of ash wood, had been expected to bring home a woman in keeping with the Jenkins tradition. Instead he had brought home Rina.

She tenderly lifted the child to her shoulder and began gently rubbing her back. Nobody knew how shocked and terrified she'd been when she found out she was pregnant. She was forty-six and thought her child-bearing years were over. Joseph was already fifteen, and she wasn't sure she had the patience and strength to go through diapering, potty-training, and all of it again. But now that she was looking at the baby, it all seemed so worth it. There was no doubt about it, this was a beautiful baby. Not because of her fair complexion or blonde hair or blue eyes, but there was something striking about her features.

Cecilia pursed her thin lips, then said sharply, "Careful, Rina, can't you see that sweet child is fragile?" She reached out her spindly, liver-spotted arms. "Gimme that baby. I'll burp her for you."

"I think I know how to burp a child, Mother Jenkins," Rina said with a deep sigh. "Like you said, I've already have one child. I've had practice."

"But Joseph wasn't as delicate as this one," Cecelia answered, her arms still outstretched, her fingers wiggling in eager anticipation.

"Why? Because this one's skin is lighter?" Rina switched the baby to the shoulder farthest away from Cecelia. "Because she's the one born with blue eyes and blonde hair?"

Cecelia slowly pulled her arms back to her sides and fixed a stony glare at the younger woman who had the audacity to challenge her. "How dare you, Rina," she said in voice as cold as her dark brown eyes. "You know I love my grandchildren no matter what color they are."

Rina ignored her, choosing instead to kiss and coo at her baby. She then put the baby on her stomach, pushed the black button on the side of the steel hospital bed to bring it to a reclining position, and closed her eyes.

"Mama," Evelyn said in her irritatingly shrill voice, "come sit down. Rina's just tired is all. She wasn't trying to insult you, was you, Rina?"

Rina wearily opened her eyes and looked up at the clock on the wall. 2:15. Thank God the afternoon visiting hours would be over in just fifteen more minutes. She carefully picked up the now sleeping baby, laid her across her chest, and began softly humming a lullaby.

"So, Rina"—Evelyn's always nervous hands fluttered in her lap—"have you and Peter decided on the name for your beautiful little girl? It's bad luck not to have a name by the third day born, you know."

Cecelia sat up straight in her chair and patted her tightly wound bun of bluish-gray hair as if to make sure it was in place. "I've already talked to Peter and we've decided to name her Victoria, after her great-grandmother," she said before Rina could answer. "She was the most beautiful and most well-respected woman in Beesville, Mississippi." She paused and looked at Rina meaningfully. "Carrying her great-grandmother's name will always remind her of what a great family she comes from—on her father's side. Something to aspire to."

"Not like my family, right?" Rina said wearily.

"Now, Rina," Evelyn interjected. "Mama wasn't trying to say that—"

"It's not our fault that your family is from the wrong side of the tracks," Cecelia interrupted.

"Mother Jenkins, it's interesting how you seem to forget you lived right next door to us," Rina snapped.

"But we didn't start out there like your family did, a dirt-poor bunch of low-life no good-for-nothings," Cecelia said with a smirk. "Our family had money and property until—"

"Until white folks strung up your father like a piece of ham and burnt and stole everything you had, right?" Rina laughed.

"And then you ended up on Chewbacca Road right along with us dirt-poor, low-life good-for-nothings."

Cecelia's eyes widened. "You think a lynching's a laughing matter, do ya, missy? You think a five-year-old child seeing her father swinging from a tree is funny?"

"No," Rina said in a cold voice. "But what I find so hilarious is that same five-year-old child growing up to worship white folks and trying her best to be just like them. Even hating African-Americans as much as them. Calling them niggas while referring to herself as colored." Rina snorted. "I don't know how you and your high-yaller clan missed the word, Mother Jenkins, but black is beautiful. And black comes in all shades. And this baby mighta been born with blonde hair and blue eyes like my grandmother, but she's still an African-American. Not a nigger and not colored, but African-American."

Cecelia jumped up from the chair and quickly strode toward the door. "Come on, Evelyn, it's time for us to leave. Peter's low-life darkie wife has obviously lost her mind so there ain't no use in us staying and listening to her hateful rambling."

"Coming, Mama." Evelyn quickly got up and gave Rina an apologetic glance before hurrying after her mother.

The two women departed so quickly they almost bumped into a nurse entering the room.

"They seem to be in a rush, don't they?" the nurse said as she walked over to Rina's bedside. "Aw, look at her sleeping like a little angel. Do you want me to take her back to the nursery so you can get some rest?"

"No, I'm fine," Rina said while softly tracing her fingers over the child's face. "And will you let whoever it is that needs to know that I've finally decided on a name?"

"Oh, good. What is it?"

Rina paused. Peter was going to have a fit, and his mother would likely have a stroke, but . . .

"Shanika," Rina finally answered with a wide smile. "S-H-A-N-I-K-A. My little angel's name is Shanika."

The train from Detroit to Chicago took six hours, which was bad enough, but the second leg of the trip—from Chicago to New York City—was almost eighteen hours. As she struggled with her luggage up the steps at Pennsylvania Station, Shanika, bone-tired, damn sweaty, and extremely aggravated, cursed herself for not taking her brother up on an airline ticket. But it would have cost more than twice what she paid for train fare, and he had his own family to worry about, especially with his wife, Ayoka, being pregnant again. Thank God her job interview wasn't until the next day. She'd have some time to rest up at her hotel room.

"Excuse me. Can you tell me where the taxi line is?" she asked one of the many police officers milling around the building. "I was told it was right outside the station, but I don't see any signs."

The officer—a beefy, dark-haired man of about forty with a bulbous red-nose—looked her up and down before answering. "They closed it down because of the President. You'll have to walk down the street and hail a cab."

"The President?" Shanika's shoulders sagged. "They closed the taxi line because of President Bush?"

The officer nodded. "He's in town so we're taking extra security precautions. Just walk a couple of blocks in any direction. You'll be able to catch a ride."

Shanika looked at her two suitcases and chewed her lip while the officer strode away without a backward glance. *Damn*, she thought, *why did I have to pack all this stuff?*

"Excuse me, miss. You need some help with them bags?"

She turned to find an African-American man, about her own age, standing in front of her. A set of earphones sat on top of his designer cornrows, and by the way he was bopping his head he was probably listening to music even while addressing her.

"Yeah, bro. I can use some help," she said with a gracious smile. "Thanks."

He looked at her quizzically, removed the earphones, and stared at her intently. "Oh, shit," he finally said with a loud laugh. "You a sista! Damn, you got that Mariah Carey thang going on for real, yo. But damn, shawtie, even Mariah ain't got them baby blues like you." He stepped back and rubbed his chin while taking a better look at her. "Yo, ma, you really had me fooled. What? Your daddy white or you mom?"

"Neither. They both have white blood and they passed a lot of it on to me," Shanika said, her hand on one hip as she appraised him. His New York Knicks jersey and baggy jeans— which looked like they were about to fall off his skinny hips any minute—were clean, and his Air Jordans, though three years out of date, were in good shape. His mocha colored face was clean shaven, and his eyes were bright. He didn't look like someone trying to rip her off, but then you never know. But hell, she didn't want to be lugging the luggage around on her own. "So you still wanna help me now that you know that I'm as black as you?"

"Aw hell, naw. You may be a nigga, but you sure as hell ain't black as me, shawtie," he said with a wide grin that revealed his pearly whites. "Yeah, I'll carry your bags. And I won't even charge you. I woulda if you was white for real, though." He picked up her bags. "What's your name, shawtie?"

"Shanika."

"Oh yeah, you a nigga for real, huh?" He let go another one of his loud laughs.

"What's yours?"

"Jason. So which way you going?"

"I've got to find a taxi."

He nodded his head toward the right. "This way, shawtie. And I know you gonna hit me off with them digits, yo. Where you live?"

Shanika had to trot to keep up with him. "Detroit. I'm just up here for a job interview."

"Shit, ma. Well, good luck. It's tight as a mug out here. I been looking for a J-O-B for a minute now."

"Damn, it's just as hot and humid out here as it is in Detroit," she complained as they walked on the street. "I'm going to melt out here."

He gave her a sideways glance and chuckled. "Oh, you that damn sweet, huh? I hear ya, shawtie. Where you heading now? A hotel? Which one?"

"No, I'm staying with . . . with my aunt in Long Island," Shanika lied as quickly as she could.

"Yeah? Well, I got a crib in the Bronx, but if you gonna be in the city for awhile maybe I can take you out? You ever been to the 40/40 club?"

"Jay-Z's club?" Shanika's eyes widened. "No. I'd like to, though."

"Well, maybe we can hook up tonight then, yo. My man be working the door and he'll let us in."

"Yeah, Jason. That'd be cool." Shanika smiled to herself. There was no way she was going to waste her time on an out-of-work scrub who cruised train stations to carry women's bags in hope of tips and had to depend on his friends to get him into clubs for free. But as long as he was carrying her suitcases, she'd play along.

She reached up to wipe some perspiration from her brow and all of a sudden felt a drop of water plop down on her forehead. "Oh God, don't tell me it's going to rain?"

A clap of thunder split the air, followed by a sudden downpour.

"Shit," Shanika muttered while pulling up the collar of her blue linen suit jacket. She tapped Jason on the shoulder. "How much farther do we have to go?"

"The corner of 30th and 8th, girl. It's the best place to flag a taxi. Right up at the corner."

It took them less than a minute to walk to their destination, but in that short time Shanika and Jason got soaked almost to the skin. Although he didn't seem to mind. What did seem to faze him was when yellow cab after yellow cab whizzed by him without stopping. Shanika stood under the canopy of a store with her luggage, watching him. When the fifth taxi passed him without stopping, she grabbed her bags and ran over to the now embarrassed and frustrated man.

"Man, I hate these whack racist mofos," he grumbled, averting his eyes from hers. "If we was uptown, I could catch a gypsy cab with no problem."

"Look. Thanks, but I got this, okay?" Shanika said, trying to sound as pleasant as possible. "You can go ahead. I'll catch it myself."

"Naw, shawtie, I got this." He tried to wave her off. He put his hand out as another yellow cab approached, and it too passed without the driver taking a second look in his direction. But the cab had to stop only three feet away because of a red light. Shanika watched as Jason stomped through a puddle to get to the car.

"Get in!" he yelled, trying to snatch the door open. The driver was quick, though, and snapped the automatic locks on.

Shanika shook her head as Jason proceeded to kick the tires, then pummel the cab's trunk.

Just then another cab neared her, and she quickly put her hand in the air. The cab stopped in front of her. She snatched the door open and struggled to get her two suitcases in the backseat before Jason could notice.

"The Ramada Inn at 30th Street and Lexington Avenue," she hurriedly told the driver.

"Hey, yo!" Jason was tapping on the closed passenger window of her cab. "Whatcha doing, Shanika? What's up with this?"

She waited until the cab driver put the car in gear before rolling down the window. "Sorry, I'm running late. Thanks for everything, though."

She didn't look back as the cab pulled off into traffic. She felt guilty since Jason was trying to help her, but she needed to get to her hotel. She'd always heard that taxis didn't like picking up black men in New York City, but this was the first time she'd actually seen it. Of course, this was the first time she'd been in New York. Obviously cab drivers didn't have as much of a problem picking up a woman. The thought that it was because she was mistaken for a white woman suddenly occurred to her.

"Did you know that man, miss?" the cab driver—who looked East Indian—asked her in a West Indian accent.

"No. He helped me from the train station with my bags," she said simply while looking at the window.

"Penn Station?" The driver peered at her through the rear view mirror.

Shanika nodded.

"Where you coming from, miss?"

"Detroit."

"Your first time in New York?"

Shanika nodded again.

"Well, miss," the driver said as he made a hard right turn

onto Madison Avenue, "you should be very careful. You were lucky. A lot of those people make a living hustling nice young ladies that just come in town. It's the way they were raised. To try and rip off people. Easier for them than to try and find work. They want to rob people or sell drugs, the lot of them, miss. And their women aren't much better. They sell their bodies or have babies so they can get on the public welfare. And they spend all of their time in the beauty salon."

Shanika's eyes widened. Okay, she *had* gotten the cab because the driver thought she was white. It wasn't the first time she'd benefited from looking white, not that she ever pretended to be white. She wasn't trying to pass or anything, she'd never do a thing like that. Never. And when she was mistaken for white and someone talked negatively in her presence about African-Americans she would hurriedly—and haughtily—announce her true heritage. But before she could say anything, the driver continued.

"Then are a lot of them in Detroit, aren't there? In fact, I've heard your city is full of them."

"Them?" Shanika said, aware of the sharpness in her tone.

"Yes. Niggers. The blacks. African-Americans."

"I call them African-Americans, and yes, the city is predominantly African-American. But I'm sorry I don't view them the same way as you." As soon as she said it she was sorry. In defense of her race she had distanced herself from it, just by using the word "them" instead of "us." That she had never done before. Her face reddened, and she quickly looked out the window so the driver wouldn't notice her expression in his mirror. Silently she asked God to forgive her.

"Here we go, the hotel is right in the middle of this block. And I don't want you to think I'm a bigot. I may have sounded like one, but I'm not. Some cab drivers won't even pick them up because they're scared. But I will, as long as it's daylight. That's why I pull the dayshift on this job so I don't have to play bias against them. I do hate it when they get in and want to go to Harlem, but I'll even take them there."

"That's mighty white of you," Shanika said quietly. She glanced in the rear view mirror and noted with satisfaction that the driver had a shocked expression on his brown face. She couldn't resist pushing it. "You're East Indian, aren't you?" she asked innocently.

"I certainly am."

"That's what I thought. But you have a West Indian accent," she said slowly. She suddenly put a bright expression on her face. "Oh, I bet you're from Trinidad! You're a coolie!"

The driver's face darkened, and he said nothing.

"You are a coolie, aren't you?" she pressed further. "My mother was raised in Trinidad, and she told me the East Indians who lived there were called coolies. She even had one as a nursemaid."

The driver pulled in front of the hotel, then cleared his throat before speaking again. "You do know that coolie is a derogatory word, don't you, miss?"

Shanika widened her eyes and put her hand to her mouth in a show of shock. "It is? No, I didn't know. I learned it from my mother. Is it racist, then?"

"It is," the driver said.

"Oh, my goodness," Shanika said, continuing her innocent act as she dug her wallet out of her handbag. "I guess it's like calling a black a nigger then? I'm so sorry. How much do I owe you?"

"That would be five-twenty-five," the driver said sullenly.

She handed him a five dollar bill and three dimes. "You can keep the change. And don't worry about helping with my bags," she told him as the hotel bellhop opened her door. "Have a nice day."

# about the author

Born and raised in Harlem, Karen E. Quinones Miller dropped out of school when she was thirteen. At twenty-two, she joined the Navy and served for five years. Then she married, had a child, and divorced—all within two years.

When she was twenty-nine, she moved to Philadelphia and got a secretarial job with *The Philadelphia Daily News*. After three years of complaining about media coverage of people of color, she enrolled at Temple University and began work as a correspondent for *The Philadelphia New Observer*, a weekly African American newspaper. Karen graduated magna cum laude from Temple with a BA in journalism, confirming her belief that the only thing she missed by skipping high school was the senior prom. She then worked as a reporter for the Associated Press and *The Virginian Pilot* before settling at the *Philadelphia Inquirer*, where she stayed for seven years.

Karen self-published her first book, *Satin Doll*, in 1999, which became an *Essence* magazine bestseller and sold to a major publisher. She went on to write three other *Essence* magazine bestselling books.

Karen lives in Philadelphia, where she heads Oshun Publishing Company, and desperately tries to ignore the empty-nest syndrome that hit after her daughter, Camille, left for Clark–Atlanta University.

You can contact Karen by e-mailing her at AuthorKEQM@aol.com or visiting her website at www.karenequinonesmiller.com.